HOUSE
OF BLOOD AND
WHISPERS

NATALINA REIS

Also by

If you liked House of Blood and Whispers you might want to check out Natalina Reis's other books.

Romantic Comedy:
We Will Always Have the Closet

Loved You Always

Blind Magic

Her Real Man

Fictional-ish

Dating the Intern

Dystopian Romance:
Heart's Prey

MM Paranormal Romance:
Lavender Fields

Infinite Blue

Of Magic & Scales

Of Scales & Fire

Of Fire & Bone

Of Tails & Mistletoe

Foxy Tails

FM Paranormal Romance/Romantasy:

Dark Feathers

Kiss of the Swan

Desert Jewel

Snow Jewel

Rebel Jewel

Contents

Dedication

Dedicated to all the kickass women who won't let anyone put them in the corner.

Disclosure/Trigger Warnings

House of Blood and Whispers is a captivating romantic fantasy tale set in a kingdom governed by a ruthless emperor devoid of morals and principles. Within this narrative, you'll encounter depictions of battles, extreme brutality, gore, explicit language, mortality, severe wounds, and sexual content, all portrayed on the pages. If you have a sensitivity to such content, please take note and ready yourself to delve into the world of the Southern Kingdom.

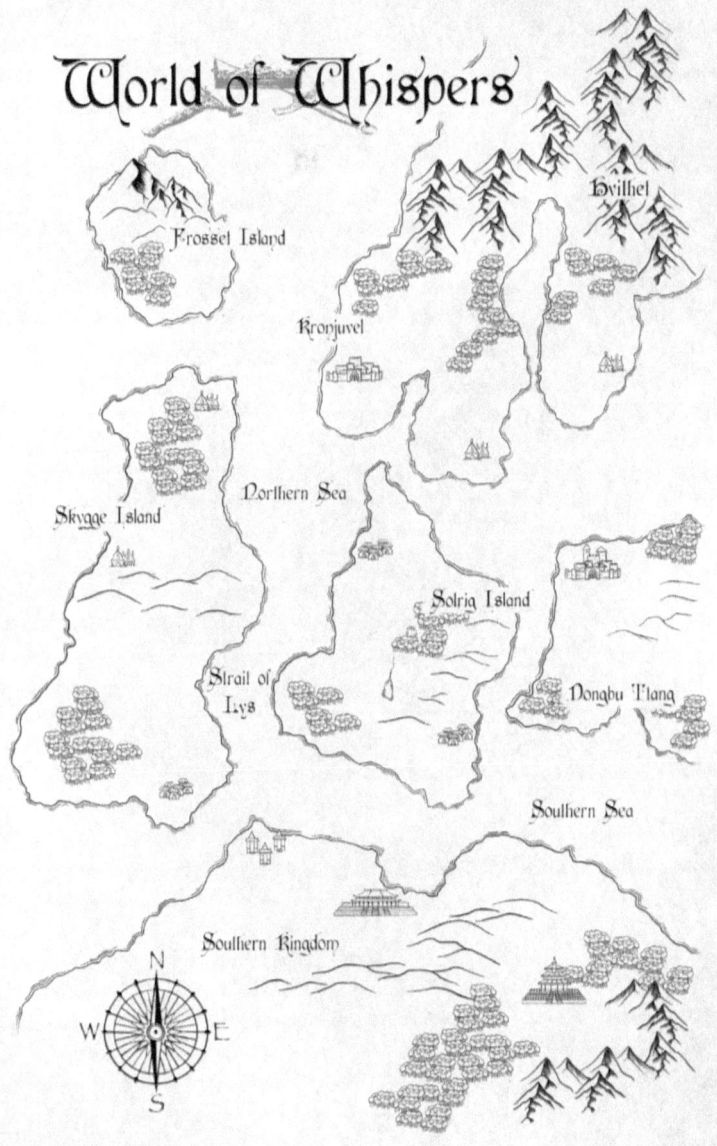

Chapter 1
Caged

E veryone calls me Cahki, an old-language word that means hard and icy. Cruel.

It'd be hard to protest that assessment of my personality as I stood in the captain's cabin, legs wide apart, braced for the few men who were still standing to attack. Bright red blood soaked my white tunic and pants and dripped from the blade of my raised sword.

Drip. Drip. Drip.

The bodies of the three men who had dared to touch me earlier were scattered on the slippery wooden floor, forming a human line between me and the men who still breathed. The captain, a burly man in his forties, stood by his bed, sputtering nonsense and waving his broken sword in front of him as he ordered his sailors to overtake me.

The remaining two had taken stock of what I was capable of and hesitated. Had they known how exhausted I was, how my legs trembled beneath me, more liquid than solid, they wouldn't have. The way every muscle of my body ached and spasmed meant one thing only: this battle was lost for me. But I wouldn't give them the satisfaction of victory so soon. I would keep them guessing until the last possible second, no matter how much pain it caused me.

I waited, sword at the ready even as my vision blurred. Soon, I'd pass out.

No food for at least three days and just the bare minimum of water had left me weak and woozy. The fact that I had managed to kill three of them gave me a sick kind of satisfaction. My dad would be proud. He had taught me well, and I would never go down without a fight to the end.

"You might be smaller than most warriors, daughter," he always said, "but you have the spirit of a fjord pirate and the fierceness of a *drage*. And with the skills I taught you, there won't be many men who can put you down."

I snorted, my sword hand shaking as I did.

"What are you laughing at, you Northern whore?" the captain yelled out. "Do you realize what great honor has been bestowed upon you by our emperor?"

I snorted again. Louder. "Honor? You call being kidnapped and taken against my will to go warm the bed of a foreign king an honor?" I spat on the floor, projecting it well enough to fall close to his boots. "I'd rather die."

"You just might get your wish," the captain said. He turned to his men. "What the fuck are you waiting for? Get her."

The men stared at each other, and that momentary hesitation was all I needed to surprise them. There was no way I could win this, but damned if I would give up.

My sword sliced through the arm of one of the sailors as if cutting through butter, and I allowed myself a moment of triumph. I might not have killed him, but he would remember me for the rest of his miserable life. Unfortunately for me, the effort did me in. My legs gave up beneath me, and I sank down to the floor, sword still in hand and a stupid smile on my lips.

Maybe they would kill me right then, and that was all right by me.

Unfortunately, I heard the captain's voice, hoarse from years of drinking high spirits, saying, "Take the bitch and put her in a cage."

Damn!

Darkness fell, blissfully quiet and oblivious. It was the closest I was going to get to death today.

Something tickled my nose, and laughter bubbled out of my dry lips before I even opened my eyes. Mom often tickled me awake, heavy sleeper that I was when I had no chores and nowhere to be. In hindsight I probably should have kept my eyes closed, because when I slowly opened them, waiting for the blur of slumber to clear, two tiny beady eyes met my gaze, challenging and icky, two of eight, I realized before I reacted.

I screamed like a banshee and smacked my nose so hard, I was sure I'd have a black eye later. Sitting up on the cold metal floor, I swatted my face several times in the off chance that the furry spider was still on my nose.

Mocking laughter made me look to the side. "Not so brave with spiders, are you, little whore?" The guard, a scrawny young man who obviously spurned dental hygiene, pointed at me and laughed again.

After spitting in his direction, I looked around. Iron bars, just slightly taller than I was, surrounded me. I looked up to find more bars stretched overhead. This square space was a cage. I was caged like a wild animal.

"Get me out of here, *jævel*," I growled, searching for my sword and not finding it. "Where's my sword?"

The man, a boy really, stood up and took a couple steps closer but stopped far enough away that I couldn't reach him. "I don't know what you called me, bitch, but I would start thinking before speaking," he said, his chin sticking out in a dare. "You have no place to go. If the emperor didn't want your kind so bad, you would have been dead by now."

"And what kind might that be? You're still wet behind your ears. What do you know about anything?" I goaded him, hoping he would get close enough that I could wrap my hands around his neck. He didn't take the bait.

"Blond hair and fair skin kind," he replied, leaning in with a huff. "You're even more precious to him with your freaky white hair."

"Oh wow, I apologize, then," I said with a mock bow. "You do know your stuff, *jævel*. Come closer and I will reward you with a kiss." The smirk died on his lips, and he blinked. "What? You've never wondered what makes women like me so special? Don't you want to try it?"

He licked his lips, and I could almost read his mind; he wanted to try it so bad, his hands shook. After a moment of silence, he took a step back and said, "No way, witch. I won't fall for your tricks."

More like he didn't want to spur the emperor's wrath by touching me that way, but I had to give him credit. He was not as dumb as he looked.

"So, am I a bitch or a witch?" I asked just to keep him talking. "You're confusing me, *jævel*."

The little turd scowled and yelled, "Don't call me that, whatever it is."

I burst out laughing, throwing my head back, and then stopped suddenly. "Make me," I growled with an eyebrow wiggle.

Unwisely, the young guard thrust his lance between the bars to hit me. Even from where I was standing, I could tell it was as blunt as a spoon, but it would do nicely. Just as he began to retract it, I grabbed it and gave it a pull. Surprised by the sudden move, the man tipped and was dragged forward until his body slammed onto the bars. I held the lance with one hand and headlocked him with the other arm, twisting his body around and nailing him against the metal rods.

"Well, well, my friend, it looks as if the tables have been turned," I purred in his ear while poking him in the back with his own lance. He tried to scream but managed only a tiny squeak. "Now, you have two options: you let me out of here, and I will do you a favor and knock you out so your captain doesn't blame you. Or I just keep tightening this hold until you can't breathe anymore. Your choice."

He mumbled something.

"What was that?" He choked as I pressed my arm harder around his neck. "Make a choice, *jævel*." I loosened my hold just enough to let him speak. He spat out a few words. "Wise choice, boy. You choose to live. Good for you." I squeezed harder just in case he thought I was bluffing. "Where are the keys to this cage?"

"In my pocket," he whispered, digging in it like a squirrel after a nut in the winter.

After fumbling for a while, he produced a large key that he handed to me. I dropped the lance but wasn't about to let him go. Stretching, I managed to insert the key into the keyhole and turn it. It clicked twice, and the door swung open.

"Good work, *jævel*," I said, stiffening my free hand before chopping it onto the side of his neck.

He went quiet and slack in my hold, slipping down until he was a puddle of human flesh on the dirty floor. I could have killed him, but he was young, and I keep my word. Most of the time.

Stepping over his unconscious body, I rushed to the door of the cabin, cracked it open, and took a look. I was in a moving ship somewhere in the Southern Sea. I had no idea how I was going to get out of here. Swimming was an option. The waters here were much warmer than the ones of the Northern Sea where I had learned to endure long hours in the water. But who knew where I was exactly? What if there were no islands close enough for me to swim to? I had no wish to continue on this ship and become a concubine to the idiot emperor who ruled the Southern Kingdom, but I also had no death wish. Jumping off this vessel was pure suicide.

But I can make them believe I did.

Beaming at the brilliancy of my idea, I snuck out of the room and slithered behind and between cargo crates to reach a nook close to the railing. I slipped out of my overtunic that was once white but was now almost grey, spattered with the dark red stains of the men I killed.

This would have to suffice. All I had to do was lie in wait and prevent my growling stomach from giving me away.

It was not a long wait. Mere minutes later, the clatter and screaming that arose from the place where I had been caged told me my guard had woken up. Men, stirred into a frenzy by the sound of the alarm, began searching for me. I couldn't wait too long.

I climbed the railing and stood up, balancing on the slippery wood. "Hey, *jævler*, I'm over here!" I yelled out, waving my arms above my head and hoping all my experience climbing icy cliffs would serve me well. "I'd rather die than bed your stupid moron of an emperor. Goodbye." I jumped over the railing, holding on to it for dear life with one hand and throwing the tunic into the waters below. As quickly as I could, I climbed back onto the deck, hidden by the crates, and sat quietly listening to the commotion I had caused.

"I see her in the water," someone said. "Should we try to rescue her?"

"Leave it be," the captain replied. "Good riddance. She was nothing but trouble."

"But the emperor would have paid us a fortune for her sort," another sailor complained with such disappointment in his voice, I was almost sorry for him.

"She already killed several of our men," the captain snapped, obviously annoyed and wanting the conversation to be over. "Let her drown. She'd probably kill the emperor, and we would be blamed for it."

Impressive reasoning for such a basic mind. He was right about that. I would totally sink a dagger into the emperor's chest as soon as I had a chance. I suppose I was doing everyone a favor by "dying" before delivery.

Now if I could only get a bite to eat, I'd be satisfied.

If at first I cursed the rain that fell mercilessly over everything and everyone in the busy harbor, I soon came to appreciate its use in camouflaging us all in a mantle of blurry grey, including my fugitive self. I was so weak from barely eating anything the past week, I was afraid I'd collapse and be trampled by the rushing people and horses coming to and fro along the quay. Out of caution, I stuck to the side of the narrow road, melting onto the wall of closed stalls and giant piles of cargo. Even though it couldn't be later than noon, it was dark and frigid. Not the kind of cold I was used to, which was icy but dry.

Instead, this kind of chill seeped into my bones and made me shiver uncontrollably, my teeth clapping together like demented clams. My clothing had been reduced to a thin layer of an undertunic and pants, neither proving to be enough of a protection, even with their fur lining, now that my outer garment was gone. The fact that I'd had nothing but stolen or discarded scraps to eat for the past few days did not help either.

I had to get out of there, find a warm hiding place, and get something in my belly. Then, I'd be able to think straight and make a plan to go back home.

Sighing, I slunk past clusters of unrecognizable people and undefined shapes, heading away from the waterfront in hopes of finding a dry spot where I could hunker down for the night. I wondered whether there were wild creatures roaming these parts, something I might catch and eat. I was not above eating a rat if that meant survival, but I hoped I didn't have to go that far.

The captain of my ship had long left the vessel, followed by a small mob of his men. He had huffed and puffed on his way down the plank, flustered and waving his short arms this way and that as if he had no control over them. The wind had picked up and had no mercy on the captain's hair, which he tried unsuccessfully to pat down and away from his face.

"The emperor will blame us, I just know it," he'd said, his rough voice carried by the wind all the way to where I was hiding. "Even though we had nothing to do with the death of the white-haired whore, we are going to be blamed."

That had brought a smile to my face. A small, but satisfying retribution for my kidnapping. Let them sweat. I only hoped the emperor was as cruel as he was famed to be and that he'd exact a harsh punishment on all of them.

Their small retinue was way ahead of me, but I could still guess the way they were heading, possibly toward a tavern where they would meet with one of the emperor's envoys. I would be heading the other way. My hair was so soaked, you couldn't tell it was white. A nice side effect of the annoying rain. In a land of mostly dark-haired people, I would not escape notice otherwise.

A few more yards into the narrow, dark streets, and I stopped, raising my nose to sniff the air. A delicious scent covered all the bad smells of the port and made my mouth water. What was that? It smelled like meat, and images of my mother's *kanin* stew immediately flooded my senses. I could almost taste the tender meat of the ice rabbit, smothered in a thick, savory sauce that warmed your stomach and healed your soul.

I licked my lips and followed the smell. Maybe they'd throw away the leftovers, and I wanted to be there to eat them. The scent had magic of a sort, making it hard to resist. I blamed it on a very empty stomach, but couldn't help but feel there was something strange about it. Tracking it all the way to an alley—the back of an inn maybe—I dropped down onto my bottom, my back against the wall, and waited. For what, I wasn't sure. Was I hoping someone would open that door and throw me a bowl of stew? Or maybe even just a bone?

The weird daze that kept me prisoner had blurred the contours of my thoughts. No matter how many times I shook my head to dispel the fuzziness that had taken residence in my brain, I couldn't clear it. It was as if something had anchored me to that spot. My legs and arms felt as heavy as my head. I couldn't shake the feeling something was wrong but couldn't muster the energy to fight it.

"We got her," I heard an unfamiliar male voice say. "*Jeonha*, come see."

My unfocused eyes couldn't quite make out who was beside me, but two dark legs appeared in front of me. "This is her?" a low voice asked. The figure crouched beside me and studied my face. "She's in bad shape."

The voice told me it was a male, but all I could discern from his body and face was darkness. All of him was dark, from the boots he wore to the hair on his head.

"Go get the carriage," the man said, standing up. "Quick."

My voice seemed to have vanished, and I couldn't move as the stranger scooped me into his arms. Fear should be filling me, but whatever was holding me in place didn't allow me to panic. Instead, just like the man who was carrying me, everything around and inside me turned dark.

And I let the darkness take me away.

It was getting old quickly, this habit of waking up in strange places and finding myself behind bars. At least this time I was in a large room, lying on a comfortable bed with soft, warm blankets over me. Once I was able to focus my eyes, I took a better look at it. Not wanting to move until I assessed my current situation, I relied on my eyes to do the exploring. The space was almost a perfect square, which annoyed me to no end. I had always had an irrational dislike for square things: too perfect, too angular. I preferred the smoothness and infinity of rounded shapes. Despite the bars on the wide double doors, the room was cozy and practical if not pretty. It was my kind of room—minus the bars preventing me from leaving. The only window, a large arched architectural beauty, was also barred but allowed the rays of the sun to fill the space with a comfortable warm glow. After the freezing cold of the night before, I was grateful for that and actually sighed in delight.

Are you stupid, woman?

I was obviously going crazy. The hunger, the cold, the exhaustion and anxiety of the past week or so had apparently damaged my brain. And speaking of which, my stomach was still cramping from lack of sustenance. My senses zoomed in on the small square table—what was the deal with all the square stuff?—and my heart almost jumped into my throat. There were plates of delicious-looking food on it, still warm if the steam wafting from it was to be believed.

My instincts ordered me to run to it and gobble it all up, but my training held me in place. What if that's what the enemy wanted? And even if they were not watching me, what if the food was poisoned? I stayed put for a moment, deliberating on my choices. They weren't good: I either starved myself and continued pretending I was unconscious, or I got up and ate and replenished my energy.

I picked the latter. After all, if I could get some nourishment in me, then maybe I could fight my way out. Or at least die happy.

Sliding my legs from under the covers and over the edge of the bed, I got up and cautiously moved toward the table. Nothing happened. No one showed up, so I moved faster to sit down and wasted no time attacking the meal in front of me. There was even a hot, sweet drink I couldn't identify but that flowed like honey over my sore throat. Instantly I felt stronger, waves of energy running through my veins and warming every inch of my weakened body.

Once nothing was left on the plates but crumbs and the seeds from a strangely tart and sweet orange fruit, I circled the room. Prowled, really. With my hands behind my back, I took wide strides around the room, studying every corner, every nook, and came to one irrevocable conclusion: there was no way out of here but through the front door that was currently blocked by iron bars that I couldn't budge.

I sat on the edge of the bed, absentmindedly caressing the soft layers of linen. It occurred to me that my clothes felt different, warmer and softer than the mess I had on before my capture. Instead of the soiled white under garments I had been wearing, I now had on a lamb soft blue tunic that covered me from neck to knees and comfortable off-white pants that hugged my legs perfectly. My feet were covered by knee-high soft white leather boots. Strange way to treat your prisoners, but I wasn't about to complain; it was the first time in over a week that I felt warm and well.

"You're pleased with the clothes, I gather."

The male voice, oddly familiar, made me snap my head up and glance at the door. At first, I couldn't discern any features, only some-one tall and dark standing on the other side of the bars, ogling me as if I were an exotic bird in a cage. Sharpening my focus, I noticed a guard beside him, sword at the ready. I smiled.

So, I still made them nervous.

"Better than wet clothes," I replied, cocking my head to the side to get a better view of the visitor. "Don't get too excited. I'm still pissed I'm here."

The man laughed, and I spotted perfect white teeth between nicely shaped lips. The skin around his eyes crinkled, narrowing his eyes further.

"I didn't expect you to be happy about it," he said, resting his right hand on the pommel of the long sword that hung from his waist. His long raven-black hair was gathered on the top of his head in a messy bun that should have made him look youthful but instead made him menacing. "But I think you'll agree this is better than the alternative."

My ears perked up. "What's the alternative?"

"You could be on your way to the emperor's bed." Well, he made a good point, but didn't he work for the emperor? "Instead, I caught you, and I have a proposal for you, if you're willing to listen to me."

A loud chuckle escaped my lips. "Maybe you should tell me who you are first, don't you think? I don't make deals with the devil." Most of the time.

"I apologize for the oversight," he said in such conversational mode, I almost forgot I was the one behind bars. "I'm Sung-jin, Crown Prince of the Southern Kingdom." He was the emperor's son? And he thought I would trust him? "And before you assume anything, I should add that I am also my father's worst enemy."

What the hell did he mean by that? How can you be the heir to the crown and yet be its enemy? I was speechless and only managed to make some weird sounds when I opened my mouth to speak.

He smirked, apparently amused by my shock. "You seem surprised," he said. "If you allow me to enter the room, I'll be glad to explain everything more clearly."

Now, that sounded promising indeed. I didn't have a weapon, but that had never stopped me from fighting. The prince was a big guy, easily towering over six feet—a giant compared to me—and even though he was covered by dark pants and matching tunic, I could perceive strong muscles beneath. I could take him as long as I kept a close eye on that mean-looking sword of his.

The lock clicked, and the guard blocked the prince's way. "Please, *Jeonha*," the guard said, an arm thrown across the opening. "You can't trust her. I heard she killed ten men on board the ship."

Slight exaggeration. More like five, maybe six men. But I wasn't going to argue with that. Rumors of this kind were good for the ego and excellent in battle. What man would not cower before a warrior with such reputation?

Prince Sung-jin forcibly removed the guard's blocking arm. "Nothing to worry about. It will be fine. Just lock the door behind me. We wouldn't want her to escape just yet."

Come to me, sweet dark lamb.

I was going to make him regret the cockiness. Why did men assume that a girl matched her size in strength? It was amazing what the right motivation made you do.

He walked inside the room while the guard did as he was told. Why was he smiling? Sung-jin was a handsome jerk who walked as if he owned the place. Well, I guess he probably did own it, but there was such confidence—arrogance—in his stride that I froze for a moment in awe.

Are you stupid, woman?

Not the first time I had asked myself that question. I shook my head, dispelling the weird vibes I was getting from the prince, and waited for him to come close enough to attack. If I could get him, I could blackmail my way out. The sword was my first target, so I assessed it. It looked heavy. I filed that information away and watched him as he stepped closer and closer.

"If you're thinking of going for my sword, think again." I froze, stunned. "It's enchanted, and you won't be able to slide it out of the scabbard, no matter how much strength you put into it."

Enchanted? This man had magic?

Something clicked in my brain. "Is that what you did to me? You used magic to subdue me yesterday?"

"Yes, and you're very welcome."

The man was not only handsome and arrogant, but he was also a freaking sarcastic asshole. Just my luck.

Chapter 2
The Plan

Her almost transparent blue eyes betrayed a dangerous intelligence. Otherwise, it was easy to think of her as harmless—just a couple inches over five feet tall and slender and elegant like a crane. This woman had fooled a whole ship of experienced traffickers into believing her helpless, and they had paid the price. Dearly. Word in the street was, she had killed at least six men, armed with only her wits and a sword. I wouldn't make the mistake of underestimating her.

"Can we talk? Or are you too busy scheming your escape?" I asked her, raising my arms in a sign of peace. "I have no intention of hurting you."

She tilted her head to one side, a movement that made me think of a crane again, wild and beautiful. Her skin was the color of white jade, and her hair, long and tied into a high ponytail, was just as white. A block of pure ice, most would say. But doesn't the white part of the flame burn the hottest?

She blinked a couple times before gesturing toward the table. "I'll listen," she said, her eyes still studying me, undoubtedly looking for ways to subdue me. "Sit, *Your Highness*."

That last part was uttered in jest. I indulged her by chuckling a bit before sitting down on one of the chairs. Watching her, I shifted on my seat, not wanting to relax too much while in the presence of this wild creature. I knew she'd jump me at any moment if she thought there was even a minimal chance of winning. "First things first," I said, resting my forearms on the table. "What is your name?"

Her pink lips were stretched into a thin line. "Cahki Aros of Hvi-thet." It was pronounced with such haughtiness, she might as well have announced she was the queen of the world. Brave, strong, and proud. A dangerous combination. "Also known as the Whisperer."

Interesting. "What does that mean? The Whisperer?"

She leaned in, and I had to resist the temptation to do the same. "I whisper sweet nothings to the men I kill." Cocking her head in that birdlike motion, she eyed me as if waiting for my reaction. When I didn't oblige, she cackled, slapping her knee and throwing her head back. "I guess the real reason will be my secret to keep, won't it? Because, my prince, I don't trust you. I don't trust anyone here."

Pleased that my lack of reaction seemed to irritate her, I suppressed a smile. "I don't blame you for not trusting me. After all, you were taken against your will by my father's orders," I said and meant it. "My father has—particular appetites, and not only for pretty girls from faraway places. One of the many reasons I fully intend to dethrone him." I cleared my throat, that ever-present emotional reaction that choked me any time I spoke of my royal sperm donor. A father, he had never really been. Not to me or my brother. "Kidnapping women to satisfy his unsavory cravings is not what anyone should expect from a good sovereign. My people deserve better."

Narrowing her eyes, she said, "And you think you are their savior?" I liked her spunk. It reminded me of Chae-yeong before she— "So where do I fit in this great scheme of yours?"

I shook out my thoughts and focused on the white-haired spitfire in front of me. "You become my wife."

Cahki froze for a moment, her gaze stuck on mine, not a single expression betraying her thoughts. But then she choked. Actually choked on air, coughing so hard, I thought she would dislodge a lung. I refrained from slapping her on the back and managed to keep my expression blank while she slowly worked herself back from the coughing fit.

"The crossing must have messed up my hearing," she finally said, her voice hoarse from the effort. "But I could have sworn you said I'd become your wife." She said it slowly, making sure she enunciated every word as if afraid I wouldn't understand her. She spoke Hangug-eo with barely an accent, and if needed, I could speak her language just as well, a Norsk dialect seldom heard in this part of the world but one I had learned from my masters as a child.

"You heard me correctly," I assured her. "You'd be my wife."

Cahki rolled her eyes, not at me, but as if she was trying to look inside her own thoughts. "How exactly will that benefit me?" she asked, body as taut as a pulled bowstring. "Because I've got to say, I seem to be the loser no matter what option I take. I either warm your father's bed or yours."

I bit my tongue just in time to stop myself from making a joke and telling her that my bed would be a hell of a lot better than my degenerate father's. "No beds involved in my case," I said instead, swallowing hard as the thought of having her in my arms at night made me shift in my seat. "It would be a fake marriage, a cover-up for the real situation."

She seemed marginally relieved, her shoulders relaxing a bit. "What would the real situation be, then?"

"You'd be my spy." For the first time since I entered the room, the Northern woman truly looked surprised. "I can't be sure the people around me are not my father's minions, so I need an outsider to do the job. The fact that you're a female and my father looks down on your gender adds an extra benefit. He will never suspect you're working for me other than under the sheets."

"Which I will never do." She was so emphatic, I almost cringed. Was I that unpleasant to look at that she couldn't envision herself with me?

Stop being an idiot. Who cares what she thinks of you?

"Right. All for show," I assured her.

"And you'll get me a weapon...?" Her blue eyes twinkled. I knew she would try to attack me as soon as I handed her a sword. She wasn't the kind to accept her fate without a fight.

I nodded, and she gave me the smile of a cat spotting a canary.

The worst was yet to come.

I may have convinced Cahki—as far as she could be convinced—to pose as my wife while working for me and against my father, but now I had to persuade the emperor to let me marry the one woman he had been eagerly waiting for. It wasn't going to be easy. Even though my father—too cocky about his own strength and paranoid of losing power through a political marriage—had long given up on marrying me off to some faraway princess, the Northern woman was a rarity this far down south with her white hair and blue eyes, catnip for someone like my father, who collected exotic specimens—his words, not mine.

After I visited Cahki, I skipped my rounds at the training field and locked myself in my room, agonizing over a plan to make it happen. Nothing came to mind. "That's great, Sung-jin. You're brilliant indeed," I finally spat out, pissed off at my own inability to come up with something. Anything.

"Well, I always thought so even though you sometimes get yourself in some pretty dumb corners." Hwarang had snuck in with his usual stealthiness and was leaning against the wall, arms crossed over his chest and a familiar mocking sneer on his lips. "Is this about the white-haired beauty?"

I snickered, running the palm of my hand over my face. "Can't think of how to convince the emperor to allow me to marry her," I confessed. "Any ideas?"

My friend, the one person in this world I trusted completely, pushed himself off the wall and came to sit across from me at the table. "When have I ever not had ideas?" he asked, and I chuckled. "The truth is, you don't need to ask for his permission. You marry her and ask for his blessing later."

Leaning over, I punched his shoulder playfully. "Right. And I'm sure he won't immediately draft divorce papers." I was certain that was exactly what would happen. "That won't work."

"Oh, ye of little faith, my friend," Hwarang said, leaning back in his chair. "I happen to know that there is a law which will prevent your father from doing that."

A little seed of hope began growing inside me. "But Emperor Min doesn't abide by any laws." His motto was that laws had been written to be broken by those who could. And he certainly counted himself among those people.

"This one will," my friend said. "It comes attached with an enchantment."

Now, that was interesting. "An enchanted law?" I had heard of those, but they were things of the distant past and no longer in existence. More myth than reality.

"The Daemeoli monks of the Southern beaches still hold on to a few." Hwarang was full of surprises. This friend of mine enjoyed his reputation as a bon vivant, a playboy, but I had yet to meet anyone as smart and as skillful with the sword. "If you get married at their enclave, your marriage will be bonded by their laws. And those always come with a hefty punishment should they be broken." It was promising indeed. "Even your royal father will not want to risk getting hexed because of a woman."

I cupped my chin, caressing a nonexistent beard. "That might just work," I whispered, my mind lost in the possibilities. "We can tell my father I met her down in the Namjjog beaches and, not knowing who she was, made her my own." My imagination was now sailing away full force. "When I found out she was the one who had escaped from the traffickers, it was too late. We had already been bonded by Daemeoli laws."

"I can make it even better," Hwarang added with a mischievous turn of his lips. "We'll dye her hair to make it believable."

Slapping my knee with a bit too much enthusiasm, I howled like a wolf, quickly followed by my friend. We were known among the nobility, especially the younger nobles and the soldiers who fought under my command, as the Neugdae—the wolves—because of our habit of howling when excited.

With my mood significantly lifted, I poured us some wine. "Let's toast to a great wedding," I said, raising my glass. Hwarang did the same. I lowered my voice to a whisper and added, "And to the end of my father's tyrannical rule."

We clinked glasses and drank the wine down in one go. I refilled our cups, but this time we sat back, ready to drink slowly while we chatted.

"How's this terror of a woman?" Hwarang asked me, wiping his mouth on his sleeve.

Despite myself, I smiled. "She's something," I said, not quite sure how to describe the wild woman from the North who had single-handedly fought a whole shipload of traffickers. "A terrible beauty of a creature. As dangerous as the wild cats of the Eastern Woods but smarter."

My friend chuckled. "You sound quite in awe of this female."

"I am not," I rushed to protest. "But as a warrior myself, I have to admire her spirit and guts. She's a teeny woman but a fiery soul. Don't let her looks deceive you."

Hwarang took another sip. "I haven't met her yet, but I can already tell she's the perfect wife for you, my friend." I threw a punch at his shoulder, but he managed to move away in time. "Congratulations on your upcoming nuptials, Prince Sung-jin. I wish you all the married bliss in the world."

I groaned. "Provided my wife doesn't kill me first."

Chapter 3
The Courtyard

A young girl in a simple gown bowed as Prince Sung-jin escorted me out of what had been my jail cell for the last few days. Sure, it was a nice, comfortable room but it was still a cage from which I had not been allowed to escape. Now that we had struck a deal, I was finally allowed to leave that gilded cage and check out this irritatingly handsome prince's palace.

The sun had just risen above the horizon, half obscured by grey clouds as the rain pattered gently on the roofs. The room opened into a hallway that led into an outdoor covered walkway. After being indoors for so long, I had to shade my eyes from the weak sunlight as I stood just outside the door.

"Where am I, exactly?" I asked, confused by my surroundings. In front of me there was a large square courtyard with a pretty gazebo in the middle. The wide space was framed on three sides by one-floor buildings like the one I had just exited from, the covered walkway running along the full perimeter. The fourth wall was just that: a tall wall with a large arched gate in the middle.

"This is Prince Sung-jin's courtyard," Hwarang answered. The man seemed to hover around the prince twenty-four-seven like a mother hen protecting her chick. I had to wonder why an adult male like the prince would need such level of motherly protection.

"What kind of prince are you that you don't even have your own palace to live in?" I exclaimed, genuinely surprised. Back in the Northern Kingdom, even minor princelings were housed in sumptuous palaces. This courtyard was cozy and pretty, but far from the luxury I would have expected for a royal.

The prince laughed. "A courtyard is what we call the group of connected buildings and enclosed garden that comprise a palace," he explained. "The emperor's palace is also in a courtyard—much larger than mine but still a courtyard."

Southerners were too complicated for my taste. "So what you call a courtyard is actually a palace?"

Hwarang huffed. "What's so hard to understand?" he said. "It's all the buildings and grounds that comprise the palace. Ours is much smaller than the emperor's, but we are several courtyards away from him, which gives us the freedom to come and go without him noticing."

Sung-jin looked at me, a subtle smile dancing on his lips. "We brought you in through our outside gate that opens directly into my courtyard and is guarded by my own men. My father's palace—courtyard—has its own gates." My head was reeling. He pointed at the arched gate to our left. "That one connects our courtyard to the path that leads to the other palaces, one for the scholars and the other for the royal concubines."

A snort made me look in the direction of the prince's friend. "The courtyard where you would be living if the prince hadn't rescued you," he said.

My hackles came out. "Rescue? You call kidnapping someone from the street against her will rescuing? What kind of parents taught you that?"

Hwarang made a move toward me, but his friend lifted his arm to stop him. "Be that as it may, Cahki, you're still in better hands than if you had been taken to the concubines' courtyard, don't you agree?"

I hated that he was right. That didn't mean I had to be happy about it. I would find a way to kill both of them and run for it. No one was going to stop me, especially now that the idiot prince had given me a weapon, a pretty but lethal dagger I wouldn't hesitate to use when necessary.

"Let me show you to our living quarters," Prince Sung-jin said, inviting me to follow him. "This building where you stayed is the guest quarters."

I began to follow him down the covered walkway. "Do you always imprison your guests?" I snorted, inhaling the wet air with pleasure after being locked up during the sea crossing in a stinky ship filled with equally smelly men and now this shorter—and admittedly more comfortable—stint in the prince's palace.

"We had it specially customized for you," Hwarang said, walking closely behind us.

I turned around to face him and flattened my palm on my chest. "Aww, thank you," I said, my voice dripping with sarcasm. "I feel so special now."

The damn man had the nerve to smile at me, self-satisfied prick. "We live to please you, my lady."

I spun in my heels with a huff, my fingers seeking and tightening around the pommel of my new dagger hidden in the folds of my dress.

Too soon. Not the right time.

I couldn't allow these assholes to ruin my plan of escape. I needed to keep calm and collected.

"As if I wanted you to please me," I retorted instead. "I haven't seen any women around for the past few days, so I'm guessing your idea of pleasing does not quite add up."

My back was turned to him, but I could still hear his breath catching and sputtering. The prince dropped a step or two behind me as if to protect me from his friend.

As we walked along the perimeter, we crossed ways with a few servants and a couple of men who were obviously soldiers, dressed in leathers and carrying swords.

"Aren't you afraid these people will tell your father I'm here?" I asked. Whatever messed-up relationship he had with his imperial father, it seemed odd to me that he was able to live what looked like a rather independent life. Wasn't he the heir to the throne? Why wasn't his father trying to marry him off to a political ally?

"These men and women are loyal to me," he said. I knew too well how loyalty could sometimes be deceiving. "I take very good care of my people and make sure their families are safe and sound away from the emperor. Besides, I only keep a low number of servants in my courtyard."

My father and mother had also surrounded themselves with loyal people, individuals who would risk their own lives to protect them. But my parents didn't kidnap women to use against the court like this prince had done. How had he earned such trust from his staff? Granted, he had been decent enough to send messages to my parents to let them know I was alive and well.

For now.

Sung-jin had stopped in front of a door that looked very much like the one we had exited from. He stepped aside and let me go in first. Even though it looked identical from the outside, it was very different indoors. It was a large space with sets of simple but beautiful furniture, separated into wall-free rooms. I studied the space, which was bright despite the rain outside, with begrudging approval. To my right there was what looked like an office of sorts with a low desk and chair and lots of books and documents on shelves. Next to it a privacy curtain half hid the bedroom beyond it. On the other side of the room, there was an area with a squat table and sitting cushions.

"Is this where I will be staying?" I asked, my fingers still clasped tightly around the hidden dagger. Not a bad place at all.

Hwarang snorted again. "These are the prince's private rooms," he announced in a tone that added an unspoken *in your dreams* to the statement.

I twisted my neck to stare at the prince, a question in my eyes.

"These will also be your rooms," Sung-jin assured me. "You'll be my wife, after all. We'll be expected to share our bed."

It was my turn to glower. *In your dreams, Your Royal Stupidity*. In my shock I pulled the dagger from the folds of my skirt into plain view. "I will bury this knife in your heart if you try anything."

Sung-jin made an appeasing gesture. "Relax," he said with a sigh. "I will be sleeping on the floor. The bed is yours."

I held my breath for a moment longer before exhaling in relief. "No touching is allowed, get it?" I said, waving the dagger between us.

He nodded, clearly exasperated. "I swear on my mother's soul," he said, and for once, I believed him. There was such an emphasis on the word *mother*, his voice catching on something that sounded like a sob. There was pain there, a hint of heartbreak too plain to be a lie.

I lowered the dagger. "Where's the kitchen?" I asked, unwilling to give him a total win but also reluctant to twist the metaphorical knife deeper into that obvious wound.

The cloud that had shadowed his beautiful dark eyes dissipated, and he pointed at the door. "I'll show you the way," he said.

And just like that, we were back on our tour of his palace. Or courtyard. Or whatever they called it.

Gods, I hated these Southerners.

Chapter 4
Layover

It figures they would reach out to a prostitute to help them disguise my white hair. Eun, the boss of The Pleasure Palace, had been hastily engaged by my idiot captor and his even more idiotic friend to come and camouflage my blatant hair and eye color. Turns out Eun is a lovely, smart woman who, after trying a couple different things, waved a white flag and told the men it couldn't be done.

"If we turn her hair black, she will be even more conspicuous," she told them. "She's too pale. The dark hair would just make her complexion even more obvious."

Duh! I could have told them that, but I am just a prisoner they want to use for their own political purposes.

In the end, they covered my head and face with a wide-brimmed veiled hat and dressed me in their silly silk dresses that cinched the area above my breasts with a tight sash, accentuating my boobs. Had males designed the female fashion in the South?

"This veil is driving me insane," I grunted, not for the first time, as we walked down the main street of a town called Busan. We had arrived about an hour ago and had left the safety and comfort of the carriage to look for someplace to eat. There was a breeze that threw the almost opaque white veil against my face, making me itchy and hot. Even though it was early spring, according to my husband-to-be, the temperature was uncomfortably warm for someone who like me had spent her whole life in the Northern fjords.

Prince Sung-jin closed his hand around my left wrist and pulled me closer to him. "Stop fussing so much," he muttered under his breath. "You're going to attract attention, woman."

My other hand tightened around the pommel of my dagger, itching to pull it out and show this royal idiot what happened to guys who dared grab me like that. But, on second thought, I needed him to be able to get out of this situation. At least for now. Hopefully I would get my chance to cut his throat further along in our journey and before we actually got married. Then I could run for it.

Hwarang pointed at a nondescript building on our left. "There. There's a tearoom," he said, not waiting for our acknowledgment before heading toward it.

We all followed, my stomach grumbling underneath the cumbersome clothes I had been forced to put on. I had never seen so much rain in my life. The skies had been bawling since we left the day before, turning everything into a gross shade of grey. The bottom of my dress was heavy with the mud that seemed to cover every road and path in town, making my already irritated self that much ornerier. I was ready to kill anyone who pissed me off, and being hungry was not helping matters. The place didn't look like much, but at that moment, I would eat just about anything.

A server showed us to a table at a corner of the restaurant and poured tea for all of us. Unexpectedly, the hot brew smelled heavenly, or maybe it was my empty stomach that made me think so. I wasted no time gulping it down and pouring myself another cup.

"Calm down, Cahki," Hwarang said, his narrow eyes twinkling with mischief. "You'll drown."

I pulled the veil apart so he could see me and growled. "If you hadn't kept me in that freaking carriage for as long as you did without food or drink, I would be calm," I spat out, my urge to pull my dagger out ever so much stronger. "Keep your comments to yourself."

The man turned to my husband-to-be and half chuckled, half groaned. "You're marrying this wild creature?" He pointed at me. "She will kill you on your wedding night." He was a bit off, since I planned to kill the prince before the wedding, but kudos for coming close. "Are you sure you want to trust this woman? She obviously has no clue how to act in a civil way, and I doubt she has any sense of loyalty."

"For your information, *this* woman has a very strong sense of loyalty," I retorted, setting the cup down with more force than necessary as the veil once again closed in front of my face. "I just choose to be loyal to those who deserve it. You're not one of them."

"What about the prince? Are you going to be loyal to him?" he asked. "Because I doubt it very much."

I then gave him the smile of a white fox eying a rabbit. "That remains to be seen," I stated. "At least, unlike you, he seems to be half intelligent."

Hwarang rose from the chair as if to hit me, but Prince Sung-jin intervened. "Stop!" he said, not bothering to raise his voice. "Enough, you two. You're attracting too much attention."

It was true. A quick glance around was met with several pairs of eyes staring at us.

"I know we don't trust each other," the prince continued, while I resumed my tea drinking. He glared at me. "You can't wait to bury that dagger in my gut." Despite my dislike for the man, I admired him for his insight. "But I am your only chance at surviving and eventually leaving the Southern Kingdom, and you are my best chance at placing a second pair of eyes on my father. We don't have to like this, but can we at least work with each other to succeed?"

With a snort, I nodded. "All right, I promise to try really hard not to kill your idiot friend, but he better leave me alone," I said, my stomach growling loudly. "Can we eat now?"

The prince waved the server over and ordered several bowls of noodles and dumplings. Southern food was strange but not bad, I admitted to myself. It definitely beat the scraps of greens and roots I usually ate when working in the mountains. Even I couldn't convince the meager vegetation of the icy peaks to grow bigger or more delicious.

When the man brought back the steaming bowls and plates piled up with soft white balls of dough, I actually drooled, sticking my nose up in the air and inhaling all the goodness.

As the dishes were set before the prince, he surprised me by gently pushing them toward me and ordering in a soft voice, "Eat."

That was a command I was glad to obey.

"I need to relieve myself," I said through the thin wood of the door. "Open up immediately."

"Is it number one or number two?" the male voice on the other side quipped in a strangled voice. The idiot was laughing at me.

"Open the fucking door, or I will scream like a banshee and alert everyone in this inn." I would do it too.

It was the middle of the night, and I could still hear the tireless rain falling against the walls. I would have jumped out the window of the second-floor room, but with all the rain, I would most likely end up splattered in the street.

For a moment, I heard nothing, but soon the clicking of the lock echoed in the silence of the night. Hwarang appeared before me with a frown on his face. "You are such a bitch," he said. I liked the fact he didn't treat me like a fragile flower. After all, I called him all kinds of unpleasant names to his face, and he didn't even blink. "Do you even really need to go?"

"Yes, I do, but it does give me extra pleasure that I can piss you off in the process," I said, snapping the veiled hat up from the small chair by the door. "Do I really have to wear this contraption to go pee?"

He nodded emphatically. "Are you really a noblewoman up North? You talk like a sailor." I did pride myself on my colorful language. I had learned from the best—my father who used to be a fjord pirate before he met my mother. "Things must be pretty uncivilized up there if the daughter of a noble talks like that."

I pulled on the hat, rearranged the veils around my head, and stepped into the hall. "I take after my father," I stated without explaining anything.

My mother was the noblewoman in the family, a lady-in-waiting for the old queen who took refuge in the fjords after the rebels had decimated the royal family. That's when she met my father and somehow managed to "reform" the old pirate into being a good husband and an excellent leader of the local community.

"He must be so proud," Hwarang commented, stepping beside me and pointing in the direction of the bathroom. "Dirty-mouthed ladies over there."

I raised my head haughtily, and when he least expected it, punched him in the stomach—not hard enough to put him out, but hard enough to smart. He humphed and bent over a little. I turned and continued on my way to the toilets. "Yes, he is very proud."

The rain had been relentless, and the roads were more liquid than solid, so the prince had decided to stay at the inn for the night and resume our travels the next day. His giant of a friend had been given the job of guarding me while I fumed behind locked doors, which both offered me a chance to tease him, to my great satisfaction, and maybe actually sleep in peace for once. Before we left the prince's palace, I slept with an eye open, afraid of who might come through the door at night. I still didn't trust either of these two men, but they seemed to be more interested in our destination than in me. Except for Hwarang, who, just like I did, found great joy in teasing me ad nauseam. But I could take it as much as I could dish it out.

Much to my surprise, the prince—not Hwarang—was waiting for me outside the toilets. "Couldn't sleep?" I asked to hide my confusion. What was he doing up this time of night? And where was the other idiot?

He gave me a weak, lopsided smile that didn't reach his dark brown eyes. "It's my turn to guard you," he said simply, stepping aside so I could pass him. "I trust you find your accommodations comfortable enough."

I nodded and walked in front of him, heading to the room. "Adequate," I said. Bullshit! After spending all that time on a trafficker's ship, this room was an absolute luxury. I was used to living in humble lodgings. My parents had never cared much for status or material possessions and neither did I. "The bed is a bit lumpy," I lied. I wouldn't want him to think I was actually impressed with the softness of the mattress, considering the inn was nothing to boast about.

He cleared his throat behind me. "I apologize, my lady, but it was the best we could do," he said politely, and I had to wonder if he was serious or pulling my leg. "Once we get to the monastery, I will make sure to arrange for accommodations worthy of my wife."

I swiveled on my heels and parted the veil to glare at him. "I am not your wife yet," I growled.

He actually chuckled. "Why do you growl so much? Were you brought up with the wolves?" Apparently Hwarang's influence was making an impact. I was not sure how to feel about it. "You're right, of course. But according to South Kingdom traditions, as soon as a man and a woman become engaged, they are already as good as husband and wife." He smiled, and I huffed, annoyed. "Without the perks," he added.

Why were my face and neck burning? I never blushed. Ever. I let the veil cover my fiery complexion and, lacking any good comeback, turned around and marched back to my room.

Once the door was locked and he couldn't see me, I leaned against the door and said, "And there won't be any perks in this marriage, Your Highness. No perks at all."

I had a sharp dagger to make sure that stayed true.

Chapter 5
All the King's Men

I rubbed my temples for the hundredth time in the past hour. The bickering between Cahki and Hwarang was driving me insane and giving me a giant headache. It had been amusing at first, but after hours of nonstop back-and-forth barbs, I'd had enough. Just as I was about to explode, I heard someone yell outside the carriage.

Pulling the curtain from the window, I peeked outside and saw a soldier on a horse riding parallel to us. "*Jeonha*," the man yelled out. "Your Highness, please stop. I bring news from your father."

Soon, the carriage had stopped, and I stepped out, leaving Hwarang in charge of keeping an eye on the white-haired creature. "What's going on?" I asked once we had walked some distance from the others. Now that we were closer, I recognized the soldier. He was one of the few I still trusted to communicate news to me with the impartiality of an observer. "Something wrong?"

The man, Dong Yun, took a moment to catch his breath before speaking. "The emperor is scouring the town in search of your bride, *Jeonha*," he finally said. "I came as soon as I heard. Someone claimed they saw her alive and on the run. He's sending his men in every direction outside the city. Some are coming this way."

"Shit," I exclaimed, bringing my fist to my mouth. Always one step ahead of me, it seemed. "Does it look as if he knows she's with me?"

Dong Yun shook his head. "He thinks she was taken by another man, but he doesn't suspect you."

"Are you sure?" I could never be certain with my father. He was a cunning, cruel man who seemed to have eyes and ears everywhere.

"I'm certain, *Jeonha*," the soldier said. "But you must speed up your journey, or his hounds will catch up with you. I managed to throw them off this path for a while, but that won't last long, and they are not far behind me."

He was right. We must get to the monastery where we would be relatively safe within its walls. I touched his shoulder and squeezed. "Thank you. You're a good man. Remind me to reward you when this is all done." He nodded, and I rushed back to the carriage.

Both Hwarang and Cahki stared at me with curiosity in their eyes. "What happened?" my friend asked. I shook my head, our usual sign that it had something to do with my father. "Hell, is he on our tails?" I nodded, sitting down and knocking on the ceiling to tell the driver to move. "Son of a bitch. Does he know? How can he—"

"No, he is just searching for her," I interrupted, sticking my head out the front window to talk to the driver. "We need to get to our destination as soon as possible, do you understand?" The man nodded and pulled on the reins to move the horses.

The carriage balked for a second and then lurched forward, throwing me off-balance. I held on to one side of the carriage and sat down next to Cahki, who watched the whole scene in silence, a worrisome fact, considering she never stopped talking.

"What happens if your father's men catch up to us?" she finally asked, her fair skin paler than usual. The woman was not stupid, and that question was rhetorical. She knew exactly what would happen.

"Let's hope he doesn't," I said, swallowing the giant knot I had in my throat. "Or we will both be screwed."

She let out a loud "Ah" and clucked her tongue. "At least you will only be screwed metaphorically, unlike myself," she said, her eyes hardening. "Don't compare our situations, prince."

Hwarang jumped in. "At least you'll still be alive," he said. "Do you know what will happen to him?" Cahki crossed her arms over her chest, defiance in her gaze. "He'll be executed. Dead. Gone."

My wife-to-be flinched, however slightly, a fact that gave me a ridiculous amount of satisfaction. She wasn't as callous as she would like everyone to think she was after all.

She glanced at me. "Is that true? Your own father would kill you for this?" I nodded. "Is he really that fucked up?"

"We have a complicated relationship," I said, not wanting to talk about it. The carriage hit a pothole, and we all bounced around, grasping at whatever we could find for a handhold. Cahki slid down the seat and crashed into my side, her hands closing on my arm just as the carriage slowed into a smoother ride. I stared at her and then at the hands that were burning through the thick fabric of my tunic. "But I will do what I can to keep you safe, I promise."

I could have sworn she blushed as she abruptly pulled her hands away and stuffed them under her legs. "I don't need your promises, prince. I rely only on myself." The brief moment of awkwardness was gone, and Cahki's haughtiness had returned in full force. I had to admire her nerve.

"The beast is back." Hwarang had been quiet for a while, but the wide smile on his face told me he had been watching the interaction with his usual nosy focus and having a good time doing so. "Can't wait to see you two get married. It will be a wedding for the books."

"What books?" Cahki asked, her arms once again crossed in front of her. "I bet you can't even read."

And here they went again!

Even wicked people often looked like angels when asleep. Not Cahki. Her lips curved up at the corners in what could only be described as a sneer even in slumber, and her white eyelashes cast threatening shadows over the paleness of her skin. She was an interesting, however scary, creature. A rare one indeed, and as much as I would be happy to never see her belligerent self again, her eyes always shiny with murderous thoughts toward me, I couldn't deny it would be a shame if she ended up as one of my father's many ill-treated concubines. To put such a rare bird in a cage, no matter how gilded, would be a crime.

A commotion outside the carriage broke my train of thought, and I moved my gaze to the window. Two of my armed guards were frantically trying to get my attention. "*Jeonha*, we have news," they yelled.

The carriage stopped, and I stepped out before Cahki woke up, leaving a half-asleep Hwarang to watch her. "What's going on?" I asked the mounted guards.

The horses were sweating and snorted as they pawed at the ground. "They are coming," one of the guards said, reigning in his horse. "The emperor's men are almost upon us."

The panic in the guard's voice was matched by the feeling that exploded in my stomach. Shit! What were we going to do? I jumped inside the carriage and grabbed Cahki's arm. "Let's go," I said. She pulled her arm back, and I added, "My father's men are coming. You have to go."

"Where can she go? There are no places to hide around here," Hwarang said. He was right. The forest here was thick but no match for my father's soldiers and their hounds.

An idea popped into my mind. I turned to Cahki and asked her, "Can you ride a horse?"

She let out a loud chuckle. "Who do you think I am? Of course I can ride a horse. Better than you, I'm sure." Why was everything a competition or challenge with this woman? "Why?"

I didn't waste time explaining what I was about to do. I jumped out of the carriage again and yelled at one of the mounted men to dismount.

My friend and my wife-to-be climbed out of the carriage to join me. "You're riding to the monastery as fast as you can," I told Cahki as the guard brought us the horse. "Follow the road. It leads straight into the monastery. Once you're within its walls, you'll be safe. Not even my dad dares offending the monks."

"We'll never see her again," my friend said. It was a strong possibility. But Cahki was smart. She'd understand that the monastery was her best chance at survival.

"You're not scared I will run away?" she asked, mirroring Hwarang's words and scowling at him.

"If you cherish your life, you'll do as I say." We had no time to waste, so I grabbed Cahki's hand and pulled her toward the horse. "Go! Ride as fast as you can." I dug my royal seal out from my pocket and handed it to her once she was sitting on the saddle. "Show the monks this, and tell them I sent you. They'll protect you."

Without further ado I slapped the horse's rear and watched as it took off at a gallop, Cahki's white hair flying behind her as she expertly steered the horse in the right direction. She never looked back.

I couldn't be sure I would ever see her again, but I had other problems to think about right now.

I turned to Hwarang and my other men. "If they catch us here, they will put two and two together later when—*if* we get married," I said. "Think quickly. We need an excuse for being here."

Both my friend and the other four men went quiet for a moment. Hwarang was the first to break the silence. "I know," he said. He pointed at one of the men. "Go get the bows in the carriage and then hide the carriage in the woods." As soon as the other man took off running, he told me, "We're here hunting for the famous white deer of these woods."

That was a brilliant idea, and the irony of it didn't escape me.

I was always surprised by how quickly my men reacted to orders. Hwarang had trained them well. In seconds, the carriage was out of sight, two of the three guards who still had their horses were on foot, and Hwarang and I were on the mounts, bows and arrows at the ready, two hunters out on a hunting expedition, to anyone who didn't know any better.

It didn't take long for my father's men—six men on powerful horses followed closely by a pack of hounds—to reach us. Their black metal uniforms glinted under the dying rays of the sun, the horses huffing and snorting as their riders pulled in their reins. I raised my hand to signal my men to stop and turned my mount around to face the newly arrived group.

"Identify yourself," the leader of the black-clad soldiers yelled out from a few feet away.

I nudged my horse closer to him so he could see my face in the dimming light. "I'm Prince Sung-jin. Who are you?"

The reaction was immediate. All the soldiers bowed as deeply as they could from their saddles. "*Jeonha*, I didn't recognize you," the leader said. His eyes narrowed. "But what is *Jeonha* doing so far from home?"

Hwarang moved up beside me. "How dare you question His Highness?" he said, his authoritative tone leaving no room for argument. "He's obviously hunting. He hopes to bag one of the fabled white deer." He pointed at the bows in our hands. "Are you blind or stupid?"

The man bowed deeper. "I apologize, *Jeonha*," he said. "I was just surprised to see you here, that's all."

I raised my hand again in a magnanimous gesture. "No harm done," I said, feigning a calm I didn't feel. "I'm also surprised to see you this far from home. What are you doing here?"

"His Imperial Majesty, Emperor Min, has sent us in search of his fleeing concubine," the man explained with yet another bow. "Have you seen her in these parts, *Jeonha*?"

"The white-haired woman who escaped the traffickers?" I asked. Then, I shook my head. "I'm afraid not. What makes you think she came this way? I would think she would try to buy passage back to where she came from."

The man frowned as if that idea had never occurred to him. "I don't think any of the ship captains would dare to defy the imperial orders," he said, further confirming my suspicion that they had never considered the possibility that a woman could indeed be that smart.

"She could have stowed away." I dug that knife deeper and was gratified to see him cringe at the thought. "No need for permission or even awareness from any of the crew."

There was silence for a moment as the soldier digested the possibility. I wasn't surprised that even my highly intelligent father hadn't considered it. Conniving as he was, he was also someone who believed women to be creatures without much of a brain, existing only to produce heirs and pleasure the males. Hadn't my mother been used and discarded the same way?

"I will leave you to your hunting now, *Jeonha*," the man said, gesturing for his soldiers to leave. "I apologize again for interrupting your sport."

I waved a hand dismissively, turned my horse, and left at a trot closely followed by my friend and all my men. I didn't look back, but I could hear the horses gallop away in the opposite direction. I would bet they were running back to the harbor to interrogate and search every ship still in port.

If my heart were not trying to escape through my mouth, I would have laughed. Now, the question was, did Cahki do as I asked her, or had I seen the last of her?

Chapter 6
Tangled

I thought about it. I really did.

In fact, at some point I veered off the road and rode the horse a mile or so away from where I had been told to go. But in the end, I knew that I'd be safer following the idiot prince's advice and just seek refuge in the monastery.

The young acolyte who opened the gate for me took a look at the seal in my hand and moved aside to let me and the horse ride in. He closed the gate behind us, and I slid off the horse, patting him gently on the neck. The poor thing was sweating and panting from the long, rough ride.

"Can someone feed and water my horse, please?" I asked the young man who didn't seem surprised by the long white hair that had escaped the bun and now fell freely over my shoulders. The veiled hat had long been lost, and good riddance. "It was a tough ride here."

He called on another monk who promptly took the reins from me and walked away with the mount. The monks were a funny bunch with their tufted hairdos and bright orange robes that only reached below the knees and had more in common with potato sacks than actual clothing. We were standing in a large courtyard framed by small one-floor wooden houses and tied together by a large, yet humble-looking, temple directly across from the gate.

"May I ask your name?" the young monk asked. He was still an adolescent, maybe fifteen or sixteen, and had very serious dark brown eyes in a small face crowned by the funny tuft of hair held in place by a wide leather strap.

My lips twitched with laughter, but I managed to control it. "Cahki is my name," I said, after clearing my throat. "Prince Sung-jin should be coming soon. You are...?"

He bowed slightly, crossing his arms over his chest. "My name is Ji-hoon," he said. "What brings you here, and what can we do to help?"

"We've come here to get married," I blurted out, surprising myself. What was I thinking? The prince was not even here yet. I could come up with a different solution to my present situation, given time. Instead, I had just locked myself into this crazy one. "I'll let the prince explain when he gets here. In the meantime, little guy, is there anything I can eat? I'm starved." After you stick your foot in your mouth, the best way to stop yourself from doing further damage is to muzzle it with food.

The boy pointed at a building a few yards away. "Of course. Please." He fell in step beside me as we took off in the direction of the nondescript house he had pointed at.

The place didn't look like much. If that was a restaurant, it was a pretty lower-end one, but this was a monastery, after all. As soon as we crossed the doorway, another monk just as thin and young as Ji-hoon came to greet us. "Welcome. Please sit outside, and I will bring you food," he said as if he knew exactly what kind of food I wanted. I guessed they must've only had one kind, then.

We did as we were told, and we sat in one of three rickety wooden tables that lined the outside wall of the building. At least it wasn't raining anymore. The weather had become progressively warmer and drier as we approached the monastery, and I was okay with that. If I never saw a drop of rain again, I'd be overjoyed.

Sooner than I expected, the little monk came out with a bowl of something steaming and a pair of wooden chopsticks. "The Father himself would approve of these dumplings," he said as he placed the dish on the table before me. I didn't know who this *father* was, but the dumplings, swimming in a reddish sauce, smelled heavenly. He handed me the chopsticks, and I wasted no time shoveling them into my mouth. The monk smiled, bowed, and went back inside, leaving me alone with Ji-hoon and the bowl of delight.

"Who's his father?" I asked with a mouthful of the hot doughy food.

For the first time, Ji-hoon smiled. His rather plain face transformed into a handsome one when his lips stretched and curved. "He meant our Father, our holy master." He pointed at a statue of a man who sat cross-legged upon a marble platform at the base of the temple's long stairway. The stone man wore the same odd clothing and hair tuft I had been seeing on the monks since I arrived.

"Shit!" I exclaimed, realizing my faux pas. "He's your religious leader? I'm sorry, I didn't realize...."

Ji-hoon shook his head. "No worries. How could you have known?" He pointed at the food. "Eat, and then I will show you to where you can rest until the prince arrives."

A nap in a comfortable bed sounded amazing. Sleeping in a bouncy carriage for the past few days didn't qualify as restful. I ate as quickly as I could without choking on the savory morsels and then happily followed the young monk to another house. On my way there, I couldn't help wondering why all the monks looked awfully young. Were all their elders in the temple or meditating somewhere unseen?

Every monk we passed couldn't be more than eighteen years old, if that.

The room Ji-hoon took me to was small and plain, but the bed was soft and warm. As soon as he left me alone, I curled under the brown blankets and fell asleep, too tired to worry about what the future would bring.

Even if it was a handsome idiotic prince.

The earthquake had a strange sound, more like the hooves of many horses against rock than the usual rolling, creaking clatter most tremors brought along. There was no place to hide in safety from where I stood on the icy cliffs of the fjord, so I did what I always had done: nothing. I would wait it out and try my best not to be crushed under giant chunks of falling ice.

The odd *clippity-clop* noise continued, closer and closer until it finally stopped. Wait! *Clippity-clop*? Earthquakes did not make that sound. Horses did, and there were no horses up on the cliffs. My eyes snapped open. Had I been dreaming all this time? I strained to listen, and sure enough, I heard horses snorting and the men talking.

My vision swam as I sat up too fast, still half asleep. I looked around, holding on to my head, trying to get my bearings. Reality came crushing down on me as I drank in the humble room and the sounds coming from outside. I was at the monastery, and the clatter outside had to be the arrival of the prince and his men.

Fully awake now, I jumped out of bed, made a half-hearted attempt at smoothing out the wrinkles in my dress, and stared briefly at myself in the blurry mirror on the table. Gods, I was a mess. My hair was all in tangles. Between the long wild ride here and my usual restlessness while sleeping, there wasn't a single smooth strand of hair in my head. I sighed and let it go. It wasn't as if I was trying to impress anyone, after all.

Opening the door a small crack and peeking out of it, I was met with two very dark eyes. I almost jumped out of my skin. "Fuck you, prince! You scared the crap out of me."

Amusement lit up his usually somber face. "Never a boring word with you, my wife," he quipped. I was not amused. "What a colorful vocabulary you have."

I opened the door all the way and scowled at him. "You would too if you had to look at your face first thing after you woke up." Not that his face was unpleasant to look at. Much the contrary. But to stare straight at his deep, piercing eyes when I thought I'd be looking at the courtyard was indeed startling, to say the least.

"I'm sure you'll get used to it once we get married, sweetheart." That last word was uttered with so much sarcasm, I could almost taste its sourness. "You got enough sleep, I hope?"

"I gather you escaped your father's clutches," I countered, not wanting to dwell on the fact that we would be married soon. Or not. There was still time to cut his throat beforehand. Or even after.

"My father's clutches were never after me," he said bitterly, "but thank you for caring." The sarcasm was back. "We must go speak with *Abeoji*." When I raised an eyebrow in question, he explained, "The Father, Master of the Daemeoli. We'll plead for an enchanted wedding."

A loud *pftt* escaped my lips. "You make it sound so dreamy and romantic." When in fact it would be bloody and doomed, or my name was not Cahki.

He shrugged. "Suit yourself, Cahki, but if we don't make a case for us being so deeply in love that we can't stand the idea of anyone breaking us apart, *Abeoji* will never agree to it, and there goes your one opportunity at freedom from my father's deviant hands."

As much as I wanted to place *my* hands around his neck and squeeze until his beautiful eyes popped out, he was right. One thing at a time. Let's deal with the emperor first, and then the son would be easier to take care of. If I killed him now, who was to say the emperor would not carry me back to his harem and destroy every chance I had of going back home? Better to wait until after the wedding, when I would be in a better position to escape.

With a nod, I stepped forward, but he stopped me. "You can't go see the Father looking like that," he said, a tiny ghost of a smile dancing on his lips. *Fuck you!* "I'll help you with your hair."

I was about to protest and say I'd do it myself, but the truth was, I had no comb or any other implement that would allow me to do it. I stepped back into the room and allowed him to follow me. I sat in front of the round rusted mirror on the only chair and braced myself for what was to come. I had always hated people touching my hair. Even my mother had to endure countless tantrums triggered by her attempts at brushing my hair when I was a child. To have a stranger do it was making my stomach turn.

"Sit still for a moment, damn it," he commanded. I had been squirming in my seat without even realizing it. I took a deep breath. "By all the gods in heaven, I'm just going to comb your hair, not pull it off your scalp."

I almost chuckled at that. "I will scratch your eyes out if you do," I replied, trying to settle on the chair. Why was I so nervous about this?

"I don't doubt it," he said, and without any warning, his hands were on my head. First, he just flattened them on the top and slid them down the length of the entangled mess as if he was assessing the scope of the damage. "Holy shit, your hair is all in knots."

I scoffed. "Well, try to ride like the wind and see what happens to your smooth black hair." That would be a sight to be seen, I was sure. I hadn't seen him with his hair loose—it always tied into a high ponytail or gathered into a bun on the top of his head—but I could only imagine the sight. *What am I thinking?* I needed more sleep. "Get on with it, prince, or we will be dead before we get to talk to the Father."

He chuckled and began running his fingers through the strands of my hair, pulling ever so gently at the knots he encountered, smoothing them with his warm palms. Shivers ran from my scalp to my limbs and gut, butterflies invading my chest and making it hard for me to breathe. As he continued his ministrations, my heart sped up, pumping an overflow of blood to my cheeks and neck. What was wrong with me? I was actually loving it and didn't want it to end despite my disgust. The prince had a magic touch indeed.

"There," he announced suddenly, snapping me out of the trance his touch had thrown me into. I stared at the mirror and was shocked to find my hair not only smoothed out from all tangles but braided behind my back. I looked like a proper lady—well, a proper woman. My dirty, torn clothes didn't quite scream *lady*. "Let's go see the master."

He offered me his hand, and I, unthinking and still bowled over by the flutters inside me, took it to stand up and follow him out of the room.

Again. What the hell was wrong with me?

Chapter 7
The Father

"What the hell were you two doing in that room?" Hwarang asked us as soon as we emerged into the courtyard. I widened my eyes in warning, but as usual, my friend took no heed. "Were you rehearsing for after the nuptials?"

It was hard to believe that such icy blue eyes could emit so much fire. Cahki's glance could have melted half of the fjords in the far North. For once I was glad not to be her target. "Do you really want to get my foot up your ass?" she snarled and stepped forward toward Hwarang, who foolishly didn't even flinch. Thankfully, our hands were still connected, and I was able to pull her back before she unleashed her fury on my stupid friend. "Because I'll be glad to do it."

A deep gut chuckle escaped my friend's mouth, and I had to wonder whether he had finally lost his mind. This was not a woman to be trifled with, especially now that she was armed. "I'm starting to like you, Cahki," he said. I was floored. What the hell was he trying to do? "All that fire beneath the ice is very attractive indeed." He turned to me. "If you don't want to marry her, I volunteer as a tribute."

The Northern beauty tried to wrench herself away from my hold, but I held steady. "Stop bickering, for all the gods in heaven," I said, my voice low enough that the monks around us couldn't hear. "We have something to do, and all this fighting is not helping."

Cahki growled, her lips furled like those of a wolf. "I will marry you, prince, but I can't promise I won't kill him at some point." I didn't doubt she would. Hwarang was playing with fire. "Let's go see the Father before I do."

As we walked across the courtyard and up the long, wide stairs toward the temple, Hwarang's laughter followed closely behind us. I shook my head and sighed. "Pay him no mind, Cahki," I told her. "He loves playing these games." Dangerous, unwise games.

Monks who were coming and going up and down the stairs stopped briefly to bow and greet us. Every time, Cahki would pause and stare at them, her brows furrowed. "Why are all the monks so young?" she asked finally. "I haven't seen a single elder since I arrived. They all look like teenagers."

I smiled. "They don't age physically," I explained, oddly thrilled that I knew something she didn't. "Their magic and cultivation keep them young on the outside."

"They don't age?" she exclaimed. "So they are immortals?" Turning her head in my direction, Cahki had her lips pursed into an "O", and, for the first time since I met her, she looked like the young woman she was, innocence in her blinking eyes. Charming.

What am I thinking?

Shaking like a wet dog, I forced my gaze to move away from her. "Not immortal. They do live longer than most humans, but they die like every other living creature. They just never look old until the souls are ready to leave their bodies." The flutter in my belly made me speed up my step. The sooner we talked to the Father, the better. Once we were married, we didn't have to be with each other as often.

"Interesting," she mumbled as she matched my stride. "Can't wait to meet this master of theirs. Does he also look like a young man?"

I swallowed the knot in my throat. "No, he is said to look ancient, but I have never actually seen him," I answered, keeping my eyes focused on what was in front of me. "Legend goes that he uses his magic to keep his monks healthy and thriving, thus his body ages much quicker than the others while his soul strengthens."

Cahki clucked her tongue. "Fascinating give and take," she said. "Now I'm really curious. Let's hurry." She took off at a run, and I stopped, stunned by her agility and beauty as she skipped steps despite her small stature. She turned back and yelled, "Are you coming or what?"

Two monks guarded the door to the temple, but they didn't stop us as we crossed the arched doorway, leaving my friend behind. It was no wonder; the sudden charge of energy that ran along my skin told me there was strong magic protecting the place. We traversed the wide, rounded atrium and headed to what seemed to be an altar on the other end, our shoes clicking on the plain white marble floor. It was a simple, if large, space with hardly any decorations or furniture. At what I'd thought was the altar, there was instead a wide, unadorned wooden throne where a small ancient man sat. The tuft on top of his head and the orange robes marked him as a monk, while his apparent old age told me this was *Abeoji*.

"What are your intentions?" The man's voice crackled as if the simple task of speaking was too exhausting. His wrinkled skin seemed to be made of old, soft leather that had seen better days.

Both Cahki and I went on our knees and bowed all the way to the floor. "Father, we thank you for receiving us today." I had rehearsed those words so many times, it felt strange to actually say them to him. "We seek an enchanted marriage from you, if you are willing to bestow it."

"Why?"

The question was unexpected, and I stuttered a bit, not sure how to answer. The Northern woman raised her head and answered instead. "There are those who would force us apart, Father."

I stole a glance at her, surprised by her words. The old man was silent for a long moment, as if thinking it over.

"In your hearts, this is what you desire?" the ancient monk finally said, his eyes opening for the first time, revealing milky eyes with no pupils. He was blind.

"It is," I replied, trying not to think of the import of that decision. Only natural death would separate us after such a union.

Another long pause.

"Then you shall have it," he finally said. "I will marry you tomorrow at noon." He closed his eyes and said nothing further.

By tomorrow noon I would be forever and irrevocably tied to a woman who wanted nothing but to see me dead.

"I will not wear such a thing." Cahki had been yelling at the poor monk for over half an hour as he tried—very much in vain—to convince her to wear the traditional embroidered white veil the South Kingdom women wore at their weddings. "Why should I cover my face on my own wedding? I want to be able to see everything clearly."

Hwarang laughed. "It's for good luck, Cahki," he explained once again. "It's a symbol of love, fortune, and fertility."

"And why would I need that? Especially the fertility bit?" she asked, a little growl punctuating each word. "There won't be any children."

After a restless night and tired from the trip, I stood up from the chair where I had sought refuge in a corner and yelled out, "Enough!" Every face turned to me, expressions frozen in surprise. "Everyone leave, please. I will talk with my bride alone." Not that I thought I could convince her of anything, but any level of quiet would be welcome at that point.

After a moment's hesitation, everyone filed out the door, throwing worried backward glances. I closed the door behind them and had to duck as soon as I turned around to avoid being hit by what I thought to be a cushion but was in fact the veil wadded up into a large ball.

"*You* wear it if it's that important," Cahki said, crossing her legs and setting her lips into a firm line. "I want to go into this farce of a marriage with my eyes wide open."

Bending down to pick up the discarded veil, a beautiful, long piece of white silk embroidered with two wild geese entangled in an embrace, the symbol of love and fidelity, I said, "If you don't want to wear it, don't," I said. "But there is a chance the Father might reconsider his decision to marry us."

She cocked her head to one side. "Because of a stupid veil?"

"Because of what the veil stands for: love and the desire to stay faithful to each other," I explained as I folded the delicate piece of cloth. "He might interpret your refusal to wear it as lack of love. This kind of marriage is binding and not to be taken lightly. He wouldn't want to be responsible for tying two people together if they are not fully invested."

Cahki digested that information for a while, biting on one of her nails, eyes lost in space. I waited patiently. If there was something I had learned about my wife-to-be, it was that there was no pressing her. The more you pushed, the more she pushed back. Give her some space, and there was a chance, however slight, that she might relent.

"All right, give me the stupid veil," she said, stretching out her arm toward me. I took a step forward and handed her the cloth and watched her as she clumsily draped it over her head and face. "Now I look like every blind idiot who marries someone they were told to." I couldn't help the little smile that tickled the corners of my mouth. She stood up and twirled slowly. "How do I look? Dumb enough for you?"

Dumb was not a word I'd use to describe her, but the veil was askew, and it was driving me crazy. I took yet another step in her direction and reached out to straighten it. She stopped moving and took a step back, as if startled. "I'm just going to fix it. It's all crooked," I assured her.

She fidgeted on her feet and then clasped her hands behind her back, unspoken permission for me to do it. The top of her head only came up to my neck when I reached out around it to tug on the fabric so that it fell more elegantly over her face. The subtle scent of mint hit me, and I closed my eyes for a deeper whiff. How could this wild creature from the icy fjords who hadn't seen a bath in almost a week smell so good? Better even than Chae-yeong.

I pulled back, my heart thumping. Why would I think of Chae-yeong as I am getting ready to marry someone I barely know? My hands shook as I stood there like an idiot, staring at a veiled Cahki and denying the truth; wasn't I doing all of this—trying to depose my father by all means necessary—because of Chae-yeong? It had nothing to do with how I was beginning to feel toward the Northern beauty. Right?

Cahki raised the hem of her veil and squinted at me. "Are you all right? You look a little green around the gills."

Part of me wanted to laugh at her usual strange choice of words, but the rest of me was in panic mode. I couldn't—*wouldn't*—develop feelings for this crazy stranger. "I'm fine," I rushed to say, turning away from her and looking for something to do that didn't involve my bride. "We should go over what we have to say during the wedding ceremony." That should keep me from trouble, I hoped.

For the next few minutes, she recited the words I taught her, her lips twisted into a sneer. "These lines are so cheesy," she protested more than once. "Why can't we come up with our own? Back home the vows are simple and more personal."

"We have to stick to the script if we want the curse to work," I explained. "Any deviation from it, and we might mess it up." She snorted but repeated the words once again before I said, "It's time to go to the Father. Are you ready?"

I heard her approach from behind me, her footsteps light on the stone floors. "As ready as any girl can be who is about to marry an idiot prince to gain her freedom." Well, you couldn't fault her for her honesty. "It sounds contradictory somehow," she mused as she walked past me and out the door.

I shook my head, a smile sneaking its way to my lips. One thing was certain: being married to Cahki would be anything but boring.

Chapter 8
The Wedding

B efore I could blink, I was married to Sung-jin.

Now I would have to kill him after the wedding, which was a bit awkward and would make me a widow at a very early age. Of course, I had to wait a while because if I did it too soon after the wedding, I would lose the protection of the enchanted marriage, but as soon as it looked as if I could make a run for it, I would cut his strong and sexy neck.

Wait! Why did I think that?

I shook my strange thoughts away and allowed the prince—my husband—to lift the veil to reveal my face to him and the rest of the world.

"Kiss the bride, *Jeonha*," the Father said after giving us his blessing.

For once, Sung-jin's expression mirrored what I felt. "What?" I exclaimed, snapping my face toward the old monk. "Why?"

The Father's wrinkled face stretched into a smile. "It's how you'll seal the enchantment," he explained. "Kiss each other now."

After an initial paralysis brought on by shock, I started to turn around to flee, but my new husband gripped my wrist and stopped me. "It's necessary," he whispered, his eyes open wide in warning. "It's only a kiss."

I did not kiss random people, and just because I had agreed to this charade out of survival instincts did not mean I was willing to kiss this man now. Even if he was unbearably handsome and had the fullest, best-shaped lips I had ever laid eyes on.

Oh, gods, I'm losing my mind.

I gulped and looked at the shriveled-up monk. "Do we really have to?" I asked, fully expecting him to say no. But he nodded with purpose, and I had to face my husband. I swallowed hard again, not able to take my eyes from his lips. I sighed. "All right, let's get this over with."

Probably afraid I'd lose my nerve, Sung-jin didn't waste any time and lowered his face to mine to cover my lips with his. They were warm and soft, barely touching mine and yet sending a storm of lightning all the way down to my toes. Our bodies didn't touch as we stood at least a foot apart. I'm sure we were an odd sight with the prince stretching his neck toward me, connected only by our mouths.

He was the first to pull away, and I almost lost my balance when he did. I kept my eyes closed a few more seconds, relishing the heat his skin had left behind on mine. Unable to stop myself, I licked my lips, desperate to taste him again. The kiss had been too brief.

It's been too long since my last lover.

That was it. It had to be. It could not be that I actually enjoyed the prince's attention or that I was attracted to him, could it? I reminded myself of my mission: keep up with this farce until I had the chance to run back home. That was all. I did not need any difficulties, especially not the emotional kind.

We stared at each other for one second too long before dropping our gazes and straightening. "Done," I declared unnecessarily.

The monk closed his blind eyes and raised both hands, palms turned toward us. "I declare you husband and wife for all eternity, whom no man may put asunder lest he or she want to rile the wrath of the gods. Go, love each other and be fruitful. May your union bring you heaven here on earth."

It was done. I was a married woman, tied to a man I did not love, a man I barely knew from a land far from my own, a prisoner on foreign soil. Anger surfaced, red hot, burning a hole in my chest and making its way up my throat. I raised my eyes to Sung-jin's, and he took a step back, startled by what he saw there.

"Well, husband," I growled between my teeth. "This is the moment when I should tell you I love you, but I don't." The burning in my chest intensified. "In fact, I hate you, Sung-jin. I hate you very much."

Not waiting to see his reaction, I swiveled on my heels and dashed out of the temple, flying down the staircase, not quite sure where I was going other than away from my new spouse. The spouse I didn't want and didn't ask for. The little girl I once was bawled. The heart of that young woman I'd been, who had foolishly wished and daydreamed about love and romance and whom I thought I had eradicated from my soul, shattered.

As the snow lily in my heart shriveled up and was crushed into a powdery mess, the adult me hardened and lusted for retribution. No happy ever after for me or Prince Sung-jin.

"Open the door, Cahki."

I had to give it to him, Sung-jin could be relentless when he put his mind to something. And right now that something was him coming in the room where I had barricaded myself after the wedding. The blasted veil was thrown across the room and lay behind a cupboard where it could remain for eternity for all I cared. I had stuck my head under a pillow and was blissfully steaming in my own juices. The prince had no idea what awaited him if I ever opened that door.

"Go away!" I barked out, muffled by the pillow still sandwiching my head. "Why would I let you in?"

"We need to talk," he said, a hint of impatience in his voice. "And also, the monks are waiting for consummation."

The pillow suddenly flew out of my hands and hit a small ceramic statue on a table. The item teetered for a moment before rolling and crashing down to the floor, exploding into sharp fragments.

"What the hell did you just say?" I yelled out, sitting up on the bed. Had I heard it correctly? They were waiting for marriage consummation. Were these monks totally daft? They couldn't seriously believe this was a real love marriage, could they?

The prince let out a loud sigh. "It's part of the ritual," he explained. "We have to consummate our marriage before they let us go."

I was out of the bed quicker than a lightning bolt from the God of Thunder. I crossed the space between the bed and the door and flung it open. Sung-jin, standing behind it, started. "What consummation? There won't be any touchy stuff in this marriage, remember?" I hoped he could understand my words from within the low growling that carried them.

He sighed again, his lips curving into a tentative smile. "We don't really have to go through with it," he said as if resigned. "We just have to make them believe we did."

My anger abated a smidgen. "How do we do that?"

"We lock ourselves together in that room for a while," he said. "Nothing complicated. They will put two and two together, and in a couple days we can leave the monastery." He paused and glanced at me, a twinkle in his eyes. "Happily married."

I spat out a loud "Ah" and moved aside to let him inside the room. "Walk right in, my not-so-beloved husband. Let's pretend we're having a great time, then, shall we?"

Being stuck in that room with an unwanted husband, however handsome, was unnerving. I could feel tiny sparks covering the whole surface of my body, and my chest was full of something I couldn't identify but that would surely suffocate me. To his credit, the prince sat as far away from me as the space would allow him to and busied himself with reading a book he had brought along with him, his long, strong fingers flipping through the yellowed pages of what was obviously an ancient manuscript. His calm demeanor was setting my teeth on edge. Even though he honored my wish and totally ignored me, something didn't sit well with me. I paced the floor, sat on the edge of the bed, even stretched out over the linens once and tried to take a nap, but nothing I did eased this anxiety inside. My fingers longed to do something, and my legs fidgeted and yearned for movement.

"Can you stay still for a while?" Sung-jin said, his gaze never leaving the pages of the book. "It's really distracting."

Thank you, husband, for handing me the perfect opportunity to let out steam.

"If you dislike it so much, you can always leave and tell the old monk you've changed your mind," I suggested, twisting my lips to the side. "Then, you can take me to a nearby port and put me on a ship to Hvithet." I brushed my hands together as if dusting them off. "Problem solved."

Again, he didn't move his eyes from the pages of the old book. "No can do, my wife. What's done cannot be undone. We're stuck with each other for the perceivable future."

Something about the calmness in his voice—and maybe how he refused to look at me—riled me up. Not thinking, I swiped a pillow from the bed and threw it at his head. He didn't seem surprised and dodged it easily, never even closing the book.

"Why, wife, you seem to be upset about something," he commented in an off-hand way, irritating me further. Sung-jin shook some invisible dust from his sleeve and continued to shuffle through the pages of the manuscript.

I growled again. Loudly, like a pissed-off fjord cat. No reaction from him. I threw another pillow at him, and he ducked for a second time. Seething, I braced my hands on my hips and yelled out, "Will you look at me, Sung-jin?"

For the first time in almost an hour, my husband looked up from the pages and glanced at me with his beautiful dark eyes. Was that a little smile I spotted? Was he mocking me? The bastard thought he was getting to me. Which he was, but I wasn't going to let him know that.

"You look beautiful when you are enraged," he said, closing the book and placing it on top of the nearby table. "But I wish you'd keep it down if we are going to pull out the illusion of married bliss."

I stomped my foot like a five-year-old, closing my hand around the pommel of my dagger. Prince Sung-jin was playing with fire. "You know I could just kill you now, right? I'm no Southern damsel in distress."

He snorted, standing up, the whole length of his tall body stretching out gracefully and yet threateningly as well. "Don't I know it, my wife." His voice was but a whisper now. "However, I feel I should warn you that, since we are bonded by an enchanted wedding, if you do kill me, you won't survive to the top of the hour either."

What? "What do you mean?" Forgetting my wrath for a moment, I focused on him as he leaned against the wall, his arms crossed over his chest.

"'*No man may put asunder.*' Those words apply to us too," he explained. "I kill you, I die. You kill me, you—" He made a cutting gesture with his hand across his neck. "It's terrifying in its simplicity. That's why we don't have to worry about my father making a play for you anymore. He holds his life dearly."

Now I was really pissed off. "You never mentioned that to me," I said, too stunned to think straight. I couldn't kill him. I fucking couldn't put an end to his miserable life without going along for the ride. What kind of hell had I signed up for? "Why didn't you?"

He upturned one side of his lips. "I thought it was implied in the 'no man may put asunder' part of the ceremony," he said as calmly as if he was talking about the weather. "And we did go over the words that we would have to recite and that would be recited to us, didn't we?"

Something inside me exploded. Rushing at him, I pommeled him with my fists, squeals of anger escaping my lips. At first, he did nothing, allowing me to hit him so hard, I was surprised it didn't knock the air out of him. I was a lot stronger than I looked, and I was using my full strength in each pounding, yet he took it without a complaint.

"Why aren't you defending yourself?" I yelled at him, so frustrated I could taste my own bile.

He held my wrists then. Gently. "Because I deserve it," he said, punctuating his words with a cough. He dropped my hands and flattened one of his own to his chest, coughing again.

"Are you okay?" I asked, forgetting about my anger for a moment. I must have hurt him. I scrambled with the ties of his tunic. "Let me see it."

Sung-jin grabbed my hands again, stopping me. "No need," he whispered. "I'm fine. I'm a soldier. I can take it."

I shook his hands away. "No, I don't want you to die," I blurted out. I glanced at him and added, "After all, I don't want to die with you." I think he smiled, but I was already busy opening his tunic to check for the damage I had done to his chest.

"Well, at least now we can tell them without lying that you stripped me of my clothes and took good care of me," he quipped, apparently still feeling well enough to make me mad.

I poked him right where I had punched him, and he groaned. "I don't have to kill you to make you very uncomfortable," I said. I had finally gotten to the last layer of clothing and busied myself opening it. How many layers did these Southerners wear? It wasn't even as cold here as in the North, and yet they wrapped themselves in as many fabric piles as if they were facing a blizzard. I froze as I peeled the last of the cloth from his chest. His white skin was already turning a mottled mess of reds and blues.

"You stupid man," I spat out, pushing him down on the bed. "I might have punctured your lungs, and you never tried to stop me."

He laughed as he fell onto his back. "Wow, wife. I didn't know you felt like that about me." The idiot was still making jokes. "But unfortunately, I'm not sure I can pleasure you tonight."

I was about to snap back at him when his eyes rolled back, and he stopped breathing.

Chapter 9
Kiss of Life

Was I hallucinating? Someone was kissing me. Hard. Almost desperately. And judging by the lovely cool scent of mint, the kisser was my new wife, Cahki. I tried to open my eyes, but I couldn't, as my eyelids were as heavy as lead, but I could feel her touch over my open mouth, her breath hot against my tongue, coating it in sweetness as her lips moved in an odd rhythmic motion, as if she was talking.

The pain I had felt inside my chest before I lost consciousness was fast abating, replaced by warmth and well-being. Something moved inside me, as if shattered and then reformed. I had never felt anything like it, a mixture of pain and comfort. Cahki's lips were soft and warm against mine, her words—because she was definitely saying something—entered my mouth with the power of renewal, of life-giving strength.

"Cahki," I whispered once my voice was working again. She stopped and pulled away, and for one insane moment, I wanted to hold on to her, anchor her to me and never let her go. Instead, I groaned and focused on opening my eyes one at a time. She was sitting next to me in bed, her face distorted by what looked like worry. I had to be dreaming still. There was no way she was worried about me, was there? "What happened?"

My vision cleared, and what worry I thought I'd seen in her expression was gone, replaced by her usual angry scowl. "You passed out, you idiot," she spat out. "Why didn't you defend yourself from my punches? Was it your male ego making you think that a weak woman couldn't possibly hurt you that much?"

I chuckled, which became more of a cough as I tried unsuccessfully to sit up on the bed. "I had every faith in you that you could punch the life out of me, wife," I said, my voice raspy to my own ears. "But I deserved it. I wanted to give you a chance of a small retribution."

Her eyes softened for a brief moment. "You're an idiot. What if I killed you? Do you think I'm interested in dying myself?"

The world swam before my eyes as I shook my head. I tried to sit up again, and this time my wife came to my rescue, grasping my arm and pulling me up until I was sitting against the back of the bed, feeling slightly more alive.

"Why were you kissing me just now?" I asked. There was no reason to beat around the bush. Despite our less-than-desirable situation, we would have to be honest and open with each other if this scheme was to work.

Her crystal-blue eyes opened wide. "That was not a kiss!"

"Fight it as much as you want, my wife, but that was most definitely a kiss." I managed a tiny smile as I rubbed the sore spot on my chest. Strangely enough, it wasn't as sore as it had been before I passed out.

Quicker than the eye, she smacked my shoulder—not as hard as she normally would, I realized. "You wish, Your Idiotic Majesty. That was a whisper." She covered her mouth with a hand as if to stop her own words. "I mean, the breath of life. You had stopped breathing."

A whisper? She had mentioned she was known as the Whisperer back home. Did this have anything to do with that? I decided to let it go for now. "Is that what they call kisses up North?"

The Northern woman grunted and stood up, then stomped across the room to sit as far away from the bed as she could. "Dream on, prince," she said. "Think what you will—it doesn't bother me." I laughed inwardly, stupidly satisfied that I had been able to rile her.

"Well, whatever it was, thank you," I finally said, amusement wiped from my face. "You saved my life."

She let out one of her little growls. "Whatever! I had to do it to protect myself. Don't make too much of it."

But I did. Before I passed out, as liquid gurgled inside my chest and the world began to blur around the edges, I had seen concern in her eyes. Real concern. She wasn't as cold as she wanted the world to think she was. There was a warm heart inside that frosty armor, I was sure of it. She might hate me—I didn't blame her—but deep inside her, there was someone who might, in time, become a true ally. Maybe even a friend.

And that, for whatever reason, made me very happy indeed.

The loud banging on the door reverberated inside my aching head. I must have fallen asleep, half curled up on the bed, covers entangled underneath me. My first instinct was to look for my new wife. I sighed in relief when I found her sleeping body on the floor, rolled into a human ball. I had to smile. I didn't know any women who could sleep like that. What kind of things had she gotten used to up North?

The banging continued, so I rolled out of bed and tentatively stood up, hoping I wouldn't be too weak. Surprisingly, my strength was back in full. My legs held steady, and my chest was no longer achy. I pulled my shirt apart to look at the bruise but found unblemished skin instead. How was that possible? After such a beating, I should at least be black-and-blue.

"Open the freaking door, lovers." Hwarang's voice came through loud and clear. "We have to get moving."

Cahki still slept on, oblivious to all the ruckus my friend was making at the door. I crossed the room to where she was and picked her up in my arms like I had done that first night near the harbor. She didn't stir as I took her to the bed and covered her with the blankets before heading to the door. Just before I opened it, I decided to remove my shirt to make our married bliss more believable.

"Shit, brother," Hwarang said as he stepped into the room. "I thought she might have killed you." He took in my bare chest and then waved a finger in my direction. "That's for the monks' sake, right? You didn't actually consummate, did you?"

I chuckled and grabbed my shirt from the floor just as two monks followed my friend into the room. "What do you think?" I whispered to him before addressing the monks, "My wife still sleeps. It was a—busy night." Hwarang snorted. "Let her sleep a little more while I go say my farewells to the Father."

The two acolytes nodded in agreement and followed me out into the courtyard and up the stairs to the temple. I had to thank the Father for what he had done. The man was no dummy, so I doubted he had fully believed our story. In fact, I was pretty certain there was no kiss requirement for such a wedding. The ancient man had been obviously toying with us, possibly testing our willingness to commit to such a marriage. But he had done it, and for that, I was grateful.

The old monk was sitting on his humble throne as if he had never left it. I bowed deeply and then waited for him to talk first as etiquette demanded. He stared at me for a bit with those unsettling white eyes, and I had to wonder how blind he really was.

"Are you happy?" It was an unexpected question that struck me dumb. "You married and protected the woman who can help you achieve your ultimate goals." How did he know that? "I allowed it because I saw something sparking between the two of you." Yes, her will to kill me as soon as humanly possible. "But my question for you is, are you happy?"

Happy with my wife? With the situation? There was no point in lying, since the man seemed to know everything. "Glad, yes, but not happy. Not yet, anyway." My words surprised me. Not yet? What did I mean by that? Was I talking about the future when I would depose my father and become what I hoped would be a better emperor?

The monk smiled, the skin around his blind eyes crinkling and making him look younger. "You will be," he said cryptically. "And so will your new wife." He paused for a moment and then let out a loud chuckle. "She's a firecracker, isn't she? There won't be any boring moments with her around."

After my initial surprise at his comment, I burst out laughing. He was right. Life beside Cahki would never be dull. Dangerous, yes, but never bland.

"I came to thank you, *Abeoji*, for your willingness to join us in marriage." I kneeled this time and bowed all the way to the ground. "May the gods in all the heavens bless you."

He waited for me to stand up before speaking. "Don't let me down." I raised my eyes to him, confused. Was he talking about my plans to depose my father? "I've joined you both for life. Make it count."

The Father obviously didn't know of Cahki's murderous goals for our marriage. I wouldn't be the one telling him about them. I nodded, a little guilty about lying to this holy man, but I intended to do my best. I just wasn't sure whether my best would be enough.

Chapter 10
Rain

The prince had somehow wrangled an extra horse from the monks after I threw a fit over having to be cooped up inside the carriage once more. I should have kept my mouth shut, because the relentless rain that this part of the Southern Kingdom seemed to be so fond of had soaked me to the bone. But I wasn't about to complain like a spoiled little girl, so I soldiered on, water dripping down from my hair to my eyes, nose, mouth and beyond. My breasts were glued to the tight undergarment they made me squeeze into, and my shoes—which had barely touched the ground since we left the monastery—felt like giant bubbles of mud under and around my feet. If I didn't hate them already, this weather would have put me off these lands forever. For once, I missed the veiled hat I had to wear on my way there.

"Why don't you wear the hat?" I swore that Sung-jin sometimes read my mind. "Or go in the carriage. You'll catch a cold."

I shook my head in protest, and rivulets of water sprang from my hair into the air. "I'm not a greenhouse flower, my husband." I always put as much sarcasm into that last word as possible. It didn't seem to faze him, unfortunately. "I can handle it as well as any of you."

There was no way he was comfortable in his soaked clothes, especially under the military breastplate he had insisted on wearing, but he exuded an air of ease and calm that set my nerves on edge. Even wet as a river rat, he looked devastatingly handsome and put together.

I hated him.

He shrugged. "Suit yourself, but don't blame me later." I would so blame him for every little thing that befell me. "We're still a couple hours away from our night stop."

"I'm used to the arctic air; this is nothing for me." Lies, all lies. Yes, I was used to days and nights in the freezing fjords of the North with little more than blankets and a meager fire to warm my bones, but at least it was a dry coldness, not this wet misery we were riding through. "Does it rain like this here all the time?"

"Just nine months out of the year," Hwarang answered. "Why? Can't Your Royal Toughness handle a little water?"

I opened my mouth to curse him out but was interrupted by the prince, who answered my question truthfully. "Only in the raining season, three months out of the year." He threw a warning glance at his friend who smirked like the asshole he was. "By next month the rains will stop."

"And then you'll wish they didn't," Hwarang added with a little chuckle. "I predict you'll be praying to your gods for a little downpour."

I really, really hated him even more than I did my royal husband.

"You're the one who will be praying I don't sneak up to your room at night," I said with one of my usual growls. My mother always chided me for them. "It's not ladylike, my love," she would say. Silly advice from a woman who had married a fjord pirate and lived in the middle of an ice kingdom.

Hwarang's hand flew to his chest as he gasped dramatically. "Did you hear that, Sung-jin?" he exclaimed. "She wants me. I swear I would never betray you, my liege and brother. Even if she threatens me with death, I will never lay a finger on her."

I screamed, enraged and frustrated. "Stop twisting my words, idiot! If I ever sneak into your room at night, it won't involve any kissing, I promise you." I hated that he was able to rattle me so easily, but at least it made for less boring travel.

Sung-jin shook his head, droplets of water flying in every direction. "For all the gods' sake, will you two just give it a break? My ears are ringing from riding between the two of you."

I glanced at him sitting on the saddle straight and steady even as the horse trotted over mud puddles and holes on the flooded road. This weird need to needle him assailed me suddenly. "Aren't you afraid you're going to rust inside that armor?"

Through the curtain of constant rain, I saw his lips quirking up at the corners. "This metal doesn't rust," he said. "I will have a set made for you after we arrive in the city. For protection."

Why did he always retort to my barbs with something bordering on the nice and caring? It infuriated me that I couldn't rattle him like I could his friend. "I don't need protection." Stupid comeback. We all knew I did. At least until I secured a way back North.

He ignored me. "This chest plate is made from a special metal that does not rust and is tougher than any weapon wielded against it. I will have one custom-made for you, no arguments." His words were like a giant final period at the end of a discussion. His royal blood came through loud and clear.

For once I didn't say anything. But if he expected me to thank him, he had another thing coming.

"Stop!" The male voice rang in my ears, too close for comfort in the upstairs hallway of the inn.

We all turned around to face an imperial guard, majestic in his silver armor that was prettier and more ornate than practical. Hwarang, of all people, placed himself between me and the guard.

"What do you want, soldier?" he asked, looking the fiercest I had ever seen him. He was a warrior after all.

"Step out of the way, sir," the guard ordered. "We're looking for that woman."

My blood froze. The moment I feared was here. No longer traveling with a veil, my white hair was exposed to the eyes of the world. I just hadn't expected to be caught on our first night on the trip back. We had purposely picked a different inn from the one we had stayed in on the way to the monastery, hoping no imperial guards would be there. Postponing the inevitable was not possible, it seemed.

"You must be mistaken," Hwarang said, still blocking me from view. "This is my friend's wife."

The guard strode toward us, unsheathing his sword, and my hand flew to the hilt of my dagger where it was hanging over my hip. "Move out of the way, sir."

Just as the guard pointed the sword at my unexpected protector, Sung-jin stepped around us to stand before the guard. "What's the problem, soldier?"

The man did a double take, surprised at first and then stunned as he recognized the crown prince. He went down on one knee and lowered his head. "*Jeonha*, I didn't see you. Forgive me," he said. "We're here looking for a fugitive for the emperor."

I had to admire the prince's royal presence, standing so tall I could have sworn he had grown an inch or two. "And what does that have anything to do with us?" he asked, never giving the guard permission to stand up.

"The woman with you...." He hesitated. "She's the one we are looking for. She's the Northern woman the emperor has bought for his harem."

Sung-jin was silent for a moment and then burst out laughing. "My wife? You think my wife is a fugitive?"

The guard blinked furiously for a few seconds, his mouth open as if he was about to say something but had thought better of it. Fidgeting in place, the man fought for the right words. "But *Jeonha*, you're not married," he finally said in what sounded closer to a squeak than words. "And the female fugitive is a Northerner with long white hair just like that one." He pointed at me as I stood behind both the prince and his friend.

My new husband made a production of turning halfway around to look at me and then turning back to face the royal guard. "I just returned from the Daemeoli monastery where I married this lovely woman. She's my wife now, not a fugitive and certainly not headed to my father's harem."

The man, still on his knee, said after a moment of hesitation, "Forgive me, *Jeonha*, I didn't know." The other two guards who had approached during their conversation also dropped to their knees, heads bowed in deference. "Greetings, *Gongjunim*," they all said in unison.

"It's not me you need to apologize to," Sung-jin said, that royal tone in his voice that made my insides quiver—in delight or disgust, I couldn't tell. He pointed at me, and I took that for an invitation to come forward.

The three soldiers bowed lower and exclaimed, "Forgive us, Crown Princess Consort." They stayed down and repeated, "*Wang-Gwan Gongju*, please forgive us."

After a moment of shock, I moved forward a few more steps and gestured toward them. "Please, stand. No need to apologize. You didn't know."

The men slowly stood, their cumbersome armor clanking. They bowed slightly, their hands clasped together in front of their chests. "Thank you, *Wang-Gwan Gongju*, you're gracious and magnanimous. Congratulations on your recent nuptials." I sneaked a glance at my husband, who had somehow managed not to crack a smile of satisfaction through the whole scene. Was the man made of ice?

The first guard stepped forward. "*Jeonha*, what do we do now?" he asked, his already pale face now positively ashen. "Your father will punish us if we return without the fugitive."

At that moment I was sorry for the poor guards. The little I had learned about the emperor told me he was ruthless and cruel. Someone would pay dearly for our marriage.

"Delay your return," the prince suggested. "Continue the search for a couple more days while we make our way to the city. Pretend you never met us, and let me be the one to break the news to my father."

The relief on the man's face was only marginal. Something told me he would still be punished and he knew it. However, he bowed graciously and thanked the crown prince before heading out of the inn.

"What's going to happen to those men?" I asked, not sure why I cared. After all, these people were my captors, very willing to truss me up like a baked hen on a silver plate and hand me to their awful ruler.

"They will most likely be beaten to within an inch of their lives," Hwarang answered, all the usual playfulness gone from his voice.

I glanced at the prince, watching him as his Adam's apple bobbed up and down his throat, his lips squeezed tightly together. "I'll do my best to have them spared" was all he said. He turned around, a dark cloud over his eyes. "Let's rest for the night. We have a long day ahead of us tomorrow."

I didn't argue this time, my stomach tied in knots as I fully realized what the prince had done by marrying me. Not only had he saved me from the hands of a terrifying monster of a man, but he had also sacrificed his peace of mind to ensure a better future for the kingdom and all his people.

I did not envy him a bit.

Chapter 11
The Emperor

The storm would hit any moment now.

I paced around my room, my hair still wet from the bath I had taken as soon as I arrived at my courtyard. To give credit where it was due, our small staff had acted as if bringing a strange woman into my palace was an everyday occurrence. Hwarang had instructed them not to mention her presence to anyone. Not that they would do it. None of them were fans of my father. Cahki, with her beautiful white hair and crass language, had quickly endeared herself to the servants, her tone of voice toward them the complete opposite of how she talked to me and Hwarang. The real thunder and lightning would come from the imperial palace, not from my loyal staff.

The word restlessness didn't quite describe what I was feeling. Hwarang had run to my father's quarters to officially let him know of our arrival, even though I had no doubt his many eyes and ears had already informed him of it. After all, trying to conceal my new wife on our way back home was like trying to tame the legendary white deer. The veiled hat was often off her head, and she had a penchant for talking to strangers and asking them questions. All I had left to do was wring my hands until they were sore and wait.

"You look worried, Sung-jin." I turned around to face my wife, fresh out of her bath and looking beautiful with her long white hair still wet and loose over her shoulders. She had put on a simple white shift over her slim body and had no shoes on her feet. "I like it."

The corners of my lips lifted. "Glad you're happy about my discomfort," I quipped, dropping into a nearby chair. "But you might want to put on some more substantial clothing because we will be summoned to my father very soon, I'm sure."

She chuckled, throwing a long strand of her hair behind her shoulder. "I thought we would rub salt on that open wound of his and let him see what he's missing." She was reckless and shameless, but inside me something stirred as she ran her hand down the front of her own body.

"Don't play with fire, wife," I warned her, heat rising to my neck. "He might not touch you that way for fear of what will happen to him, but if you tease him too much, he wouldn't think much of killing both of us out of spite." I swallowed hard as my eyes met the smoothness of her bare neck. I waved a hand at her to hide the rush of blood to my cheeks. "Go put on something appropriate."

She snorted. "Your people are so prudish," she stated, turning to the dresses I had one of the female servants lay out on the bed. "At home we are so much more easygoing."

I stood up. "I'll call a servant to help you dress."

"No need. You do it." My feet froze in place. What was she asking me to do? I turned a confused face toward her. "What?" she asked. "It's not like I'm naked. All you need to do is lift this damn heavy dress over my head and help me with the ties. Why bother the servants?" Her lips stretched into a wicked smile. "You're my lawful husband, after all, aren't you?"

Cahki was a devilish creature. Did she know how my body woke every time she walked into the room? Was she aware of the heat that ran through my veins at the sight of even an inch of her skin or the sky in her eyes?

Nevertheless, I wouldn't give her the satisfaction of knowing I was attracted to someone who would sooner see me dead than in her arms. "Sure, why not?"

I took the dress she gave me and lifted it up. I was a full head taller than she was, but I still had to step close to be able to slip the dress over her. Too close. My chin touched the top of her head, and I stepped back as if touched by fire. She tilted her face up in surprise. Our eyes met, and I almost dropped the dress as my fingers went numb. We were both still for a moment, and I could have sworn I heard my heart slam against my chest.

She was the first one to talk. "Are you going to stand there all day? Your arms will hurt."

Damn! I looked like an idiot with the dress hanging from my raised hands. I hastily slipped it onto her, grateful that it covered her eyes in the process. I needed a minute to regain my composure.

"Will you pull this thing down? I can't breathe." Her annoyed voice was muffled by the several layers of fabric of the dress that now covered her whole face. I gave it a gentle tug, and it slid down into place. She blew a loud exhale. "Shit. How do your women put up with this crap every day?"

I had no answer, so I circled behind her to tie the dress, my fingers brushing her skin under the thin cloth of her undergarment, my heart still thudding away like a horse out of control.

Despite my shaking fingers, I finally finished tying all the laces of her dress. I took a long breath. "There," I said unnecessarily. "You need shoes and your hair done." She opened her mouth, but I stopped her. "I don't do hair. I'll call the servant."

Was I imagining things, or was that disappointment in her eyes? "No need. I can do it myself."

I sat back down and watched her as she combed her hair into a long braid before coiling it on the top of her head and securing it with a simple white jade pin. Either by accident or artifice, two long strands of hair came loose from the bun to frame her fiercely beautiful face. Cahki had picked the simplest of the dresses and wore no ornaments on her ears or neck, yet she looked stunning, a ray of sunshine in the bleak rainy season.

A loud knock on the door snapped me out of my paralysis. It was Hwarang.

"Brace yourselves," he said as soon as I opened the door. "The storm just turned into a typhoon."

We had gone over what to tell my father a million times on our way back from the monastery, yet I couldn't help wondering if, once under the stress of being interrogated by the cruel man who ruled my kingdom, Cahki would cave and mess it all up. She didn't seem the kind to be easily intimidated, but the emperor could scare a monster.

Despite the urgency of the summons, we had been waiting in the throne room for over thirty minutes while my father obviously made the point about who was in charge. Cahki was beginning to fidget, her feet squeezed into satin shoes she was not used to and a dress cinching her tightly above her breasts.

"Stop fidgeting," I whispered to her as we stood in front of the steps leading to the throne, an ostentatious chair made of gold and enclosed in a giant crown made of gold spikes. My father would never be accused of being subtle.

"My feet fucking hurt," she whispered back. "Where the hell is your father?"

As if on cue, one of the ceremonial guards yelled out, "His Majesty, Emperor of the Southern Land." My father, dressed to the hilt in expensive furs, velvets, and gold-embroidered cloth, came through the side door and climbed to his throne. My stomach churned as I watched him slowly make his way up the steps, not once deigning to glance our way. Even as he sat down on the padded throne, his eyes never turned in our direction.

Cahki did it before I did: she fell to her knees and bowed until her forehead touched the floor. I followed suit, glad that for once she had actually paid attention to my directions.

We waited for what seemed like an eternity, our foreheads and knees aching against the cold marble floor. He would make us well aware of the error of our way.

"Get up," he finally ordered, sounding annoyed as usual. We did as he asked and stood beside each other, arms touching but not daring to blink. "Care to explain why you are now married to my concubine, son?" he asked.

I bowed my head slightly before saying, "Father, I had no idea she was headed to your harem when I met her while on a hunting trip." The lie came easily, and despite the nerves that made me quiver inside, the more I spoke, the easier it became. "I fell for her, and since we were in Daemeoli territory, I decided to get married there."

Satisfaction filled me as my father flinched at the mention of the monks. "Daemeoli? You got married at the monastery?"

Nodding, I continued. "Yes, Father. I was so taken by the beauty of my wife that I decided to make our relationship permanent." I put extra stress on that last word. "We would love to have your blessing, Father." About as much as we would love to be dipped in honey and fed to the bears.

My father squinted. "What kind of wedding did you have?" He leaned over a bit as if anticipating the answer.

"An enchanted wedding, Your Majesty," I answered, refraining from looking too happy. "Can we have your blessing? Since I inadvertently stole one of your concubines, my wife will gladly serve you in other ways to make up for it."

I could almost hear Cahki growl, but she stuck to the plan and said, "Your Majesty, I would be honored to serve you in any way you see fit." Except the way he really wanted. Sex with an enchanted bride would bring him definite pain, even death. Even my deviant father wouldn't risk it.

The emperor grunted. "I will think on it and let you know," he said. "I'm displeased with you, son. Check in with the Discipline Master. I've given orders for your atonement."

I knew it was coming. My father would never let something like this slide without some kind of retribution. But in the big picture of what I was hoping to accomplish with this marriage, this was a small price to pay. "I accept your wisdom. Thank you for being so forgiving of my wrongdoings." I bowed again. He dismissed us with a wave, and we wasted no time getting out of there as quickly as we could.

"Who the hell is the Discipline Master?" Cahki asked me as we rushed down the steps from the throne room and into the main courtyard.

"The minister in charge of doling out punishment." I knew that was a nonanswer, but I didn't want to talk about it with her.

She stopped suddenly, making me skid on the stone floor to look at her. "What do you mean, punishment?" Cahki stood with her hands on her hips, suspicion in her eyes. "You told me this was a sure thing. That your father wouldn't be able to touch me or hurt me in any way."

I gulped. "That's right. He won't touch you." Why was I so reluctant to tell her what was about to happen? It wasn't as if she cared about me. Given the opportunity, she would most likely join forces with my father in this matter. "That doesn't mean he can't punish me for having gone against him."

"What kind of punishment?" She had gone very still, which scared me. Cahki was not the quiet, unmoving kind. It was like the quietness of a volcano before eruption.

I lowered my eyes and turned to resume my way across the courtyard, but she reached out to grab my arm. I sighed and glanced at her. "Not sure yet, but it will probably involve a whip or a cane of some kind."

Her mouth fell open. "He's going to beat you up?" The shock in her voice made me happy, fool that I was. Was it possible she actually cared a little?

Nodding, I said, "At the very least. He may have me put in the sensory deprivation box as well."

My new bride was silent for a long moment, her eyes searching mine as if expecting me to suddenly burst out laughing and tell her it was all a joke. It wasn't. My father was a cruel man who cared about one thing only: himself and his power—so, I guess, two things.

"Go back to our quarters," I told her. "I will send Hwarang to look after you while I'm—" I faltered. Healing? Licking my wounds? Too weak to walk to my own place?

Cahki shook her head. "You don't give me orders, husband," she said with the fierceness I had come to know well. "I'm coming with you."

Chapter 12
Punishment

I didn't know what was harder to believe: the fact that a father would order such a punishment for his own son, or that Sung-jin accepted it as unavoidable.

My new husband rushed to the Ministry of Discipline as if he were running towards a coveted reward. "It's better to get it done and over as quickly as possible," he said, not looking at me as we approached a large dark building that screamed pain from every black brick of its windowless walls. "The sooner I recover, the better."

"Recover?" I screeched rather than asked, my stomach fisting and threatening to empty itself over the cobblestone of the courtyard. "What exactly are they going to do to you?" An odd sense of panic rose in my chest. Why was I so concerned with this? It wasn't as if we were really a couple or that I had any intentions of sticking around for long.

"We'll find out soon," he said, beginning to climb the ominous stairs leading to the Ministry of Discipline. Even the sign featuring the name of the building was bleak, with faded white lettering over a pitch-black background. "Are you sure you don't want to go back to your room?"

Incapable of further speech, I nodded and followed him up the steps. The building was as dark inside as it was outside, lit only by flaming torches that lent a strange odor to the air. The guards at the doors bowed and greeted the prince, but Sung-jin didn't reciprocate. He was on a mission, heading toward whoever the Master of Discipline was. We didn't need to go far. At the wall opposite to the entrance, a small man with a prominent nose sat behind a large table packed with papers.

"Master," Sung-jin said as soon as he reached the table. The man raised his eyes to the prince, a wicked smile stretching across his lips as he recognized him. "I'm here for my punishment."

How could Sung-jin be so calm? I would be raving mad at the injustice of it all, but my husband seemed to have accepted—almost embraced—it.

The man stood up, confirming my first impression that he was very small indeed, shorter than I was and even thinner. This was the Master of Discipline? He looked as if he couldn't hold a sword, much less exact physical punishment on anyone else.

"His Majesty the Emperor has given me his orders, *Jeonha*," he said in a sticky honeyed voice. I disliked him instantly. "He has ordered fifty lashes with the paddle, all in one session."

My heart jumped out of my mouth. "What the fuck? No one can survive that."

Both the master and the prince stared at me. "Who is this? And why is she here?" the master asked, his disdain for females clearly plastered on his face and tainting his words as he scanned me from head to toe.

The prince pointed at me. "This is my wife, and she insisted on being present today." The little man opened his mouth to protest, but my husband interrupted him. "You will abide by her wishes." The authority in Sung-jin's voice caused goosebumps to erupt all over my skin. "She is the crown prince's new consort, and you *will* show her the respect she has the right to." Heat invaded my cheeks and I hoped he couldn't see it.

The master bowed slightly, his mouth twisted in disgust. "Of course, Your Highness. Shall we proceed to the discipline room?"

Sung-jin turned to follow the man. That's when he grabbed my hand and pulled me along. The touch of his skin set me on fire, but I didn't pull away. Instead, I closed my fingers tightly around his and followed a step behind, my heart beating so loudly, I was sure the disgusting little man in front could hear it.

After fiddling with a gigantic set of keys hanging from an iron circle, the master unlocked and opened the heavy wooden door and invited us to enter. I couldn't help having the feeling we were walking into the gaping mouth of a monster of some kind as we stepped into the dark room beyond. Once inside, my eyes adjusted to the dim light, and I saw what were obviously tools of torture, some of which had not been cleaned yet and were covered in dry blood.

I pulled on Sung-jin's hand and whispered, "Can't you use your magic and convince him not to do this?"

He shook his head. "My father would find out sooner or later, and then it would be even worse," he whispered back. "Might as well take care of it now."

"You sound like you're talking about something trivial," I protested a little too loudly. "This place doesn't bode well, my dear husband."

The Minister of Pain, as I had titled him in my head, gestured toward a long, low wooden bench narrower than a man's girth. Sung-jin dropped my hand and began removing his top tunic, dropping it to the floor and then shrugging off the undershirt. Suddenly the prince was standing half naked before me, and the fire in my veins flared as if fanned. He was as handsome without his clothes as he was with them. His chest and arms were shaped by lean but well-toned muscles that continued down his torso and into the waist of his loose pants. But when he turned around, his bare back now in view, I gulped; ugly, thick scars crisscrossed the muscles on his back this way and that in a variety of colors that proclaimed their different ages. Where had he gotten those? They didn't look as if they had been caused by sharp weapons.

Sung-jin stretched along the bench on his belly and waited. I was just about to ask him what he was waiting for when two burly guards walked in. The first one carried a rope, the other a thick long-handled paddle that was almost the man's height. The one with the rope crouched by the bench and proceeded to tie Sung-jin's wrists together underneath it and then his feet. I wanted to scream, tell them to stop, but the prince had turned his face toward me and begged me to stop with his soulful dark eyes.

It got worse.

As soon as he was tied and immobilized, the second guard stepped forward and raised the thick wooden paddle in the air over Sung-jin. I did scream then and ran forward to stop him, but a pair of strong hands circled my waist and held me in place.

"You aren't helping him," a voice whispered in my ear. It was Hwarang, who had somehow sneaked into the room without me noticing. Then again, my eyes hadn't left my new husband and the tool that was about to lash into his bare back.

I screamed, nevertheless. "Stop! He's the crown prince. How can you do that to a human being?" Hwarang held me fast no matter how many times I kicked him.

The paddle came down hard.

Again.

Again.

I screamed and cried until my voice was hoarse and eyes blurry. It didn't make a difference. The paddle kept slamming onto his back, over and over again until his old scars opened up and bled and new wounds erupted from cracked skin. Sung-jin didn't make a sound. He buried his face on the wood as his body bounced off the bench every time that damn paddle pounded his body. At some point between the twenty-fourth and the thirty-first lash, the prince's body went slack, the muscles on his arms relaxing and his hands drooping beneath the bench.

He had passed out.

I fell to my knees, taking Hwarang along with me, and sobbed. There were still twenty lashes to come. He was as good as dead.

There was no way he would survive such a beating. No matter how strong he was, that was not the usual paddle used by parents to discipline their children. The one that kept coming down on Sung-jin's back was at least a couple inches thick and a good five inches wide. The blows were delivered in a rather indiscriminate way, sometimes hitting his buttocks, but often targeting his lower back. I watched, horrified, as the paddle came down on his upper back and across his shoulders a few times. My new husband's organs would be liquefied by the time they were done.

"Let me go, Hwarang," I pleaded. He was still holding on to me, determined not to let me throw myself at the man paddling the prince. We were both on our knees now, his arms securely around my waist. "He's your best friend. Are you just going to watch him die?"

"I'll explain later," he whispered in my ear. "He'll survive, I promise."

His words made no sense to me as I watched the executioner bring down the paddle one last time. Blood oozed from the open wounds, and his skin was a mottled mess of bruises in the few places it wasn't cracked. He was still unconscious, his face so pale, he was almost transparent.

"The punishment has been dealt," the obnoxious Master of Discipline pronounced in a self-important voice. "You're free to take him home."

Hwarang didn't let me go until the master and his minions were out of the room. He knew I would throw myself at them and let them know exactly how I felt. As soon as they left, the arms that held me in place relaxed and let me go. I crawled to the platform where Sung-jin lay, dragging my skirts through the blood that dripped from his body. I rested my ear on his back. Miraculously, he was still breathing, however shallowly, and his heart sounded as strong as that of someone who had not just been beaten half to death. This prince was tougher than I had thought.

"I'll carry him," Hwarang said. He helped me up to my feet, my satin slippers sliding on the wet floor beneath me. "Are you okay to walk?"

Normally I would have stabbed him with my glare, but I didn't have the energy. I was emotionally drained and annoyed for allowing myself to feel that way. I simply nodded, wiping my bloody palms on my dress.

Hwarang lifted his friend as if he weighed nothing, and it occurred to me for the first time that he might also have magical powers. I waited for him to go through the door before following him out of that horrible place. I didn't remember how exactly we got to Sung-jin's palace, but as soon as we arrived, a gaggle of servants rushed to Hwarang's aid. Sung-jin was laid stomach down on his bed, and a doctor was immediately summoned. "Not the imperial doctor," Hwarang instructed. "The healer in town."

I sent a servant out to get me warm water and clean bandages. We might not be a real couple, but I was not about to see my ticket out of the Southern Kingdom bleeding to death before me. I shooed a protesting Hwarang away and began cleaning the prince's wounds. It wasn't my first time doing something like this. When you live in a semi-independent kingdom run by a fjord pirate in a mostly frozen part of the world, you learn basic wound-dressing quickly. If the pirates or the old queen's men didn't get you, chances were that ice will.

"How come he survived this?" I asked, my hands busy as I dabbed the wet cloth on a particularly virulent scar that crossed the prince's back from the right shoulder to the left side of his waist. "No human should have been able to do so. Is Sung-jin not fully human?"

Hwarang pulled a chair closer to the bed and sat down, wiping his bloody hands on a clean towel. "Of course he is," he said, his dark eyes narrowed to slits. "I was protecting him with magic."

I raised my eyes to him, surprised. "Magic? What kind of magic? And why would the emperor let you do it?"

He offered me a sad smile. "The emperor doesn't know about my magic," he explained. "At least, not the full story. Sung-jin and I thought we should keep it a secret, and I'm glad we did." He threw the stained towel into the discard bucket. "I can create a sort of protective armor—a barrier of sorts—that won't completely prevent the blows, but it will soften them. He obviously still got hurt, but his organs inside are not destroyed." He stared at his own hands as if expecting them to do something. "That last blow to his upper back would have cost him a lung if I wasn't protecting it."

The idiot was not as useless as I had thought. I hated to admit it, but I was glad Sung-jin—and I—had a friend like him in his court.

"Thank you," I whispered reluctantly as I went back to cleaning the wounds.

Hwarang leaned closer, cupping a hand behind one ear. "What was that?" he said, blinking his eyes. "I thought I heard you thank me."

Throwing a wet cloth at him, I said, "Don't get too cocky. This doesn't mean I like you. Or the prince."

The cloth missed him. "Why, it seemed to me that you do indeed care for your husband," he said, an impish smile on his face. "You sure cried a lot for someone who claims not to care."

I hated him.

"Look, Hwarang," I started, leaning closer to him, daggers in my gaze. "If you ever mention a word of this to the prince, I will cut off your balls and feed them to the pigs." He flinched. "Get it? I was only worried that if he died, I wouldn't have a way back home." Half-truth. As much as I hated to admit it, there was more to it. Seeing the man suffer like that had done something to me. Something deep and irreversible.

"Can we keep my body parts out of the equation?" he said, twisting his lips in disgust. "I won't say a word, but maybe you should be more honest with yourself. You are not as immune to my friend's charm as you claim to be." I raised my hand to hit him, and he pulled away. "You could do a lot worse that having Sung-jin for a husband."

I opened my mouth to reply, but a man dressed in long white robes entered the room, a large square box in his hands. "Where's the prince?" he asked. "I'm Chul Kwok, the town healer."

I stood up to reveal the prince behind me. "I cleaned most of his wounds but had nothing to treat them with, doctor," I explained, discarding the last of the stained cloths.

The man set the box on the table and opened it to reveal a well-stocked medicine bag. He examined the many vials inside until he found one that he seemed to think was the right choice. "This is *Dang-Gui*. It should do the trick."

I watched the healer apply a powder to every wound on Sung-jin's back before turning his attention to the skin under his pants. The healer pulled down on the clothing, revealing more wounds on perfect buttocks. My face burned with embarrassment—not because of the prince's bare butt, but rather due to my physical reaction to it. Was I losing my mind? The man was bleeding from terrible wounds, and I was lusting over him?

"Who will be taking care of his wounds after I leave?" the doctor asked.

"I will," I volunteered, Hwarang's smirk immediately making me regret it.

The healer handed me another vial of the same powder and instructed me on how to do it. "This is angelica root. Apply it twice a day. Do you understand?"

I nodded. I knew what to do. That wasn't why I was so flustered. My one and only worry was how I was to treat him without letting him know my whole body tingled at the sight of his.

Chapter 13
Wounds

I couldn't believe my ears. There was no way in hell I was going to allow my new wife to treat my wounds. Especially not the ones below my waist.

"Stop being stubborn," Cahki said, leaning over me. I scooted further up the bed until my back hit the low wooden headboard. I yelped as my fresh wounds rubbed against the hard surface. "See? You're being stupid. It's not like I'm attracted to you. I have seen plenty of men's butts up North."

I did not doubt it for a second. But this was my ass we were talking about. "Tell the doctor to come do it," I insisted, slapping her hand away from me. "Or Hwarang. He has dressed plenty of my wounds in the past." Some from battle, but also too many inflicted by the Master of Discipline under the orders of my father.

Cahki glowered at me. "He's busy and your wounds need to be treated." She grabbed the edges of the blankets and began pulling them from my fierce grip. "Be a good prince, and turn around so I can do it."

I was still weak from the beating, and she was freakishly strong for her size. With a last push, she took the blankets off the bed and stood beside it, her hands on her hips and a fake pout on her lips. I looked wistfully toward the door one last time, hoping Hwarang would walk in and rescue me from my wife's hands, but no such luck.

"I have a vested interest in your health, my prince," she said, helping me turn around onto my stomach. "If you die or get too weak to be of any use, I lose too. I love my skin a bit too much to let that happen."

I sighed, resigned to expose my ass to her. She touched my skin right underneath the waistband of my pants, and I braced myself for the pain, but she was surprisingly gentle, peeling the silk fabric down and away from my skin. I could feel how the cold air was making it pucker. Cahki pulled away for a few seconds before I felt her touch again, dabbing the angelica powder along the edges of the open skin. Much to my mortification, I hardened against the bed at her touch. I whispered a small prayer of thanks to the gods that all my wounds were on the back side of my body.

A few minutes later, she had moved up to my back, lifting my shirt to reach the skin beneath. "Has your father always treated you this cruelly?"

The question surprised me enough to make me choke on the words for a moment. I took a deep breath. "Always."

"And your siblings?" Her touch was magic, soothing more than just the wounds. Despite all our differences, I felt at home when I was with her. I had never had a home, but this feeling had to be what it was like.

"I have a younger brother." The words were out before I could stop them. Could I even trust her? This was the same woman who wanted me dead and gone as soon as she could escape.

"Where is he?" Cahki asked, continuing her gentle ministrations on my back.

"Away," I answered quietly. Her hands stopped, but she didn't say anything, waiting for me to further explain. "Away from my father. I'll keep him there until he's old enough to endure the emperor's cruelty. My father thinks he died."

Cahki resumed her treatment, working her way up my back. "How old is he now?"

I swallowed hard, my eyes burning as I recalled my little brother being brought up by strangers in a strange land. "He's sixteen."

"Do you see him often?" she asked, her warm fingers brushing over my skin, a tingling trail following their track. I had the odd sensation that my skin was knitting itself together.

"No, he's too far away, and I have my responsibilities here." It sounded like an excuse even to me. The truth was, I was terrified my father would send his minions to follow me there. I couldn't risk having my brother's whereabouts known to the emperor. I had been able to weave a story of his demise and keep the truth from our father.

Silence fell and stayed for a while. I could have sworn Cahki was whispering something under her breath. A prayer? Or maybe she was talking to herself. My wife was not what she had seemed when I first met her, shivering and wet in that lonely corner of the harbor. There were so many more layers to her than those she allowed others to see.

Warmth covered my back like a soft blanket as she pulled the sheets over me. "All done," she said. "Is your father the reason for all of your scars?"

"Most of them," I confessed. "Some were honorably attained in battle."

"Man!" she exclaimed, standing up. "Why do men always have to attain honor solely with battle? Aren't these scars you've got from disobeying a tyrannic ruler just as honorable?" I opened my mouth to protest, but she interrupted me. "Men!" With a huff she walked out of the room.

What had I done now?

"Your dear wife is driving everyone insane," Hwarang declared, slamming his sword onto the table. "Warm up water. Make that bread softer. That's not how you make that lotion." His voice had gone up a few octaves. "For someone who wishes you dead, she sure takes good care of you."

The reality was that Cahki was protecting herself by healing me back to health. Nevertheless, I couldn't be more thankful for her care. She had been so attentive, and thanks to her, my wounds were healing a lot faster than ever, and my strength was almost fully restored.

"Where have you been?" Better to steer away from the subject of Cahki. She seemed to have a weird relationship with my best friend.

"Checking in with our spies," he said, dropping into a chair and crossing a leg over his opposite knee. "Your daddy has been busy since the skirmish at the border."

My ears perked up, and I scuttled backwards a bit on the bed. "What do you mean?"

"He's been conscripting soldiers in every village and prison from here to the border."

Now, that was interesting and disturbing. Why would he need more soldiers when our army was by far the biggest and strongest this side of the ocean? "Why?"

Hwarang shrugged. "Good question. Unfortunately our spies couldn't ferret that info out of their contacts. Maybe your fair lady can. We all know your father has a weakness for females."

Heat rose to my cheeks. "In bed. He's only interested in one thing," I snapped at him, hot liquid anger burning my insides. "I won't allow him to touch Cahki."

My friend lifted his arms to appease me. "No, I don't mean that," he assured me. "He knows something bad will happen to him if he tries. He might be a monster, but he likes himself quite a bit." Hwarang chuckled at his own joke. "I meant you should use her charms to extract that info off the emperor or one of his closest minions."

It was my turn to laugh. "Have you met my wife yet? Charms? She's as prickly as a desert flower."

He nodded in agreement. "And just as beautiful."

It was true. She was. And female beauty, especially the unusual kind, was like catnip for my royal father. Cahki was also highly intelligent and cunning. I had all confidence she would prove to be an awesome asset to our mission. But I had begun to have misgivings about placing her in harm's way. There was no such thing as safety around the emperor. He was known to kill even his most trusted ministers, some of whom were rumored to have shared his bed. He was devious enough to come up with some loophole to the conditions of the enchantment in our marriage and hurt Cahki.

"We have to proceed with extreme caution, Hwarang," I told him. "I don't want anything bad to happen to her."

A sly smile stretched my friend's lips. "Oh, so you do care for her," he quipped.

"I promised I'd protect her," I protested. "Our marriage might not be a real one, but I still made promises to the gods."

"Those promises meant nothing, and I will decide what I'm willing to do or not do." Cahki had walked into my room without us noticing. She stood by the doorway, hands on her hips and wearing her usual scowl. "What makes you two idiots think you can either order me around or protect me? I've been my own protector for a long time."

I stole a moment to take her in. All of her: the transparent blue of her eyes, the snowy avalanche of her hair, her slim, well-shaped figure. My gut burned.

"You've never dealt with my father," I protested weakly.

"In case you haven't heard, I dealt with a ship full of male buffoons," she retorted, crossing her arms over her generous breasts. "Your father is not a big concern."

But he was. The traffickers didn't have magic. My father did. Over the years, he had surrounded himself with men who had magic to make up for the lack of his own.

"Don't be too cocky, wife," I warned. "And never, ever underestimate his cruelty and intelligence."

Those two traits had cost me too much already. Had I not been so confident in my own cunning and powers that I fell right into his trap and lost not one, but two loved ones because of that? It had been a warning, my father had told me, a warning about rebelling against him in any shape or form. "It brings heavy consequences, my boy," he had told me back then, his hands still stained with the blood of my mother. And I didn't heed him even then, walking right into his web of malice.

I shook my head to dispel the memories. No, I would not let that happen to Cahki. No one else would lose their lives because of me.

"Came to treat your wounds," she announced, showing us the small tray with the usual bandages that she had put down on a small table. "Get out of my way, Hwarang." She practically barreled her way past my best friend and sat down on the edge of my bed. "And don't even start with the usual moaning about this idiot doing it, because I will not put my life in his hands." How could such pale, transparent eyes be so fiery? She glanced in Hwarang's direction. "And I might not be able to kill the royal idiot, but I have no problem killing you. So I suggest you keep your distance."

Who were we to disobey such an imperial order?

Chapter 14
Emperor

I hated that I was this nervous.

I'd been summoned by the emperor. An army of servants invaded my quarters with trays covered in makeup, clothing, and shoes. After a torturous hour of being brushed, wiped, massaged, and painted like a doll, I was escorted out by a couple of pompous men whom I guessed served the ruler.

Halfway to the imperial palace, Hwarang intercepted our small procession. "Where are you taking the crown prince's consort?" he asked, placing himself in our path. A tiny smile danced on my lips. Sometimes I liked his less-than-subtle style.

"We have orders from the emperor to bring her to his presence," one of the overbearing servants said, his head slightly bowed. "She's to serve His Imperial Majesty, starting today."

My heart stopped for a moment. I hoped to all the gods that he didn't mean what I thought he meant.

Hwarang raised a hand to stop the servants from continuing their march to the palace. He asked the question hovering in my mind. "What exactly do you mean by 'serve'? She's no concubine, and she's under the protection of an enchanted marriage."

The other servant bowed a couple times. "We know, lord Ki." Hwarang's family name was Ki? "We don't mean serving that way," the servant assured him. "The emperor wants her by his side, that's all. As a companion of sorts."

Everything I knew about this horrible tyrant told me he did not want a companion. So, what exactly did he want with me? Then again, wasn't this what my new husband was hoping for? That his father would take me into the imperial palace so I could spy on him?

Hwarang threw me a worried look. "Does the crown prince know about this?"

"A messenger was sent to him an hour ago," one of the men said. "He did not refuse."

I wasn't sure whether that was a sign that it was safe or if he had been so scared of what his father would do to him, he had no balls to refuse him. Sung-jin didn't strike me as a coward, so I chose to believe it was the former.

"It's all right, Lord Ki." I emphasized his name and was rewarded with a frown. "If my husband thinks it is safe, who am I to disobey?" The quirk of his mouth told me he knew I was bluffing. Hwarang might be an asshole, but he knew I wasn't your regular damsel in distress. I had no doubt he would run to his friend and find out exactly what was going on.

"Maybe I should tag along," he said, his head cocked to the side.

"I'm afraid the emperor wants to see her alone," the other man said with enough authority, you'd think Hwarang was the servant.

With a tiny nod, I agreed to the terms, and Hwarang nodded, too, stepping aside for us. "I will be close by," he whispered for my ears only as I went past. Despite my dislike for the man, I was glad he would be near and ready to protect me if needed. Not that I would ever admit it.

The remainder of the way seemed to be encrusted in tiny, sharp pebbles that pierced through the soles of my feet and into my very heart and soul. I had faced monsters and demons in the frozen fjords of the North. I had to deal with frostbite, avalanches, starvation, and illnesses of all kinds. Never once had I been as anxious as I was now, walking toward the sumptuous imperial palace. What would the emperor want me to do?

Emperor Min—as I found out he was called—was sitting on the same throne where I had seen him the last time, overdressed and wearing an elaborate head contraption that probably stood in for a crown but looked more like a beehive with several spikes poking through on either side and delicate gold chains hanging from their tips. It was ridiculous, but I couldn't laugh. I did as Sung-jin taught me and dropped to my knees to kowtow to the tyrant.

"May Your Imperial Majesty Emperor Min live forever." *In hell, where the other demons lived.*

He grunted. "*Il-eona*," he said. "Get up. No need for ceremony. You're my daughter-in-law now." Fighting the urge to puke, I did as he said and stood up, my legs weak beneath me. "I'm still pissed my son stole you from me, but like the old saying goes, it's spilled milk. You can still be an asset to my palace even if I can't touch you."

Well, so much for subtlety.

"Hear my edict," he said, and another pompous old man stepped forward with a rolled manuscript that he handed to me. I wasn't sure if I was supposed to open it, so I just waited for further instructions. "I'm guessing you can't read." *Fucking patronizing prick.* "It says that you are to come to the palace every day unless otherwise instructed by me. You are to perform menial tasks such as making my tea, serving me meals, giving me massages, and whatever else I deem necessary. Understood?"

Did he really believe all women were dumb? I nodded, biting my lower lip so I wouldn't say something stupid. "*Gamsahabnida*, Your Majesty, for giving me the honor. Do I start today?"

He shook his head. "No, I have some important guests coming," he said. "You will come tomorrow and serve us tea."

So I was now a glorified servant. Better than a concubine, I guessed. I nodded and bowed deeply. "I will be here. Thank you, Your Majesty." He shooed me away as if I were a nuisance, and I backed up a few steps before turning around and leaving the throne room. I wanted to run, but I controlled the urge and walked slowly away from the royal dick who gave me the willies.

As soon as I was at the bottom of the great staircase, I did run. I was going to let my husband know exactly how I felt about being his father's fucking maidservant.

"Are you sure he can't touch me in any way?" I asked for the twentieth time as we sat around the table for our evening meal. Sung-jin was still recovering from his wounds, so we stayed in his room instead of eating in the dining area, which was bigger and more public. "I didn't like the way he was looking at me when I served him tea today. I swear he licked his lips like a fucking wolf eying a sheep."

Hwarang, who barely ever missed a meal with us, chuckled, a large chunk of bread stuck between his teeth. "I bet he did, the old slime. The enchantment doesn't extend to gestures or expressions, you know. I'm sure he's still having wet dreams about you."

My husband kicked his friend under the table. "This is my wife you're talking about," Sung-jin said. "A little respect."

I leaned over the table and batted my lashes at Hwarang. "Why do you think that? Are *you* having wet dreams about me too?" I had never seen such an explosion of red on the face of someone as tanned as Hwarang. His skin was a soft shade of honey, the complexion of someone who spends most of his time outdoors. I almost felt guilty for making him blush so furiously. Almost.

Sung-jin coughed, trying in vain to hide a chuckle. "You two are impossible," he said. "Can't you be in the same room without bickering like siblings?"

"Siblings?" I exclaimed, straightening on the chair. "As if I could ever have a brother this dumb. My parents are too smart to spawn such an idiot."

Hwarang composed himself pretty quickly, I had to admit. "And my parents would never give birth to a wild creature like you anyway." There was nothing wrong with being wild. I was rather proud of it and took it as a compliment.

The prince sighed. "Can we get back to what's important?" he asked, rubbing his brow. "I feel a headache coming on."

I was on my feet and behind my husband's chair before I could think about it. I had been caring for him for the past couple weeks or so, and somewhere along the way, I seemed to have decided it was my responsibility. I told myself it was because caring for him was safeguarding my own life, but my investment in his well-being was starting to irritate me. All he had to do was complain about an ache, and I was there, whispering to him. How pathetic.

"So very touching," Hwarang said with a smirk. "She runs to her beloved husband at the least sign of pain. I'm a little jealous."

My protest was interrupted by Sung-jin's grunt. "I want you to be extra careful, Cahki," he said after throwing an icy glare at his best friend. "Try not to be caught alone with him. He's cunning, and I wouldn't put it past him to find a loophole in the enchantment's terms. Be very careful, and always carry your dagger with you."

I instinctively reached out for the weapon hidden in the folds of my skirts. I had another smaller knife tucked and tied against my thigh. I wasn't going to take any unnecessary risks. "I'll slit his throat if he makes a move toward me, I swear. Dirty old man."

Sung-jin covered my hand lightly with his across the table. "I trust you can protect yourself, but—"

I pulled my hand away, uncomfortable with the heat his touch stirred up inside me. "There will be a feast in two days' time," I told him. "He wants me to entertain the guests with dancing."

Hwarang guffawed. "Can you even dance? You're not particularly graceful."

I killed him with my glare and replied, "I am the best dancer in Hvithet." It wasn't a brag, just a fact. Not that there were a lot of dancers back home. Living in such an icy kingdom did not make for the perfect environment to cultivate the arts. Our people were far too busy with where the next meal might come from or protecting their livelihoods from the few rogue fjord pirates who worked for the queen to take the time to learn poetry or graceful dancing. Dancing happened mostly at festivals and other celebrations and was normally a boisterous affair, having little to do with the arts and a lot to do with the amount of alcohol being consumed.

My husband let a brief look of delight cross his features. "Really? That, I'd love to see."

Caught by surprise, I stuttered for a moment. "Well, y-you won't." I straightened the folds of my skirt, giving myself some time to gather myself together.

I couldn't see the expression on his face because I didn't dare look at him, but his voice was gentle and quiet. "I just might," he said in almost a whisper. "My father invited me to the feast."

Holy shit! It was one thing to dance for an odious old man I wished death on more than anything. It was another thing altogether to dance for the man I was now married to.

Chapter 15
The Dance

My father had gone all out. The party hall was a lavish festival of colors and lights, from the bright red-and-gold lanterns hanging from the high ceilings to the sparkling silky cloths covering the tables on either side of the room. Plates and bowls, piled artistically with delicious and rare foods, decorated every surface as servants dressed in yellows and reds hurried from one table to another, pouring wine from gold-encrusted ceramic pitchers into the equally fragile-looking goblets in every guest's hands. Spirits ran high throughout the whole meal presided over by the emperor, who sat in his usual display of wealth upon a raised dais at the head of the two long lines of tables, but I couldn't share the excitement.

"Stop frowning," Hwarang told me, a glass of wine in his hand. "Your father is going to think you are not enjoying yourself."

"He'd be right," I said, my crankiness seeping out with my words. Cahki had been summoned to the dressing room to prepare for her performance, and my stomach was tied in knots, as I was afraid of what my father might be plotting with this whole exercise. In the few days that my wife had been serving him, not one bit of useful information had been revealed by him or his cronies. I was starting to think this had been a terrible plan that might very well end with Cahki's demise.

"You're normally good at pretending for your father's benefit," Hwarang said, hiding his lips with the glass. "Why can't you do that now?" Unconsciously I stared at the door to the side of the dais from which the dancers would be emerging soon. "Ah, you're worried about pretty Cahki," my friend concluded. "Don't forget that she's just as lethal as she is beautiful. She'll be fine."

I snapped back, much to my chagrin. "My father is putting her on display for all these disgusting men to drool over. It's demeaning." Why was I this angry? Even Cahki herself didn't seem as discomfited as I was. "She's my wife, after all. My father has no right to do this."

Hwarang shoved a large goblet of wine into my hand. "Watch your volume, friend. You don't want your father's cronies to hear you spewing treason, do you?"

He was right, of course. I seemed to be losing my mind, especially on what concerned my wild wife. When it came to her, I had lost all sense of caution or composure, and it was driving me crazy. I had always been good at staying cool under any circumstance, but Cahki had somehow cracked that veneer.

Applause and a rumbling of excited voices snapped me out of my thoughts. My father had risen from his throne and was addressing the guests before him. "Treasured guests, I have a special treat for you tonight," he announced, and my stomach churned, bile rising in my throat. "I introduce you to my new daughter-in-law, an exotic beauty from the far North, here to entertain you all today with a dance." He extended his arm and pointed at the side door where a female dressed all in black stood.

"Cahki," I exclaimed under my breath, swallowing the knot in my throat as I followed her progress from the door to the space between the lines of tables in front of the dais. I barely recognized her. She was shrouded in black cloth from top to bottom, not an inch of skin showing. Even her face was covered by a black veil that obscured her features and her eyes. What was she up to?

Stealing a quick glance at my father, I knew he wasn't pleased. He had expected the usual dancing fare with pretty, colored clothing and lots of bare skin. My wife was playing with fire, but then again, what had I expected from the force of nature that she was?

Cahki walked gracefully to the center and bowed deeply to a scowling emperor before signaling to the musicians to start playing. The music gradually grew in momentum, wafting up to the high ceilings before echoing back to us at the tables. She waited a few bars before beginning her dance. At first, she moved only her arms, undulating them like the wings of a crane, long and graceful, and I almost expected her to take flight right there in front of us. Then her body followed, her hips moving slowly as her feet began an intricate pattern on the floor.

I couldn't help it; I glanced at my father again to find him entranced as if Cahki had somehow put a spell on him. His mouth was slightly open, and his eyes followed her every move.

The music became louder and faster, the drums now joining the fray, and Cahki began peeling off the layers of her clothes. My heart exploded. Was she going to strip in front of my father? In front of all these men? First, she removed the long black scarf that covered her shoulders, revealing yet another layer of black. I let out a deep exhale of relief, but it was short lived because she immediately removed another layer.

And another.

I held on to the edge of my table for fear that I would jump onto the dance floor and hide her from all the greedy eyes that followed her every move. Like a butterfly peeling off the layers of her cocoon, Cahki emerged from her black coverings as a creature of exquisite allure. Not bare, as I had feared, but clothed in shades of blue and green, silk and glittering lamé flowing with her movements in a perfect imitation of the fluid beauty of butterfly wings. The paleness of her bare arms and face complemented the brightness of the fabrics enveloping her, but the true star of the show was her hair. Cahki had pinned a couple of her white strands on the top of her head with a tiny crown-like barrette and allowed the rest of her wild mane to cascade down her shoulders in waves of snow.

The emperor and his visitors couldn't take their eyes off her, and neither could I. Inside my gut, an out-of-control fire had ignited. I swallowed hard.

My wife was astoundingly beautiful, and, whether I liked it or not, I wanted her more than I wanted to depose my father.

"Close your mouth," I ordered, using a finger to physically lift my friend's chin up a notch. I couldn't blame him for the reaction. The whole room was in a state of awe over my ridiculously alluring wife. Cahki was indeed dangerous, a beautiful sharp blade disguised as a butterfly. I wondered if my father could see her sharp edges beneath the mask.

Hwarang cleared his throat and looked properly embarrassed by his obvious gawking. "Wow, your wife is—" He too couldn't find the right word to describe her. "Your father will definitely drool over her now."

That was the problem as much as the goal of this exercise. If my deviant father thought of Cahki as only a sexual object, he'd be more apt to let slip bits of info in front of her, but on the other hand, it also meant that, devoid of suspicion, his dirty mind would be undressing her every time he saw her. The thought turned my stomach.

Cahki was still bent into a deep bow when I stood up and rushed to her side despite Hwarang's attempt to stop me. She threw me a surprised glance, but it was too late. I bowed to my father, whose slimy smile had been replaced by a scowl.

"What do you want, Prince Sung-jin?" the emperor asked in an obviously angry tone. "Why soil your wife's beautiful performance with your presence?"

It's your thoughts, Father, that soil it, not my presence. I clenched my jaw, stopping the words from escaping my lips. Instead, I bowed again. "Princess Cahki and I have prepared a surprise dance for you, Father, as a token of our loyalty and gratitude." Cahki's face turned toward me, her eyes widening. "If you'll allow us."

It took a few seconds for my father to agree to it, but eventually he waved his hand in assent. I offered my wife a hand, and she straightened, her eyes piercing me with the sharpness of well-honed blades. I'd never be able to live this one down. Bending, I whispered in her ear, "Trust me. Do you know the Dance of the Geese?" The confusion in her eyes told me what I should have already known; why would a Northern woman be familiar with the traditional wedding dance of the South? "Just follow my lead. It's a dance about love and fidelity."

The musicians began playing at my signal, and I muttered a little prayer to all the gods in heaven. To her credit, Cahki recovered quickly, holding on to my hands for dear life.

Our eyes locked, and that was it; the world beyond us vanished.

The music danced around us, caressing our ears and skin, and our bodies began to move along. The Dance of the Geese was a simple dance, a combination of twirls and spins, retreats and advances, hand-holds and strolls along the dance floor. Like our connected hands, our eyes never parted as we danced our way to the end of the melody, when our bodies crashed together harder than the dance required. My arms went around my wife's waist to keep her from losing her balance, and our faces came dangerously close. Dangerous, because I was insanely yearning for a taste of her lips.

Awkward silence filled the banquet hall as we stood in each other's arms, paralyzed by some kind of magic long after the melody had stopped. Hwarang coughed. Loudly.

The trance was broken, and I almost dropped my wife as I pulled away from her suddenly. I cleared my throat and hid my eyes, a flush of heat rising to my cheeks. Turning toward my father, I bowed, not daring to check on what Cahki was doing.

"Father, I hope our two performances pleased you and your honored guests," I said, hoping the tingling I felt inside and outside my body did not reflect itself in my voice. "We thank you for your graciousness."

A quick glance at Cahki beside me told me she was also bowing to the emperor. "It was an honor to dance for you, Your Majesty."

My father dismissed us with a barely audible "Go" and a wave of his hand. He was not happy with my performance. *I* wasn't happy with my own performance. What in heaven's name had come over me to do something so stupid? Putting on a show that clearly marked Cahki as mine for all to see was not a smart move. I had poked the wasp's nest, and I was sure I'd pay for it one way or another.

Eerily enough, Cahki barely said a word for the rest of the banquet as she sat beside me at the table. Even Hwarang's usual jabs didn't stir anything from her. I wasn't used to a quiet Cahki, and it made me anxious.

At the end of the night, the guests filed out of the banquet hall, zigzagging in their drunkenness, slurred voices echoing between the walls and into the dark night outside. Hwarang went ahead of us, a bit drunk himself and howling. Cahki and I were the last ones out.

Halfway across the now deserted courtyard, Cahki grabbed my arm to stop and turn me to face her. "What the hell was that, Sung-jin?" Well, at least she hadn't addressed me as idiot. "What possessed you to do that? Your father was throwing daggers at you all through the dance."

What could I say? I had no idea why I did it. At least no idea I could accept. I shrugged.

"Are you stupid?" she continued, her voice rising into the darkness. "Have you already forgotten the beating? Are you begging for another one? You might not be so lucky this time."

I wanted to assure her there wouldn't be any more beatings, but knowing my father, that would be a lie. "I'll be okay. I'm used to it."

Cahki's white hair shone by the weak light of the moon, and that strange tingling feeling invaded my being again. She hit my chest with her fist just hard enough for me to feel it. "Idiot! You may be used to it, but I don't need the stress of watching you nearly bleed to death again."

My heart softened. "I didn't think you cared," I admitted in a quiet voice. A stubborn smile popped onto my lips. "I thought you would welcome my demise."

She was quiet for a moment, her eyes still full of fire and her lips pressed tight together as if she wanted to stop words from flying out. Just when I thought she wouldn't say anything, she exclaimed, "Asshole. If you die, I die, remember? Don't get all sentimental about this."

And there she was, the Cahki I had grown to know and admire.

Chapter 16
Stained

The world might not have ended, but it sure shook under my feet. What was I thinking? Why had I gotten so worried about my fake husband that I almost bit his head off when he challenged his father? The implications of what I felt were too much for me to handle. So I did what I normally did: I ignored it and focused on what was important—survival.

"You're sure that's what he said?" Hwarang asked me yet again, his eyes narrowing to mere slits and his arms crossed tightly over his chest. "I mean, Hangug-eo is not your native language."

I shot him a few flaming glares before turning my attention to my spouse, who was always more reasonable than his idiot friend. "My knowledge of your primitive language is excellent, as you well know."

It wasn't a boast. I was indeed fluent in Hangug-eo, just as I was in three more languages. Growing up in a perpetually frozen kingdom with only the company of mountain goats, snow wolves, and retired fjord pirates was not as exciting as it sounded. I was chronically bored, so I learned new things from the few-and-far-between foreign guests and immigrants whom I stumbled upon. The fact that I learned their languages pretty quickly had never seemed to faze my parents, so I never thought much about it myself. But Hwarang and the prince seemed surprised when I told them how I'd learned Hangug-eo. Weird.

"He's amassing soldiers along the border," Sung-jin said, summarizing what I had just shared. "And this bit of info came from the mouth of the Minister of War."

I nodded. "From the horse's mouth. He got a sharp look from your daddy, but even the emperor is starting to forget I am a living being with ears." I had made myself invisible, at least when it came to serving tea and pastries to the emperor and his minions. I made sure to wear plain clothes like the other female servants so not to call any undue attention to myself, and it was paying off. The Minister of War had visited this morning, and while I poured never ending amounts of *boricha*, a sweet brew of barley tea with honey, he had become careless and let slip what sounded like a huge piece of information.

While this was not new to us, it did in fact confirm earlier intel. I couldn't care less about their politics, but this involved my survival, so, like it or not, I was invested now.

"Before he revealed that nugget, Minister Ha had been whispering about 'the Northern vermin' and 'the Southern lack of naval power,'" I continued. I scratched my head. "Do you think he's talking about the northern territories of the Southern Kingdom or my Northern Lands?" The thought had just now erupted in my head. What if the fucking emperor was planning something against my people?

Hwarang shook his head. "Nuh, can't be. The Northern Lands are too far and too hard to get to," he said. "Not to mention that there's nothing up North the emperor would covet."

I snorted. "White-haired women?" If that was the case, he would be sorely disappointed. I was the only white-haired woman I had ever met. My people were fair, but their hair coloring ranged from black to golden, not white. Even the old folk's hair was not snowy white like mine.

Sung-jin covered his head with his hands. "There has to be something—something he really wants. We must find out before it's too late." I agreed, but I wasn't sure how exactly we would manage that. It wasn't as if I could just walk to the slimy ruler and ask him. Sung-jin raised his head. "We have to be more diligent and keep our eyes and ears wide open. No distractions."

I understood the urgency and his frustration, but I was also the one who had to act like a servant all day for a man who would be more than happy to force himself on me if the enchantment of my marriage were not firmly in place.

"Easy for you to say," I spat, anger clouding my best judgment. "You're not the one prancing around a deviant, serving him tea and biscuits while he undresses me with his eyes."

The prince visibly deflated, his shoulders hunching forward into the posture of a much older man. "I'm sorry," he whispered, eyes moist with emotion. "I really wish there were another way. I hate that you're exposed to his disgusting thoughts every day. I can't sleep at night, just thinking of what could happen if he one day decides to test the enchantment. I'm so sorry."

His sincerity hit me like an avalanche. I wanted to refute his words, called his bluff, but the truth was, he meant it. Heartwarming honesty wafted from his lips like a sweet yet bitter perfume. Lies I could deal with, but this? How did I react to the concern of someone I'm supposed to hate and wish dead and gone?

"It's not like Sung-jin has an easy time, either, Cahki," Hwarang reminded me, jumping to his defense. "The emperor doesn't trust his own son, and the prince must walk a fine line and play a part just as you do. You saw what happened before. How can you think he has it easy?"

I didn't. Not anymore. I had witnessed firsthand how cruel his father was. But I wasn't used to caving in, to accepting defeat, so I yelled out, "All fine and dandy, but he doesn't have to feel the emperor's lascivious glares all day, does he?"

It wasn't fair, I knew. Sung-jin was still healing from the beating despite my daily whispers. His flesh had been so abused in the past that it took a lot longer to renew itself, to knit itself back together. I didn't want to make my treatment too obvious, so I was taking it slow, much more slowly than I normally would, and definitely slower than he needed.

"One day, I will make it up to you, Cahki, I promise." He wasn't bluffing, and at that moment, the intensity of his dark gaze melted my heart and made other parts of my body burn with equal fervor.

I so wanted to hate him, but by now that was the farthest thing from what I truly felt for my prince.

Filthy old man!

My skin was crawling, and anger rose in my throat like a stream of flames I couldn't put out. Anger at myself for feeling so dirty when I had nothing to do with it. Anger at Sung-jin who had put me in this position for the sake of political games. Wrath at the emperor who had no respect for women, no respect for anyone but himself.

I ran across the two courtyards that separated our palaces, ignoring the incessant rain that blurred my vision and soaked my bones, with only one thought in my mind: to put as much space as possible between me and my father-in-law with his leery glances and shameless morals. How could anyone be so deviant, so horrible as to think that what he did was acceptable? The fact that he was the emperor did not make him a god, impervious to human shame and morality.

My foot snagged on a crack in the mosaic floor of the Garden of Serenity—what a joke! It should have been named Den of Depravity instead. My ankle twisted, and my shoe got stuck, but I didn't care. I yanked my foot out, ignoring the pain and leaving the silk footwear behind as I limped the rest of the way home. For once I thanked the gods for the awful rain that covered my tears, tears I hated wasting over such an incident. I was stronger than this. I had faced blizzards alone in the frozen mountains, fjord pirates blinded by greed, and wild animals frenzied by hunger. Not once had I shed a tear, and yet here I was now, crying like a little lost girl because of how a cruel and vile man had made me feel.

I pushed the door open to our main hall and walked across the tiled floor, leaving small puddles of rainwater along the way. I needed a bath, a long, hot bath, and a large scrubbing brush. I needed a new skin. Mine felt slimy and tainted.

Sung-jin was in the room, sitting at his desk, working on something like he often did. I didn't even look at him, aiming for the bathroom just beyond him, my face still dripping with a mixture of raindrops and tears. I didn't quite reach it before he jumped out of his chair and came to stop me.

"What's wrong?" he asked, urgency so clear in his voice, it made my heart clench. "What happened?" I made to ignore him and push the door open, but he held on to my arm. "Tell me. Did my father hurt you? Did he touch you?"

"Let me go, Sung-jin." I hated how I sounded so pathetic, tears still rolling down my face and snot collecting on my upper lip. "I don't want to talk now. I want a bath." I hiccupped a couple times, tiny sobs escaping my lips despite all my efforts to repress them. "I feel dirty."

The prince was silent for a moment, his eyes searching for an answer in mine, but I couldn't tell him. Not yet. Maybe never. "Let me run the bath for you, Cahki." He whispered his plea. "Let me do this for you, please."

I wasn't going to fight him. We both walked into the bathroom, and he rushed to the large bathtub to run the water while heating it up with his magic. I threw my cloak into a pile on the floor and kicked my remaining shoe into a corner, wincing as my ankle reminded me of the earlier twist. Sung-jin looked at me with watery eyes and fidgeted in place. "What's wrong with your foot?"

Shaking my head, I shrugged my outerwear off like an unwanted skin that puddled around my ankles. "Nothing. I twisted it on my way here." I wanted all these clothes off me, gone, burned. I began peeling off my undergarments, disregarding the laces and closures. With one pull, I ripped the diamond-shaped silken piece that covered my torso from me and threw it onto the pile.

Sung-jin averted his gaze. Like I cared!

His eyes didn't hold the malice his father's did. His gaze on my bare breasts did not stain me like his father's leering of my clothed body had. I had never been ashamed of my body until that sickening man had sat on his equally horrible throne, jerking off while I danced for him. I should have known when he dismissed all the other servants from the room. I hated myself that I didn't see it coming.

I climbed over the edge of the tub without bothering to remove my underpants. I'd remove them later. I sank all the way in and then slid my body down and along the bottom until even my head was under water. When my lungs began to burn, I emerged to find frantic hands reaching out to me.

"You're scaring me, Cahki," he said, cupping my cheek with one of his hands as he kneeled beside the tub.

I slapped his hand away. "I hate you. I hate you so much." The hurt in his eyes didn't faze me. I was angry and I needed someone as a target. "You brought me into this situation. You are just as much to blame for your father's odious behavior as he is. At least he has no moral compass, but you do. And yet, you still brought me into this."

He dropped his arms and swallowed, his Adam's apple bobbing up and down. At that moment I saw the boy he had once been, lost and lonely, aching for the love of a father who was incapable of it. Guilt filled my gut.

I took a deep breath. "Wash my hair, Sung-jin," I begged in a whisper, tears streaming down my cheeks. "Wash the stain away."

Silently, my husband poured warm water over my head and washed my hair, gently and slowly, rubbing the soap into each white strand, massaging my scalp until the tension in my body began to let go and I was able to breathe normally again. He rinsed it with more warm water and soothed my nerves with his magic, caressing each muscle with his mind and giving me a moment of peace, of relief.

"I'm sorry, prince," I finally said, my eyes closed and my body relaxed within the warm embrace of the water. "I don't hate you, and I don't blame you for your father's sins. I was just angry, and you were there. I'm sorry."

Silence was all I heard for a moment or two before his rich voice reached my ears. "No, I'm the one who's sorry, Cahki. You were right to be angry at me. I have much to make up for, but I promise you, I will."

I believed him. Right there, in that moment as we kept each other company in a steamy bathroom, half dozing off from the effects of his magic, I not only believed him but hoped I would be around him long enough to see it come true.

Chapter 17
Falling

I'd never seen Cahki this vulnerable. The white-haired beauty from the North was normally nothing like this broken creature in my arms. Cahki was confident, feisty, an indomitable spirit, a force of nature who could annoy you to the edge of insanity and laugh about it. There was no middle ground to how I felt about her; I either wanted to throttle her or kiss her.

At that moment, as I carried her to bed, I wanted to kiss her.

But she had been violated by my father. He may not have physically touched her, but he had nevertheless made her feel used and dirty. My father, the mighty emperor, had done it again. He had deeply hurt someone close to me without much thought or concern.

I had done the best I could to soothe her with my magic, just enough so she could relax, leave the nearly cold bathwater, and slip on the nightclothes I had pulled out for her. When I scooped her into my arms to carry her to bed, I had been met with no objection. The Cahki I knew would have fought me. This version of my wife submitted to my hold, leaning against me like a child and allowing me to lay her gently on the bed.

Anger had built inside me to the point I thought I'd explode. I wanted to run to the imperial palace and tell my father exactly how I felt about what he had done—no, I would *show* him how I felt. But then again, it hadn't worked the last time. All my raving and threats about Chae-yeong had fallen on deaf ears, and when I got physical, all he had to do was call his guards and have me dragged down to the Discipline Hall for a good beating. I was powerless against him.

For now.

I covered an unusually quiet Cahki with one of the silk duvets and had started to retreat when she clasped my wrist. "Don't go," she whispered, a touch of despair in her voice. "Stay with me, please."

After a moment of hesitation, I stretched out atop the coverings beside her, my face turned to hers, and smiled. What else could I do? Drawing her into my arms would be too invasive after what had happened. Kissing her would be even worse. So I'd just lie there, keeping her company until she could rest. I thought I had protected her well by marrying her under the enchantment spell, but my father was crafty, especially when it came to finding novel ways to get what he wanted. And he never took anyone else's feelings into account. Not even those of his own flesh and blood.

We must have fallen asleep. When I opened my eyes, it was getting dark already, the dying light of the sun valiantly struggling to illuminate the bedroom. Beside me, Cahki was still sleeping, her lips contorted in pain, or maybe anger, and yet still beautiful, a rare flower in the desert of my life. I reached out to her face and brushed a couple of fingers over her cheek. She winced, and I pulled away. If she had disliked me before, there was no hope of any cordiality between us after what had happened. I was my father's son, after all. As much as I hated it, it was not something I could change. But I could—and would—strive to rid the world of the emperor's rule.

Cahki stirred, mumbling something I couldn't understand. Her eyes opened, their transparent blue shining in the dim light as they lingered on mine for a moment.

"How do you feel?" I asked, unsure of how to proceed. Would she kick me out of the room and her life? I wouldn't blame her.

She blinked a few times and then sat up, propping her back against the cushioned headboard. "I'm all right," she said. "Angry. Very angry."

Nodding, I sat up as well. "I don't blame you." My gaze fluttered to her lips, pink, full, and inviting. Shit, I so wanted to kiss her. "I'm sorry for what he did. He's a disgusting human being."

Cahki smiled then. "That he is," she agreed. "But you're not to blame and shouldn't apologize for his actions. You're better than he is. So much better."

Her true spirit seemed to be returning, just as a rosy blush colored her previously pale cheeks. "I hate him," I blurted out. "I hate him for what he did to you, what he did to my mother, what he did to Chae-yeong—" I had said too much. I bit my lip and looked down. "I just hate him."

There was silence for a while, but I didn't dare look at her. "Who's Chae-yeong?" she asked finally.

I was afraid she'd ask. I didn't want to talk about it. Doing so would only bring painful memories, thoughts I would rather forget or at least hide in some dark corner of my mind. "She was my fiancée," I answered anyway. I knew she'd ask more. "I don't want to talk about it, Cahki. Not now."

We sat in silence for what it felt like a long time, the waning light of the sun filling the room with long shadows, and the pitter-patter of evening showers beginning to echo against the windows. I almost jumped out of my skin when Cahki cupped my cheek with her hand. I lifted my eyes to look at her, my mind percolating with questions that she didn't give me the chance to ask. Her face drew nearer, and before

I could react, her mouth had covered mine, her soft skin yielding beneath my lips, warm and exciting.

The kiss was over before I knew it, and I sat there like an idiot, staring at her, waiting for something, anything. I fully expected to see the usual cold mocking glint in her eyes, but instead there was tenderness, softness in those blue orbs. Expectation, even.

It took me only a moment to decide. That brief kiss had not been nearly enough.

I leaned toward her and, shaking in anticipation, I kissed her.

I expected her to pull away, punch me, push me off the bed, but instead her lips yielded to mine as if they had been meant to all along. My hands wrapped themselves around her waist and pulled her closer just as hers knotted behind my neck. Her taste was a sweet wine that went straight to my head and left me intoxicated, unable to stop myself even as that quiet, rational side of me told me how unwise this whole thing was. Cahki did not like me. Why should she? I might have offered her a safety net, but it was far from freedom, far from what she'd wished for. She had been forced into a marriage she didn't want to the son of her worst enemy, only to turn into a pawn in palace politics. In very dangerous political games.

Worst of all, I had placed her under the scrutiny and the daily presence of my father, a man I knew too well to be a degenerate. How could she ever like me? Why would she ever accept me?

Yet, she had allowed the kiss, my feverish exploration of her mouth. Later I would wonder why, but in the moment, all I could think of was the way her touch made me feel, how the warmth of her body crushed against mine made my heart beat faster. How the taste of her mouth made me drunk with a feeling I hadn't been familiar with in a long time. Not since Chae-yeong. Not since I had closed my heart to anything sentimental, anything that would make me vulnerable to my father, anything that would turn into a weakness. My mother had been my first weakness. I should have learned then—learned that whoever I loved would automatically become my father's target, his leverage against me. It took what happened to Chae-yeong for me to realize I had to build an armor around my heart if I wanted to ever have the upper hand where the emperor was concerned.

Cahki was thawing out the ice inside me, one inch at a time. It was a dangerous game for me and for her. Was I really falling for my wife? Or was I just infatuated with her looks, her wild personality, the challenge she personified?

In the end, I was the one who pulled away, a groan leaving my lips as they broke contact with hers. "I'm sorry, Cahki," I said, yearning choking me. "I shouldn't have done that."

Cocking her head to the side, she studied me for a few seconds, her brows knitted together. "You speak as if this was all your decision, and I had no choice." The edge in her voice was back. "Do you really believe I'd let you kiss me if I didn't want you to?"

No, of course I didn't. I was in shock that she'd allowed it to happen, but it still felt wrong that I, the son of the man who had just assaulted her, would feel free to put my hands on her. I shook my head, not able to articulate the words I wanted to say.

"Let me tell you, idiot prince of the Southern Kingdom, you were not the one making that decision," she said, and somehow, her words sounded like a compliment rather than an insult. "I kissed you first, didn't I?"

I nodded, still tongue-tied.

Cahki bookended my face with her hands and took a long look at me. "You're very handsome, my husband, and I haven't had sex in a long time." Heat rose to my cheeks under her soft palms. "Stop overthinking everything. Sometimes a kiss is just a kiss."

What the hell did that mean? I was so confused by her statement that I almost missed that the old Cahki had returned, biting and cold. Or at least that was what she wanted everyone to believe she was. I had seen enough glimpses of a very different woman not to fully buy into that mask. Yet, I still heard myself ask, "Really? Is that what it was? Just a kiss?" I clamped my mouth shut, but it was too late.

Her perfect lips curved into a wicked smile. "Why, did you think it was more than that?" Her mocking tone was as sharp as a well-honed dagger to my chest. "Did the little prince think I was kissing him because I'm falling for him?" She tilted her head to better examine my expression. She let out a loud cackle that didn't suit her at all, and I hoped she was lying. Gods protect me, I wanted her to be lying through her teeth. I needed her to tell me she was in fact falling for me just like I was falling for her. She narrowed her eyes and dropped her hands. "Oh, for all the gods in heaven, you did, didn't you? You thought I was falling for you."

My skin felt bereft now that she wasn't touching me any longer. How could I be so stupid, so naive? For years now I had trained my heart not to feel, not to be ensnared by another soul. How could someone like Cahki, cold and a tad cruel, be the one to break through that layer? Chae-yeong had been a warrior, too—tough when she needed to be, soft when we were together. My wife reminded me of her when she stood up to danger as if she were an immortal with no fear of harm or death. But there were other times when they couldn't have been more different. Chae-yeong and I had been close, two bodies but one soul, it seemed at times. Cahki would sooner plunge her dagger into my belly than develop any warm feelings for me.

"Don't fool yourself, my husband. Just because I took care of you when your father beat you to a pulp does not mean I like you," she continued, each word a new shard of glass embedded into my gut. "I did that because we are now connected by the damned enchantment. Taking care of you is taking care of me. Don't get your pretty little head all confused."

I couldn't speak, and I was certain my usual mask of indifference had all but melted away. Like it or not, this white deer had crushed me with just a few words.

"After what happened with your father, I just needed a bit of loving," she said, her lips still twisted into a smile that didn't fit her. "But one pretty boy is just as good as the next, so I will turn my attention to your dumb friend, Hwarang. I bet he won't be so picky."

She slid off the bed and left the room, still in her nightclothes and barefoot. I sat there for a long while, stunned and angry at myself. Cahki was right. I was stupid to even consider that the kiss had meant anything to her past the pure physical comfort it brought.

The problem was, it meant a whole lot more for this stupid little prince.

Chapter 18
Cold and Cruel

G uilt was eating me from the inside out. Outside it was still raining—did the rain ever stop in this place?—and my bare feet and the hem of my white nightgown were caked with mud. I didn't care. It grounded me at a moment when I couldn't understand my own feelings. Around the corner of the building that held our quarters, there was a small niche on the wall, half protected by the overhanging of the roof. Whatever used to be housed there was gone, so I took up residence, bringing my legs up until I could rest my aching head on my knees.

Where was this guilt coming from? I had done nothing wrong. In fact, I was the one who had been wronged, time and time again, for the past couple months. First, I had been wrenched from my own home up North, then taken across the ocean to serve a disgusting ruler, married his son, and was now being kept like one of those high-end courtesans who stirred up a lot of obscene thoughts in men like the emperor. Why was I the one feeling guilty?

I tapped my forehead on my knees. "Stupid, stupid." The look on Sung-jin's face when I told him it had been just a kiss had broken me, and I didn't understand why. Yes, he was not this horrible man I had thought him to be at first, and we had developed an awkward friendship of sorts. But that was all.

Or was it?

I should have stopped the torrent of words, but my survival instincts kicked in, and harsher, colder ones left my lips. Gods in heaven, I even told him I would go after his best friend. But I couldn't—wouldn't—let him believe I liked him. He was still the enemy, however in a different class than his father. He was still holding me prisoner in a kingdom too far from home, with little hope of ever returning. But he was kind and courteous, always making sure I had everything I needed, that I was safe and comfortable. Last night he had helped me bathe, comforted me, and let me sleep in his arms when I was terrified of how I felt. Those were not the actions of a foe, no matter how much I'd prefer to view him that way.

I had repaid his kindness with cruelty, my words barbed with poison. Their effect had been painfully clear by the haunted gaze in his gorgeous eyes, the sudden dip of the corners of his lips. I had crushed something within him, something I suspected he didn't reveal to anyone. Yet, when he was trusting enough to be vulnerable before me, I betrayed that trust and used it as a weapon against him.

My name fit me after all. Cold and cruel.

The truth was, I was scared; scared of these new feelings warming me from the inside. Something in me yearned for Sung-jin. I couldn't lie. I enjoyed his company, and when he had been beaten to the doors of death, a part of me had nearly died with him. Not because of the enchantment, but because I liked who he was. I loved that he wanted to fight for his people despite being under the rule of such a powerful and cruel father. He was a good man, and he had carved a space for himself inside my heart.

That scared me most of all.

My parents had always told me, "You keep your heart protected, girl. Don't let anyone worm their way inside it. When you fall in love, you become vulnerable. You become a weapon against yourself." I had never quite understood it, considering how they had married for love all those years ago, but I agreed to do what they had advised. We lived in such isolation anyway, so it wasn't as if I had young men or women keeping me company. The chances of me falling in love were minimal, having only fjord creatures as my companions and prostitutes when I needed release.

But I now wondered whether they were right. My heart was indeed opening to this man, and I did feel exposed—hurt even—by his rejection. He had pushed me away from a kiss that had me flying so high, I could see the whole planet from the stars. He had apologized for the kiss as if it had disgusted him.

"What are you doing here?" The male voice snapped me out of the paralysis of misery. Hwarang stood next to me, wearing a wide straw hat from which a stream of rainwater cascaded. "You're soaking wet."

Still wallowing in self-pity and guilt, I shrugged, only half aware of the cold creeping up my legs and numbing my feet.

"You'll be sick," he said unnecessarily. Doubtful, as I very rarely got sick, and being cold was never an issue for me. My body was conditioned to adapt after a lifetime in the Northern fjords. "Come on. Let's get you inside."

He moved to help me off my perch, but I slapped his hands away. "Don't touch me!"

Hwarang didn't even flinch. "Don't be stupid. It's not like I'm going to go for my best friend's wife." His words brought back my last conversation with Sung-jin and with it a new wave of shame.

"Like he'd care," I snapped. The memory of the prince's rejection erupting in my mind. "He'd probably be glad he didn't have to worry about me anymore."

A burst of laughter broke the monotony of the rain.

"Is that what you think?" he asked. "I thought you were smarter. That man would kill anyone who laid a finger on you, no questions asked."

I shrugged again. "Well, yeah. I'm his ticket to deposing his father."

He laughed again, shaking the rain off his hat. "That has nothing to do with how he feels about you, dummy."

Lifting my face from my knees, I gave him a hard stare. I was in no mood for his usual teasing. "Oh really? And how exactly does he feel about me?" I snapped. "I'm like an exotic cat you keep around to attract the beasts of prey. It's working too. His father has taken quite a hands-off but I'll-swallow-you-just-the-same interest in me."

That caught his attention and wiped the smile off his face.

"Did the emperor do something to you?" His words were a low growl. "Does Sung-jin know?"

I nodded. "What can he do? His father didn't really touch me. Not with his hands anyway." It didn't make it any less disgusting, but I suppose it was a blessing.

Hwarang offered me his hand. "Let's go. We need to stop your husband from doing something really stupid."

What would Sung-jin do? He was powerless against his father. If marrying someone the emperor wanted for himself had gotten him almost killed, what would happen if—?

I jumped to my feet, wincing at the cold floor and the tingling of blood finally flowing through them.

Sung-jin was in trouble.

We both ran around the bend to the room we shared, only to find it empty.

"He's going to the emperor!" Hwarang exclaimed, pale as a ghost. "Get dressed."

I wasn't going to waste time putting on clothes. We needed to get to my stupid husband before he saw the emperor.

The short distance between our palace and the emperor's felt never-ending. As we turned around the corner that led to the imperial courtyard, we saw a group of people walking across it in our direction.

"Sung-jin!" I yelled, taking off running. The prince was being escorted by two guards, which could only mean one thing. "Stop! I want to talk to my husband."

Surprisingly, the guards obeyed me and waited for us to reach them. Sung-jin half hung from their hold, a large angry bruise across his face.

"Where are you taking him?" Hwarang asked.

"The dungeons," one of the guards replied. "The emperor has ordered him to be held and punished for three days for challenging him."

Sung-jin gave me an apologetic shrug. Stupid man! I had never asked him to be my protector.

"What did you do?" I asked him, fully aware of what he must have done. Guilt flooded me again.

"I just had a little disagreement with my father over his treatment of you," he said. "Go home and don't go to the palace for a few days. Tell them you're sick."

The guards resumed their walk, but I followed them. "What are they going to do to you?" Dread filled my stomach with acid.

"Nothing serious, really," he lied. "I'll be home in three days."

Hwarang held my arm, stopping me from following further. "Let him go. There's nothing we can do for him right now."

I shook him off, but he was right. "What will they do to him?" I watched as the guards half dragged my husband away from us.

"Whip him, starve him, and then return him home." He sounded so matter-of-fact, as if talking about the weather. How often did this happen to the prince? "He won't be as hurt as he was the last time, I promise."

"Why did he do this? He knows he won't win against his father."

Hwarang sighed. "Do you understand now how he feels about you?"

The answer was a resounding no. Why would he risk his life to protect someone who might be an asset but was also a liability? It wasn't a wise political move.

Sung-jin's best friend slapped his forehead. "Holy fuck, Cahki. How stupid can you be?"

I stared at him, confused.

He scowled at me. "He's in love with you, dummy. Head over heels in love."

Hwarang's words still rang in my ears, as loud and shocking as when he first uttered them the day before.

I bathed and got dressed, all the while musing about everything that had transpired within a day. Sung-jin was being kept in the dungeons, exposed to indignities and pain I could only guess at. Sung-jin, my husband, who, according to his friend, was in love with me. Not that I believed him. The man had pulled away from my kiss as if afraid he'd catch the plague. How did that translate into any kind of love?

More pressing in my mind was the fact that he was a prisoner, and I was not going to let him suffer for me again.

I had a plan.

Admittedly not a great one, but it was something. If I couldn't get him out, I could at least keep him company.

My father was fond of saying that every man had a price. So I was willing to bet that if they were offered enough money or valuables, the prison guards would be willing to turn a blind eye to what I wanted to do.

Hwarang was waiting for me outside in the courtyard. "Did you find anything?" he asked.

I showed him the loot, a mixture of small objects collected from around our palace that I was hoping were as valuable as they looked.

Examining them carefully, he nodded. "These will do nicely. They're worth much more than any of those guys make in a year." I almost dropped the makeshift bag. Hwarang let out a bitter chuckle. "Yes, these guards make close to nothing. Another thing Sung-jin wants to change. The lucky devils will be able to sell those items on the black market, and no one will rat them out. Our emperor does not inspire much loyalty."

We crossed the courtyard, heading to the dungeons. My cloak hid a bag of food and medical supplies that I was hoping would go unnoticed.

"Are you sure about this, Cahki?" Hwarang asked as we crossed through the large doorway to the prison. Two guards stopped us and asked for identification.

"I'm the crown prince's consort," I announced, gathering as much haughtiness as my nerves would allow. "I'm here to see my husband."

One of the guards held an arm in front of me to stop me. "The orders are to keep him isolated."

I stole a glance at Hwarang, and he nodded. I opened the ends of the scarf I was using as a bag and allowed the guard to peek inside.

"All I'm asking you is to let me spend the night with my husband, nothing else. I'll be out before the change of the guard and back during your shift with more goods."

The eyes of both guards widened into perfect circles, and I could almost see the wheels in their brains turn, making plans for the wealth being offered to them. They stared at each other for a moment, then nodded and moved aside to let me in.

"You get half of this now, the other half when I leave in the morning." They didn't argue with me as I handed them an armful of treasure.

Hwarang helped me put the bag together again. "You be careful. Sung-jin wouldn't forgive me if something happened to you."

I shrugged. "I'll be fine. Come get me in the morning."

Before I could change my mind, I turned around and followed one of the guards to the cells in the basement. The deeper we went, the stronger it smelled of a mixture of moldy earth and unwashed bodies. Moans reached my ears as we landed at the bottom of the stairs in a large circular foyer from which several corridors sprouted. The guard took a right turn, and I followed him down a dank, dark hallway bordered by cells that were little more than open spaces with floors covered in hay and encased in metal bars from the bottom to the top.

Sung-jin was inside one of those. Some of the moaning I heard could be coming from him. The wet chill of the air and the dread in my gut made me shiver. All the cells were empty, contrary to what I'd thought, and the sounds of pain fading behind us had come from a different corridor. I took a deep breath as the guard finally stopped before a smaller cell, roughly the size of an oversized cage that stood in the middle of a wide, circular room. He jiggled the large keys around his waist until he found the one that fit the lock.

"You have my husband inside here?" I couldn't believe it. I could almost accept that the emperor wanted to teach his son a lesson, but sticking him in this barred box was simply inhuman. The cell was barely big enough for an adult male to stand up in and not wide enough for anyone to lie across. The room was sunken in dark shadows, and I couldn't see the inside properly.

The guard had the decency to throw me an embarrassed glance before turning the key in the keyhole. "Emperor's orders," he whispered. The door swung out. "Are you sure you want to spend the night here? It's not fit for a lady." Gods, even the guards were more scrupulous than my father-in-law.

"Yes, I'll be all right," I assured him, stepping inside. I had been in worse conditions when up in the fjords by myself. A night in this box wouldn't kill me. "Come get me before the change of the guard."

He nodded and locked the door behind me, shaking his head before leaving. I squinted, getting my eyes used to the dimness of the cage while looking for Sung-jin. Why wasn't he speaking? He must have heard us talking. My heart clenched. Blinking furiously and cursing the extended amount of time it was taking my eyes to adapt, I took a few steps further inside the cage and almost tripped over a body.

Dropping to my knees, I was terrified to realize it was Sung-jin lying in a fetal position, unconscious. "What have they done to you, Sung-jin?" I asked, a tiny sob escaping with the words. I rolled him onto his back and peered into his face, searching for signs of life. "Damned darkness!" I folded myself over him and placed my ear over his mouth, sighing in relief when I felt a whisper of air. He was alive.

I removed my cloak and the things I had hidden underneath. Thankfully, I had listened to Hwarang's advice and brought a small torch. I pulled it out from the hidden pouch inside my cloak and lit it. Light, however wan, flooded the small space, and I could finally see my husband clearly.

Sung-jin was so pale, he was almost transparent, the veins on his face and neck a network of visible lines and his lips a discolored bluish hue. Placing the torch on the floor beside us, I untied his tunic, a ratty garment made of scratchy burlap, to look for injuries. Hwarang had mentioned he'd be whipped, so he must have wounds that needed to be treated before they got infected. His skin was icy cold but covered in a sheen of sweat.

Fever!

Before anything else, I grabbed my water skin and poured a few drops between his lips. Most of it poured out, but eventually he began to swallow it. His eyes fluttered open. "Cahki?" he whispered. I offered him more water, and he accepted it without complaint. "What are you doing here?"

"Came to take care of you," I said, covering the skin and putting it aside. "Are you hurt? What did they do to you?"

His hand stopped me from removing his tunic. "You shouldn't be here, Cahki. Go away." His voice was raspy, as if he hadn't used it in a long time. "I'll be fine. Go!"

I braced my hands on my hips. "My idiot prince," I said, anger adding *oomph* to my voice. "You should know by now that you can't tell me what to do. Being my husband and a prince does not make you my boss, understand?"

Sung-jin stared at me for a while and then burst out laughing. "You should see your face, Cahki," he said between bouts of chuckles. "You're really a wild thing."

"Just shut up and turn around so I can check your back," I ordered, hoping my emotions wouldn't come through. He obeyed, still laughing, and I removed the tunic to examine his back. New wounds were carved across his skin. Not as severe as the last time, but wounds, nevertheless. "Fuck! When are you going to stop getting yourself in trouble, Sung-jin?"

His muffled voice teased, "Do I hear a note of concern?"

I flicked one of the wounds, and he groaned in pain. "You wish, Your Stupidity. Stay still so I can treat the wounds." He stopped moving and relaxed onto the cold floor. Underneath the tunic, he had on a pair of thin pants and nothing else. He had to be freezing. I worked as fast as I could, spreading the healing balm over the broken flesh and whispering. At first, he flinched and muffled a few groans as my fingers tracked the open wounds, but as they began to heal, he went quiet, and his muscles softened under my touch.

"Turn over," I told him when I was done. "How do you feel?"

Gingerly, he turned around. "Feels great," he replied, surprise coating his words. "You're a miracle worker."

I snorted. "As if." I handed him my cloak. "Put this on. It's cold in here, and you are running a bit of a fever." I helped him drape the heavy cloak over his shoulders and tie it in front. "Now, you rest," I ordered, leaning against the bars and calling him to my side. "Lay your head on my lap and sleep."

His breath hitched and a timid smile spread slowly on his lips. "Why?"

"Why what?" I knew exactly what he was asking me, but I was going to play dumb, as if being with him in those dungeons was as normal as the rain that never stopped falling in this gods-forsaken kingdom.

"Why are you taking care of me? I thought you hated me." My cruel words to him came storming in and filled me with shame all over again.

"I don't hate you, stupid," I said, avoiding his eyes. "Now, shut up and lie down. I could use a nap as well."

He didn't say anything, but even in the weak light, I could see his tiny smile turn into a grin. And strangely enough, that filled me with unexpected joy.

Chapter 19

Darkness

H er scent filled me with infinite pleasure, an extreme sense of well-being. I could only imagine that the heavens smelled the same as Cahki. Cradling my head on her lap with her legs stretched out in front of her, she rested one hand on my shoulder. I lay curled up on my side because there was no room in that cage for my outstretched body. Whatever my wife had done to my injuries, it had worked like a charm. The pain and burning I had felt before her arrival had faded into the mild discomfort of a scratch. With Cahki's cloak over me, I wasn't as cold as before, but shivers still shook my body.

I turned my head just enough to look at her. She seemed exhausted, her eyes closed and mouth slightly open. Her chest rose and fell as her breathing slowed. She was asleep. I watched her for a while until my eyes became too heavy.

The lack of natural light in the cell prevented me from knowing how long I had slept, but when my eyes finally opened, I was shaking like a leaf. Cahki's face hovered over me, her blue eyes closed but her lips moving, a whispering of incomprehensible words washing over me. A moment later my shaking subsided, and I felt almost myself again.

"The fever still lingers," my wife told me, the blue of her eyes shining in the dim light. "But I think I was able to get it under control. Can you sit up?"

With her help, I sat up with my back to the bars. The movement made my head swim, and I had to close my eyes for a few seconds to find my balance again. I leaned against Cahki, my head resting on her shoulder.

"Thank you for being here," I told her in a soft voice.

I couldn't articulate how grateful I really was. I was used to my father's punishments, but that didn't mean I was impervious to them. He knew that sticking me in this dark, lonely cell was the worst type of torture for me. Ever since my teens, I had been scared of the dark—not the actual lack of light, but what memories it held for me. Any time I was in a place like this, echoes of my past came back to haunt me.

"You don't have to thank me," she said, touching my forehead to check for a fever. "You've helped me in the past, so it's only fair I do the same."

I wasn't buying it. Whether she wanted to admit it or not, we had a connection of some kind. Ever since my father had me beaten, she had been there for me every time I was in need of a friendly face.

"What were you whispering right now?" I asked her, curious to know whether this was how she had gotten her nickname. "Is it a prayer? A curse?" I chuckled softly at my joke.

Her hand dropped into her lap, and she didn't say anything for a bit. "I have a special gift," she finally said. "That's why they call me the Whisperer."

I raised my head from her shoulder to look her in the eyes. "What gift is that?"

She hid her gaze and fidgeted with her hands. "I can heal," she confessed. "I can whisper people, animals, even plants into health. That's how I treated your wounds after your beating and the ones you just got yesterday."

Magic. She had magic like me. I could manipulate people's actions and do small things that weren't even worth mentioning, but she could actually heal. No wonder I had bounced back so quickly from my injuries; she had been working on it all along. I had simply thought her skilled in medicine and that her whispers were just a quirk of her unusual personality.

"Why didn't you tell me?" I asked. Her gift seemed like something she would like to share.

"My parents taught me to keep it a secret," she said, finally lifting her eyes to me. "They told me I couldn't tell anyone because it was dangerous. People would kill to use my powers, they said." Her eyes widened as my lips stretched into a smile. "You won't tell anyone, will you?"

Of course I wouldn't tell anyone, but what was making me smile was the fact she had trusted me enough to tell me her secret. I wasn't sure why it brought me such joy, but it did. "I won't mention it to anyone, not even Hwarang," I promised.

Cahki smiled then, and I swear the room lit up around us. "Don't think that just because I told you about this and took care of you in this disgusting place, it means I like you," she said. "Because I really don't."

Love might never be in the books for the two of us, but she couldn't fool me any longer. Her self-proclaimed hatred toward me was a lie, and nothing had ever made me this stupidly happy.

Cahki came back to my cell the next night and whispered me back to better health. My fever was now fully gone, and with the nourishment from the food she had spirited in, I was quickly returning to my former self. But the best part of the whole thing was her company throughout those lonesome, coal-black nights. With her there, the terrifying memories that I had carried with me for most of my life of waking up in the dark one night, wet and confused, were kept at bay. Memories of being in bed, paralyzed by fear, knowing someone was lying beside me in the dark. The feeling of the sticky wetness on my clothes and my hands haunted me to this day. Even before I was sure of what it was, I knew it was something frightening and heartbreaking. I had scrambled around for a light of any kind, but none was to be found. So I waited for dawn, for those first rays of light to seep into the room just enough that I could identify what was going on.

I groaned, wishing that train of thought gone, but it was too late.

"Sung-jin? Are you all right?" Cahki had been napping beside me, her hand loosely resting on my thigh. "Are you in pain again?"

I shook my head, hating myself for waking her up. "Sorry. Just a nightmare."

She sat straighter and searched for something in my eyes. "What were you dreaming about? Your father's punishments?"

I chuckled bitterly. "Believe it or not, his beatings are not the worst he has ever done to me," I said. "He's done far more."

Quiet for a moment, Cahki bit his upper lip. "Like what? What could possibly be worse than almost killing you?"

She had no idea, and I hoped she would never experience the fullness of my father's cruelty. "One day, when I was sixteen, I woke up bathed in blood." Cahki started, her lips ajar. I wasn't sure why I was telling her this. Other than Hwarang, I had never told anyone. "It was the middle of the night, and I couldn't see anything because he had made sure to close all the shutters and taken all other sources of light away. I knew something was wrong since I couldn't even conjure up a magic glow, but I wasn't aware of the enormity of it all until the sun came up, and light came through the cracks in the windows."

"Whose blood was it?" my wife asked, eyes glistening in the dusk.

"My mother's." My voice faltered as the memory exploded in my mind. I had been lying in bed all night next to my butchered mother. "He had slit her throat and wrists and left her to bleed to death beside me." At the time, I couldn't understand why I didn't remember it happening—until I found out my father had drugged me which explained my inability to magick a glowing light. I learned his lesson: you did not challenge your father, or else. "I had begun questioning his practices and effectiveness as an emperor and was foolish enough to voice those concerns. My father could have killed me, but I was his only remaining heir, so he killed my mother instead. Message received loud and clear: obey him or lose everyone I care about."

Lost inside my head, I didn't notice that Cahki had covered my hand with hers until she began rubbing her thumb over my skin. Shivers ran through me, both from pleasure and gratefulness. "I will help you fight him," she said in such a small voice I barely heard it. "I will do all I can to depose the son of a bitch."

My eyes sought hers, and when they found them, it brought a smile to my face. Cahki always sounded so fierce, so determined. One of the many reasons, against all odds and my best efforts to the contrary, I had fallen for her. "You're beautiful, wife." The words escaped my lips before I could stop them, so I waited for her reaction.

I half expected her to smack me or storm out of the cell in a huff, but instead she leaned in, cupped my cheek, and kissed me. At first it was a mere touch of lips, a tiny peck of gratitude, perhaps. But it soon caught fire, our mouths and tongues tasting each other, teasing and demanding. The flames spread to the rest of my body and settled in my gut, making me hard and hurting for release.

"Cahki," I whispered against her lips, breathless. "You don't have to do this."

She bit me. Not hard enough to really hurt but enough to draw blood. "That's what you get for rejecting me, husband," she announced, cleaning a drop of my blood from her lower lip with a finger, murder in her gaze.

I didn't bother wiping my lips. I had brought her into the mess that was my life without any regard, at first, for her safety, so I deserved it. "I'm not rejecting you, Cahki," I said, finding it hard to breathe. "There's nothing I want more at this moment than to make you mine, but I'm in a fucking prison cell. What kind of man would I be to take you under such circumstances? I wouldn't be able to live with myself afterward." I took a deep breath. "I'm not rejecting you, wife. I'm respecting you."

Cahki, her long white hair standing out from the darkness of the cell, studied me from under half-closed eyes. "Respecting me?" she echoed in a quiet voice. I nodded, unsure she would take that as the compliment I intended or twist it into something negative as she often did. She was quiet for what felt like hours before she added, "All right. Respect it is. I will also respect your feelings and not push further."

I sighed—of relief or disappointment, I wasn't sure which—my thin pants straining against an erection that didn't agree with my thoughts and my words.

"I'll tell you what, Your Stupid Handsomeness," she started again, her gaze rolling over every inch of my body from my feet to my mouth. "I will respect you until you get out of this cage, but after that, it's no-holds-barred, my husband. You. Will. Be. Mine."

Chapter 20
New Plan

"**H**is Imperial Majesty, the emperor, requests your presence," the servant said, making the word *request* sound more like *order*.

I had managed to avoid the crooked emperor for the few days Sung-jin had been jailed, but I knew that sooner or later, I would be summoned. The very thought of seeing the same man who sat on his throne masturbating while I danced for him made me want to throw up. But I had made the decision to do what I could to help my husband defeat the monster he had for a father, and if that meant having to pretend the emperor's actions were flattering rather than debasing, I'd swallow my disgust and do it.

"I'll be along shortly," I told him, clasping my hands together to stop them from shaking. I had to pull myself together before facing my father-in-law. The emperor had to see me as harmless and helpless against his kinks but also singularly dedicated to his son so he wouldn't forget the enchantment tying us together—and keep his monstrous hands off me. "You can do it," I told myself after the servant had left. "You have survived blizzards and savage animals—you *so* can do this."

By the time I arrived at the door to the throne room, I had somehow managed to get my emotions under control. I only hoped I could keep calm throughout the whole thing.

I strode confidently down the long hallway until I was standing at the bottom of the steps to the throne platform. I bowed and kept my eyes on the floor before me. "May you live a thousand years, Your Imperial Majesty," I said, my fingers discreetly crossed inside the folds of my skirts.

"Get up," that most hated voice said. I raised my eyes to find his dark face, handsome but overshadowed by the evil in his heart. "Why haven't you visited me for the past couple days?"

Straight to the matter at hand. I could deal with that. "My profound apologies, Your Majesty," I said, hoping my acting skills were believable. "My husband was jailed, so I didn't think it would be proper for me to be out and about."

He grunted. "Yet, you were seen walking around the palace courtyards."

Damn! His spies had spotted me. "I did try to visit Sung-jin a few times." Half-truths were better than lies. "But the guards wouldn't allow it."

"And so they shouldn't," he said with a slap on the arm of the throne. "I ordered him to be isolated."

I went down on my knees and bowed all the way until my forehead met the cold floor. "I know I did wrong, Your Majesty, but he's my husband, and I was anxious about him, like all good wives should be." Would he buy it? I added for effect, "I wasn't thinking straight."

After a moment of silence, he told me to get up. "Silly of me to expect a woman to understand the situation," he said in his usual condescending tone. "No problem. The guards did their jobs. Good."

I got up onto my feet slowly, making sure I didn't look directly at him. I even managed a few tears. Let him think I was scared or humbled by his forgiveness. The truth was, I didn't want to look at him and be reminded of what I had been forced to watch a few days ago: a powerful man with his pants down around his ankles, pumping himself hard while I tried to keep it together, whirling around the room like a drunken butterfly. Bile rose to my throat again, but I pushed it down. I wasn't going to let him see me squirm.

"Put yourself together, woman," he ordered, gesturing toward me. "Sung-jin will be out today. No need for tears." I made a big production of wiping my eyes on the edge of my wide sleeve. "Go now! But be here tomorrow as usual to resume your duties."

I bowed again, relief washing over me. "Thank you, Your Majesty." I backed up a few steps before turning and almost running out of the throne room, away from this evil man.

Sung-jin was being released later today, and I wanted to make sure everything was ready for him. I felt like a new bride—which I supposed I was, since our marriage was a fake one and had never been consummated—a fact that made me extremely irritable; why should I be anxious about having my fake husband home again? It wasn't as if I loved him. I didn't.

Did I?

No, of course I didn't love him. I was attracted to him. Very much so. After all, he was a beautiful man with his narrow, dark brown eyes and a long curtain of inky silk for hair. And his lips were perfectly shaped, beautifully full and kissable.

Where was a fan when you needed one?

I was frantically looking for something to fan myself with when Hwarang walked in. "Do you ever knock?" I asked, my crankiness fully obvious in my tone.

He threw his hands up. "Whoa, woman, the door was wide open." He had a gift for always acting as if *he* were the victim. "I came to see if you needed help with anything before my brother comes back."

Hwarang had been my rock for the past couple days, and as much as I loved teasing him, I had to admit I couldn't have done it without him. "Can you check the kitchen and make sure they have his favorite food?" I asked him, giving up on my search and turning my attention to the incense burner instead. "And ask one of the servants for a lavender stick."

Cocking his head to the side, Hwarang cupped his chin and smirked. "For someone who doesn't care, you're sure going the distance to please your husband."

I melted him with my glare, but he didn't even blink. "Stop being an asshole," I told him. "I agreed to help you guys with your imperial issue, and to do that, I need to make sure Sung-jin is okay." It was a flimsy excuse, but it was all I could come up with at the time. I shooed him with my hands. "Go, go! Check it out."

The day stretched far too long before us. My anxiety had swelled to an explosive level by the time I finally heard Hwarang yell out for me from the courtyard, "Cahki, we're back."

I sprang from where I was sitting to open the door, my heart almost jumping out of my chest. Sung-jin was home.

My husband's arm was draped over his best friend's shoulders as Hwarang helped him walk. Why was he limping? There had been nothing wrong with his legs last night when I stayed with him.

Sung-jin—who I swear could read my mind—shrugged awkwardly. "My father wanted to make sure I'd remember this," he said as he limped his way across the threshold. "So he sent one of his men to break my leg this morning."

How could anyone be this beastly?

"It's his way of making sure Sung-jin can't lead any military campaigns from now on," Hwarang explained, worry creasing his brow. "Brilliant in its wickedness."

I was frozen in place, speechless. Then I growled between my teeth, "One day I will steal a boning knife from the kitchen to gut Emperor Min in cold blood. And I will enjoy every minute of it."

"I can heal it," I told him once Hwarang left to go fetch the food. "But everyone will notice if you go from disabled to walking around normally."

If the emperor found out Sung-jin was still fit and able, all hell would break loose. Whoever the guard was in charge of breaking the prince's leg would most likely be executed for a job poorly done, and the emperor would be even more irate and suspicious than he was now. New and crueler punishments would certainly follow.

"This may work for our benefit," Sung-jin said, propping his leg on a chair. The handsome idiot was pale from the pain but still putting on a cool front.

"How can this mess—any way we dice it—be beneficial?" As far as I could tell, no matter what we did, we would be stirring up more trouble.

"You heal my leg, but I keep up the pretense of being disabled," he explained, rubbing his knee. I had to check his leg soon. "That way, my father thinks I'm not much of a threat to him anymore, and we'll be able to move around more freely."

It was a good plan except for the fact that his leg was indeed broken and that the pain he was in came through loud and clear in the shadows carved beneath his eyes and the pallor of his face.

"Let me check your knee," I demanded, reaching out for the leg of his pants. He flinched even before I touched him. I rolled his pants carefully up to his knee.

"Fuck your father and all his minions," I exclaimed at the sight of his badly broken shin bone.

"You really talk like a pirate," Hwarang said as he walked in with a tray full of food. His gaze roamed to his friend's leg, and he froze. "Holy shit! They did a number on you."

That was a gross understatement. Sung-jin's knee had swelled up so much, it was unrecognizable. I couldn't feel a pulse on his leg, which could only mean one thing: there was no blood circulation below the knee. I had to act fast, or he could lose his leg or even his life.

"You have a broken tibia and a dislocated knee," I said, covering his knee with my hands as gently as I could. "Hwarang, get behind Sung-jin and hold him." I looked up at my husband and warned, "This is going to hurt."

"What are you going to do?" Hwarang asked, blinking in panic. "You're not a doctor."

Sung-jin held on to his friend's arm. "Do as she says. Trust her."

Hwarang put the tray down on the side table. "Are you kidding me? This is not a scratch or a bruise. What makes you think she won't botch the whole thing and make it worse? Has she ever set a broken bone?" he protested.

"For fuck's sake, stupid, hold on to him, or he'll lose his leg." We were running out of time, and wasting what little we had in an argument was counterproductive.

Hwarang glanced at the prince, who nodded. "I don't like this," he muttered, placing himself behind his friend. "Don't like it at all."

Once my husband's shoulders were firmly secured by his friend, I closed my eyes so I could feel the injury, counted to three in my head, and snapped the joint back into place.

If our stories about his injuries would not be believable enough, the blood-curdling scream Sung-jin let out would most definitely do the trick. People in town must have heard it.

Sweat dripped from the prince's forehead, and his pallor got worse. For a minute I thought he would pass out, but he held on, breathing deeply and steadily. I didn't want to admit it, but my admiration for him grew exponentially.

"Are you all right, brother?" Hwarang asked him. The prince nodded silently.

"He'll be okay," I assured him. "Give him a minute to calm down, and then let's carry him to his bed."

Hwarang threw me the most lethal of glares. "You better not have hurt him," he said in a low menacing voice.

"I didn't hurt him, idiot," I said, rubbing my hands together to produce some heat. "I've just set his knee. Now he needs that fracture to be taken care of."

Hwarang stepped forward to argue with me, but his friend stopped him. "She knows what she's doing. Let her be."

"Just because you are blinded by love, doesn't mean I am too." Love? What was Hwarang talking about? There was no love between us. "One of us has to stay objective."

I threw Sung-jin a silent question, but he avoided my eyes. "I am being objective, Hwarang," he protested. "Cahki knows medicine." That was a lie, of course. My gift could not be classified as medicine; it was closer to magic than science, but I knew he was trying to protect my secret.

I hung my head and hunched my shoulders with a dramatic sigh. "Just tell him, Sung-jin," I said. "He's like a dog with a bone. He'll never drop it unless we tell him the truth."

Hwarang bounced his gaze between me and my husband, his brow furrowed. "What truth? What are you talking about?"

"You tell him while I go prepare your bed," I told the prince and left the hall.

To heal such a break, I would have to expend quite a bit of my energy. With the emperor expecting me at his palace the next day, I had to be careful with how much I spent so that I could function on the morrow, even though I could always use the excuse that I had been taking care of my husband to justify my fatigue. I looked for cushions inside the cabinets and found a couple I could use to prop his knee just enough to alleviate his pain while he rested. I most likely would end up sleeping on the floor so I could keep an eye on him through the night.

The consummation I had been planning all day would have to wait until he was feeling better, which was probably a blessing in disguise. Why was I so eager to tighten our relationship all of a sudden? Nothing good could come of it. As soon as he succeeded in deposing his father, I would be on my way north, never to see him again. Why was I insisting on getting closer to him?

Whatever the answer to that question was, the fact remained that I was more than a little perplexed and annoyed by my own disappointment.

Chapter 21
Confession

I t was hard to resist the temptation to wrap my hands around her waist and draw her to me. She was so close, hovering over my body as she whispered my leg whole again. I still couldn't understand how it worked, but I could actually feel the bone knitting itself together. It wasn't a pleasant feeling but not exactly painful either. Cahki's head hung over my leg, her eyes closed and her lips moving with whatever words she used to summon her magic. She was beautiful, her disheveled hair falling over the sides of her face and onto my leg.

My gut tightened as I remembered our kiss in the cell just a night ago. Had she been serious when she told me she would have me for her own? Or was it just a ploy to distract me from the harsh reality of that dark space?

Hwarang had left, still not fully convinced Cahki could do what I had told him she could, that just like us, she had magic. Healing powers were unheard of in the Southern Kingdom, and he had always been protective of me, the big brother I had never had. Only two years older than me, Hwarang had assumed the responsibility of being my protector early on, and I had never been able to change his mind about it. I wasn't going to complain. Thanks to his willingness to do whatever he could to help me, a lot of the beatings I had been subjected to by my father didn't have as big of an impact as they would otherwise. Hwarang had hidden his magic powers since childhood and had always used them to lighten the effects of the punishments. One day, I hoped to be able to repay him for all he had done for me.

"Why are you looking at me like that for?" Cahki was finished with whatever she was doing and sat back on the bed, curling her legs under her bottom with her knees touching my bare leg.

I coughed to hide my embarrassment at being caught gawking at her. "Nothing," I lied. "You just look impressive when you whisper." Impressive? Was that something you told the girl you were in love with?

"I'm pooped," she declared, sliding her legs off the bed. "I will sleep on the floor tonight." Since our arrival at the palace, I had given her my bed and slept on a mat on the floor a few feet away from her to give her some privacy.

I grabbed her wrist and held her in place. "Why the floor? You should take the bed," I said.

"You're in it, stupid," she said, rolling her eyes. "And you're the one who's sick."

I gulped, swallowing the sudden knot in my throat. "We could share," I suggested, only half expecting her to consider it. I rushed to clarify. "It's a big bed." It was, but it was still only one bed. She would never take the offer.

Cahki hesitated for a moment, her eyes studying me as if looking for possible hidden reasons for my offer. "Okay, we'll share. I'm too bone-tired to sleep well on the floor."

I couldn't believe it and wavered between elation and apprehension. It was hard enough to have her sit next to me in bed, I could only imagine the divine torture of having her lying beside me.

Sliding off the bed, she collected a couple of steamed buns from the tray Hwarang had left in the room and came back to bed. "Here, have a bun," she said, handing me one of them. "You need food to get stronger." She took a big bite of hers and sat on the edge of the bed. "What did Hwarang mean when he said you were blinded by your love for me?"

Cahki didn't believe in subtlety.

Heat rose to my cheeks as I looked for an answer that wouldn't embarrass her or myself. I knew she cared more than she was willing to admit, but love? It was too long of a shot. "You know Hwarang. He likes to shoot his mouth off." Even I thought that was a weak excuse.

She shook her head. "No, he was serious," she said, taking another bite of the bun. "But was he talking about lust or actual love?"

My heart dropped a few inches, swelled up, and exploded inside me. I *was* in love with her. Yes, lust was there, too, but it went much deeper than that.

"No matter, I'm too tired to worry about it." With her usual abandon, Cahki threw herself on top of the bed beside me with a loud sigh of contentment. "Cozy," she declared, pulling on my pillow so she could lay her head on it. "So much better than the floor."

She flopped onto her side, facing me, her face so close to mine, I could feel her warm breath. Silence enveloped us, the only sound that of my heart thumping away in my ears. Her intense blue eyes burrowed into mine, searching. I wanted to look away, but I couldn't. I needed to swim in those lakes, dive deeper and never come up for air again.

"Love," I heard myself whisper. She lifted her head an inch or so from the pillow. "Not lust. Love. I think I'm in love with you, Cahki."

Was I really doing this? I had just fully realized that my love for her was a truth I couldn't escape from, but why tell her right now? Our lives were complicated, entwined in ways that might turn sour for both of us. Cahki viewed me as a forced ally, someone she would help because it in turn helped her get closer to returning to her kingdom and her family. That was it.

Her head fell on the pillow again, her eyes softening. "How can you be sure?" she asked. "Have you ever been in love?"

I nodded, acutely aware of the proximity of her lips. "Yes, once."

"Where is she?"

"Dead." It had been almost five years, yet the wound was still fresh. Chae-yeong had been my first and only love. Until Cahki. "Another one of my father's punishments."

Shifting a little, she licked her lips and said, "One day I'll kill him for you."

As horrible a sentiment as that was, it was the sweetest thing anyone had ever said to me. I kissed her, her soft lips fitting perfectly against mine as if they had always been meant to be joined. Cahki didn't move. Just as I was about to pull away, her arm came around me, drawing me closer. I couldn't hide my yearning from her any longer as our bodies met, and our tongues slid against each other's.

There was no denying it; I loved her and hated myself.

Loving her was cursing myself to misery. One day, if we survived my plan to defeat the emperor, she would leave, and my heart would once again shatter like a thin sheet of ice. But for now, I wanted to believe this could happen, that we could be a real couple with common dreams and a future together.

For now, I would pretend that loving this fierce female would not be the biggest mistake of my life.

The fire roared inside me. Despite part of me knowing how unwise loving this woman was, my heart was all in. And so was my body, it seemed, judging by its reaction to her touch.

Cahki's hands were just as wild and adventurous as she was, fingertips brushing over my shoulders, my chest, and crawling under the edges of my clothes to touch my bare skin. She grunted, exasperated.

"Too many clothes," she said, struggling to open my tunic. "Why do you wear so many layers?"

I chuckled. "Tradition," I explained, reaching out to help her with the ties. "Southerners are pretty...." I searched for the word as one of the knots came undone.

"Prudish?" Cahki offered. I had to laugh. "Or hiding something?" She unfastened another knot. I gasped in anticipation. "Fuck it!" she exclaimed before she sat up and ripped the other knots with a strong pull. The seamstresses would be wondering what had happened to that tunic. She peeled the fabric from my body and studied me. "You're beautiful. Why would you hide behind so many clothes?"

I wanted to sit up and free her of her clothes, too, but my leg sent waves of pain up my hip and spine every time I moved. I grunted, clenching my jaw. Oblivious to my frustration—or not caring—my wife continued her exploration, fanning her fingers over my bare chest and sending a shower of shivers through my whole body. She moved down to my belly, making small maddening circles with the tips of her fingers, bringing life to every inch of my sore muscles.

"Does it hurt?" she asked, bending over me and replacing her fingers with her lips. "I don't want to hurt you."

My leg did hurt, but I didn't care. My desire for Cahki was stronger and more urgent than the need for pain relief. I needed a release of another kind, one that only the wild creature I called my wife could give me. I shook my head. "No, you're not hurting me."

She kissed each ridge of my abdominal muscles, running her tongue over them before turning her attention—and impatience—toward my pants. It took her no time to untie the knot at my waist. I braced myself for the pain, expecting her to pull on the pants as wildly as she had pulled on the tunic, but she was surprisingly gentle, slowly peeling them off me until I was naked before her. Being this vulnerable would normally set me into a panic, but with her it felt right, as if this was where I was supposed to be—no hidden agendas, no secrets, just plain, bare me.

Cahki watched me for a while, her eyes roaming over every inch of my body, lingering here and there, her gaze an invisible caress. I had been with women since Chae-yeong, strangers-in-the-night type encounters that held no meaning. This was different.

"You're hurt, so let's take it easy," she said, running a hand over my abdomen, teasingly close to my erection.

I wanted to scream, "No, let's not slow down. I don't care about the pain," but she was right. There was no way I could fully love her with my leg broken like this. Her whispering had gone a long way to make it better, but it was still far from healed.

She pulled her nightdress over her head, not bothering to untie the laces, and threw it to the floor. She wasn't wearing anything underneath. My mouth watered even as a smile erupted on my lips. She really didn't like our Southern clothing standards. My wife, the rebel. I liked it.

"Help me sit up," I requested.

With a quizzical look, she proceeded to help me up, my back supported by the wall. As she held me with her arms beneath mine, her breasts brushed my lips. I might have imagined it, but I thought I heard a gasp. Instinctively, I caught one of her breasts in my mouth and ran my tongue over her nipple. There was no mistaking it this time; she moaned and pressed herself closer to me, fanning my fire.

I held her left leg and brought it over my lap so she was straddling me. Cahki hovered over me, not touching me yet making me explode with yearning. My hands went around her waist, sliding down her narrow hips, her outer thighs, her buttocks. I groaned against her breast, still suckling, and slid a hand between her legs to caress her softness. Cahki threw her head back and moaned, pressing herself down onto my hand but being careful not to sit on my lap. I wanted her too. I wanted to be inside her. My grunt of frustration quickly turned into a yelp of surprise when Cahki closed her hand around my erection.

"I can pleasure you without pain," she said, her lips over my ear.

She set out to prove it, sliding her hand along my length, first gently, cautiously, but soon with all the power and passion I knew she had in her. I matched her moves with those of my fingers over and then inside her folds, in and out, faster and faster, my tongue still dancing over her nipple until we were ejected to the skies above—a meteor shower of sensations that left us both breathless. We leaned on each other, spent and sated.

Moments later when we lay side by side, her beautiful face against my shoulder and her hair spilled around her like a halo, I couldn't help but smile. Cahki was not all edges and sharp corners. There was softness underneath her fierceness, just like I had guessed. As I watched her sleep, her white eyelashes fanning over her ivory skin, my smile faded away, my heart shattering into a million fragments.

I had declared my love for her, but she had not once said she loved me back.

Chapter 22
Whisperer

S ung-jin had been acting weird all morning. It was more than
awkwardness over what we had done the night before. He kept
avoiding my gaze, as if afraid I would hurt him. He had told me he
loved me. Did he expect me to tell him I loved him too?

Except I didn't know if I did.

I did care for him, but I had never been in love before. My only
romantic partners had been male prostitutes from the local brothel.
How was I supposed to know what love felt like? Was this constant
worry about his health a sign of love? Or the heat and tingling feeling
in my gut whenever I touched him? The truth was, I didn't know
whether I loved him or not, and by now, I had grown to respect him
enough not to lie to him about something so important.

I shook my head, dispelling those thoughts. There was no time to
waste. I was expected in the palace, gods protect me!

"Be careful," Sung-jin, my husband and now lover, said, the first
few words he had uttered all morning.

Turning briefly around, I waved and smiled. "Don't worry. I'll be
fine. Got my dagger with me." I was hoping that would put him at
ease. The fool could barely walk and had a father who hadn't hesitated
to disable him for life, yet he still worried about me. My heart clenched
a teeny bit.

"I'll send Hwarang around in a while," he told me, a wince of pain twisting his lovely features as he tried to move his leg.

I sighed, tempted to turn around and take care of him instead of catering to his awful father, but I knew that wouldn't end well for me or Sung-jin. "Try not to move too much," I said instead. "I'll take care of your leg when I come back."

He made a grunting sound that I took as assent and left.

A nervous energy was running through me like electricity from a storm. I was scared. Not that the emperor would hurt me, but being exposed to more of his disgusting sexual activities was not something I was looking forward to. With the fear there was excitement. One of the servants had told me that morning that the emperor was expecting some guests. During such occasions, information sometimes slipped, and I was itching to find out more about why my father-in-law was planning to attack the Northern Kingdom, a place that held no value to him at all.

Dressed in my plainest clothes, I arrived at the imperial palace just in time to witness the arrival of a couple of dignitaries I had seen before. One of them was the Imperial Army General who controlled the armed forces for the emperor, and the other was a minister who visited often and tended to have a loose tongue, especially after a few drinks. I made a mental note to put some alcohol in his tea and see what happened.

Other than a lascivious glare or two, the emperor largely ignored me as I busied myself serving tea and pastries to him and his guests, later adding several carafes of wine to the beverage offerings. I came and went quietly, willing myself invisible, and when I was out of the room, I made sure I was hidden somewhere close enough to listen to the conversation.

As expected, after a few glasses of wine, their tongues began to wag more freely. I pressed myself against the balustrade where I was hidden and listened. There was indeed talk of invading the northern territories, subduing or bribing the fjord pirates into working for the empire until they could find the one thing they were searching for.

But what was it? They kept referring to it as the vessel. What the fuck did they mean by that? Some valuable cup? A ship of some kind? I strained to listen more closely.

"How can we be sure this vessel actually exists?" the general, who was the only one who seemed to be controlling his drinking, asked.

"It does. My spies in the North confirmed it." There was no room for arguing as the emperor lifted his cup with a drunken air of authority. Then he folded over himself, leaning toward his conspirators. "It is said that whoever or whatever this vessel is, with one drink of its blood, you can revive the dead."

My whole body went cold.

"Can you imagine the advantage we would have over our enemies if we could revive every dead soldier in the battlefield?" the emperor asked no one in particular. "I would truly be the ruler of the whole world."

My legs went weak beneath me, and I had to hold on tighter to the balustrade. I couldn't let them see me.

"Do we have intelligence on who this vessel might be?" the general asked.

"Not a name per se," the minister replied. "But we know what they call it."

With my heart exploding inside my chest, I dug my fingers onto the marble, breaking a few nails. Could it be? Could they have found the secret that had been so carefully protected and hidden from the world?

The minister, a bald man in his fifties, leaned even closer. "They call it the Whisperer."

My legs did give out on me then. Strong hands held me up, preventing me from making a ruckus and alerting the three men in the room. "Are you okay?" Hwarang whispered from behind me.

I had never been so grateful for his presence. I put my index finger in front of my lips and pointed at the men sitting around the small table. I returned my attention to what they were saying, afraid I'd miss something vital.

"How does that work, though?" the minister asked with a hiccup. The wine was working its magic. "Wouldn't that kill the Whisperer?"

"Not if we attach the creature to a machine and siphon its blood regularly to store it for future use." My stomach rumbled and my breakfast threatened to make a reappearance. "That way, the creature will be kept alive and producing blood for as long as we need it."

The silver lining was that they obviously had no idea who this Whisperer was or even whether it was a human or something else. The bad news was that the secret my parents had striven to protect for so many years was out, and the emperor, in his greed, was on its trail.

Hwarang held on to me as we made our way to the door, tiptoeing out like thieves. I wanted to shrug him off, but my whole body shook, and I couldn't trust my legs to support my full weight. So I leaned on him and allowed myself the comfort of his strength and loyalty to my husband. Intoxicated as they were by now, the emperor and his minions would never notice I was gone.

The world had just been turned upside down again, and this time I had no idea how to turn it the right side up.

"There's no reason to panic," Hwarang said. It said a lot about how both Sung-jin and I were feeling if Hwarang was the one keeping his cool. "They don't know you've heard them, and this invasion they're planning won't be happening for a while. My sources tell me they are still a long way from having enough troops for something of that magnitude. You don't build a strong navy overnight."

He was right, of course, but the very idea that the emperor and his closest minions knew about my existence—even if in a very vague way—made me break out in hives. And by the looks of him, Sung-jin was not feeling any better.

My husband wiped his face with a hand and sighed. "How are our allies doing?" he asked Hwarang. We had allies? How did I not know this?

Hwarang threw me a look before answering, "We're not ready yet, but it's looking good." He nodded my way. "Are you sure it's okay to talk in front of her?"

Knives flew out from my eyes straight to his heart. I opened my mouth to protest, but Sung-jin beat me to it. "Cahki is my wife and an integral part of the whole thing. We can trust her."

Hwarang hesitated for a moment, bouncing his gaze between me and the prince. "No offense, Ice Princess, but you haven't always been the friendliest of allies."

No matter how right he was, it still stung that he didn't trust me. I realized I had come to think of him as a friend rather than an enemy, and that thought froze the nasty words getting ready to leave my lips. For a second. "You, King of the Idiots, are one to talk. I wouldn't trust you as far as I can throw you." Not true. I did trust him, ever since the day he had used his secret magical powers to protect his best friend.

"Can you guys just stop for a second?" Sung-jin sounded exasperated. "This is not the time for bickering like children."

We both shut our mouths and retracted our imaginary swords.

Hwarang resumed his reporting. "The Eastern Kingdom has amassed enough weapons and soldiers, but the Western Kingdom still has a way to go," he said. "I'm in negotiations with the Island Nations. They have a strong navy. If they are willing to help us, we could cut off your father's attempt at invading the Northern Kingdom."

"Why are all these nations willing to fight against Emperor Min?" I asked, surprised by how deeply this whole rebellion plot ran.

Hwarang snorted. "Have you met him?"

"They know he will invade their territories as soon as he is able," Sung-jin explained. "Better to be proactive and go on the offensive than waiting like sitting ducks."

I couldn't agree more.

"I think it's time for you to tell us more about this magic healing thing you got going on," Hwarang said, crossing his arms over his chest, the muscles of his arms visible under the stretched-out fabric of his sleeves.

I glanced at the prince. "It's okay," he said with a shrug. "I have set up a containment spell around this room. No one will hear us." My husband was full of surprises.

"It's a long story," I said, still unwilling to bring back the nasty memories attached to my tale. I'd been so perfectly happy living a regular life in the Northern fjords that I had almost forgotten who I really was. *What* I really was.

"We have no place to go," Hwarang said, a smirk on his face. "Your beloved husband is laid out with a broken leg, and I have no duties until much later today."

I sighed. The emperor was going on an official visit to a military camp outside the city and was busy preparing for the trip, which freed me from my afternoon duties at his palace. I had no excuses to postpone this conversation.

"How much do you know about the history of my kingdom?" I asked the two handsome men staring at me, one lying in bed and the other leaning against the bedpost.

Sung-jin replied, "The basic history: Queen Risberg and her consort, Count Eskelson, were dethroned by her sister Inger Risberg about twenty years ago. There was a lot of upheaval and many deaths among the nobility. Story goes that Inger is ruthless and got rid of all of those who might question her right to the throne."

I nodded. "She had whole families killed on the off chance they may rise against her rule," I said. "Ruthless doesn't begin to describe her. Now that I think about it, she's not much different from your father." Thankfully I had little to do with the court, living in the fjords, which was a place that only those who had been born there and the pirates were built to survive. "The previous queen had three children, two boys and one girl," I continued, my heart sputtering a bit at the memory. "When the coup went down, her two sons—one was fifteen and the other around ten—were immediately executed along with their parents."

"And the girl?" Hwarang asked, crossing his ankles.

"She was only five at the time and happened to be in a different part of the palace. A nanny was assigned to watch her and bring her up as was the custom in court back then." That wound inside me that had been closed and almost forgotten all these years was cracking open again. "The queen picked one of her most trusted maidservants to do the job and set her up in a remote area of the palace where the child could be raised free from the mechanics of court and be groomed for a political marriage later in life."

Sung-jin's eyes searched mine, a glint of understanding in their watery depths. He knew what I was getting at. "Edel, the maid, held a special place in her heart for the princess and protected her like a fjord cat. One day when the girl was about three, they had a visitor—an old woman who called herself Elli."

I took a deep breath, pacing myself. I had told this story exactly once in my life, and that was only because my mother wanted to make sure I'd remember it correctly.

"Edel didn't know the woman and wondered how she had managed to evade all the soldiers that guarded their side of the palace. The woman told the nanny that she was there to bestow a special gift upon the child, but that it was one that was hard to bear." Visions of my mother telling me this story by a roaring fire made my eyes water. "Edel tried to stop her, but the woman spoke some words and touched the girl's head anyway, giving her the dubious gift of bringing the dead back to life."

Hwarang had forgotten to look like an adult and stared at me with the expression of a ten-year-old listening to a story of wonder. "Is that even possible?"

I nodded. "The old woman, who, it turns out, was a goddess, gave this child the power to heal with her voice and the ability to resurrect those who were dead." I took another deep breath, my eyes burning. "There was a caveat—as always seems to be the case. Whispering to heal could only be done for short periods of time so as not to deplete the girl's life energy, and the resurrection issue—well, to bring some-one back to life, the girl had to offer some of her own blood."

"If ruthless men like my father got a hold of this girl, they would enslave her for the rest of her life," Sung-jin concluded, his face paler than usual.

The prince's best friend pushed himself from the wall, uncrossing his arms. "Well, the emperor doesn't even know it's a girl, so there's no danger. At least not imminently."

"Yes, there is a great deal of danger, Hwarang," Sung-jin replied. "The girl is here."

Hwarang's mouth fell open. "What? How do you know that?"

I stepped forward, feeling queasy. "Because I *am* that girl."

Chapter 23
Healing

I wanted to hug her. But this was Cahki, and I wasn't sure she would appreciate me showing what she would view as a sign of weakness in front of Hwarang. But I would hold her later when we were alone—I would hold her tightly in my arms until every muscle in her body relaxed and softened.

"What do you mean you're that girl?" Hwarang asked, squinting. He had dropped his arms and stepped forward a few inches.

Cahki snorted. "Are you totally dumb, Hwarang? You know about my whispers. How can you still not connect the dots?"

Now that I'd known her for a while, I recognized her at-tack-first-defend-later strategy for what it was. She hid her real feelings well behind her surface callousness, and who could blame her? She spent a lifetime hiding a major part of herself.

"But this whole thing of bringing back the dead. Are you a necro-mancer?" Hwarang's eyes burned with a mixture of curiosity and awe. Maybe even a bit of fear. He had hidden talents as well that he had kept secret his whole life as a weapon against my father and a way to protect me.

Cahki stole a glance my way. "It's supposed to be used very spar-ingly—the gift, I mean. Only when circumstances demand it." She swallowed hard. "Death must have occurred very recently, within no more than a couple of hours, for it to work. But every time I use my blood for such thing, a part of me dies."

"What do you mean?" I asked, fear filling my heart.

"I may temporarily lose the ability to speak or see," Cahki explained, and my heart fell a few inches. "There's always a price to pay for the use of magic." She took a few steps forward and sat beside me on the edge of the bed. "You know that. What happens when you use your magic?"

"I feel weak for a few hours and need to recover by meditating or resting," I replied. My magic wasn't very powerful, but it still took a toll on my energy level every time I used it.

"It's the same with me," she said. "That's why I couldn't heal your leg in one session. If I did, I wouldn't have been able to go to the imperial palace the next day because my life energy would be spent." *And we wouldn't have been able to be intimate either.* The words were left unsaid, but I heard them anyway. "Bringing back the dead is the strongest kind of magic and also the most demanding. It's possible to recover, but it takes time. I've used it twice in the past; once to save an artic fox that had bled to death and another time when one of the prostitutes in the brothel had a heart attack. It took me over a month to recover my eyesight and strength that last time."

Hwarang pulled out a chair and sat down, his brow furrowed. "So, if the emperor siphons out your blood without giving you the time to recuperate, you will end up dying?"

Cahki nodded. "I'll lose all my senses first, one at a time, until my life energy fades away completely."

"We can't let that happen," I said, timidly seeking out her hand over the covers. She didn't pull away, allowing me to wrap my fingers around hers. "We must act faster. Gather our sources and attack before my father is strong enough to do what he's planning." I squeezed her hand. "And we must keep Cahki's real identity under wraps at all costs."

Hwarang sighed. "Her position as the emperor's handmaiden won't make it easy." He was right. I hated myself for being the one who had placed her in such a dangerous position. "Or it could actually work well for her." Both Cahki and I looked up at him, an unspoken question in our eyes. "The emperor doesn't think of women as intelligent enough, so all he sees when he looks at Cahki is a sexual object incapable of rational thought, much less as the holder of such strong magic." He cupped his chin in a comical imitation of a philosopher of the past. "How does the old saying go? The best hiding place is in plain sight."

It wasn't much of a comfort, but it was something. My friend was right; my father's disdain for females could serve us well as long as we could keep my miraculous recovery a secret.

"Hwarang has a point," I told Cahki, our hands still connected. "We will have to be extra cognizant of acting as if I am disabled so we don't raise any suspicions of your gifts. And you, Cahki, have to do your best to blend in with the background."

She nodded, her lips still pinched.

"In the meantime, I will speed things up on my front," Hwarang added. "I will talk to the Island Nation representatives again and be clear about the urgency of the uprising. Knowing the emperor is indeed plotting an invasion of the Northern Kingdom will put a fire under their asses." He stood up, moving the chair aside. "You, lovebirds, enjoy the rest of your day together. I will go speak to my contacts."

I didn't dare look at Cahki at the mention of our developing relationship, but she didn't move away from me. I took that as a good sign. Maybe we actually had a future together.

As soon as my friend had left and I dropped the defensive barrier, Cahki climbed onto the bed, kneeling beside me. My heart thumped like a mad rabbit, but all she said was, "Time for treatment." Disappointment flooded me as she pulled the bed linens off me and leaned over my injured leg. She examined it with the proficiency of an experienced doctor before declaring, "Another couple whispers should do it."

At the moment, I couldn't care less if I ever walked again if it meant she'd lie down, hold me, and never let me go. My heart was bursting with love for this wild creature I had married just as the fear of losing her paralyzed me.

"Will you kiss me?" The words escaped me unbidden. "It's okay if you don't love me. How could you, after what I did? Tricking you into marrying me, tying you to this insane and dangerous plot. How can I ever expect you to care for me?" Now that I had spoken, I couldn't stop pouring my heart out to her. "But I love you just the same and always will, Cahki. Can you forgive me?"

She watched me for a long moment in silence, her eyes probing but not cold. I knew I had seen warmth in them many times before, no matter how much she wanted to hide it. I knew there was something, maybe not love, but definitely something there for me.

"Why aren't you saying anything?" I pleaded, torn by her silence.

Quiet as the mist that covered the ocean in the morning, she scooted closer, her gaze still locked with mine. Placing her hands on my shoulders, she pushed me down onto the bed until I was lying flat, and her face hovered over mine. So sure that she was getting ready to whisper her healing magic, I let out a small sigh of disappointment.

"I've already forgiven you, Your Stupidity," she whispered, her breath warming my lips. "Why else would I do this?"

Her head dipped lower until her mouth was on mine, hungry and sweet, devouring me whole, heart and soul.

With my lower lip still stuck between her teeth, Cahki began her whispering. That now familiar feeling of bone restructuring and sinew stitching itself together spread over my broken leg from my hip to my toes. I let out a quiet moan, half from disappointment that her mouth was not on mine anymore, half from the strange healing sensation.

"Does it hurt?" she asked, putting a few extra inches between our faces so she could look me in the eye.

I shook my head. "No, I just wasn't prepared." For the healing or the kiss? I wasn't sure. "It's all right."

Cahki watched me for a few seconds and then resumed her whispering, her lips hovering over mine but not touching them, a sweet torture that was wreaking havoc on my senses. A few more moments of that, and I would be throwing caution to the wind and pulling her onto my lap.

"Don't even think about it," she said in between whispers. "There will be time for it later."

I grunted, not sure whether I was more annoyed about her reading my not-so-pure thoughts or the fact that I had to wait. But I obeyed, lying as still as I could while her breath caressed my face and her hair tickled my neck.

I may have fallen asleep, because I wasn't immediately aware she had stopped. She dropped down beside me on the bed with a loud sigh, and I had to bring myself back from wherever my mind had gone to focus on the present. I turned my face toward her and frowned. Her eyes were closed, and her breath was shallow and rough, as if she had run a marathon.

"What's wrong?" I asked in a panic, turning onto my side to better look at her.

Cahki never opened her eyes. "I'm fine, just tired. I need to sleep to recuperate from the healing."

I hated that taking care of me took so much out of her. It felt as if I were sucking the life out of her even though she'd assured me she could—and would—recover completely after a good night's sleep, maybe two. I draped an arm over her and pulled her closer until her head rested comfortably on the flat of my shoulder.

"Sleep in peace, wife," I whispered, my lips brushing her forehead. "Let me take care of you for a while."

All thoughts of consummating our marriage flew out of my head. The important thing now was for her to be strong again. What if my father came back early and summoned her? She would be too weak to drag herself to the palace, much less dance or serve my father the blasted tea he so adored. I uttered a little prayer under my breath as Cahki cuddled closer to me.

Gods, it felt so right to have her glued to my side, her head on my shoulder, her hair spilled over my arm and chest. It was pure perfection of the kind I had never experienced, not even with Chae-yeong. Cahki's face had softened, all her sharp edges wiped from her face by slumber, exposing the core of her heart: wild but warm. I closed my eyes, too, relishing her heat against my body. When she moved her leg and placed it over my broken one, I cringed in anticipation of the pain, but there was none. Whatever she had done, it seemed it had totally healed it. There was no pain, no numbness, and when I tried to move it, I could do it with ease.

"That's going to be a problem." Hwarang's voice startled me, and my eyes flew wide open.

With my index finger over my lips, I told him to quiet down. "Don't wake her up. She needs rest. What are you talking about, and why are you back so soon? I thought you were going to talk to the Island Nation representatives."

Hwarang pulled up a chair and sat down. "I sent a pigeon message to Lord Kappas to set up a meeting in the near future," he explained. "Now I wait and see. But the fact that your leg is healed will be a major problem for us all."

I knew I would have to fake my disability in order not to raise any suspicions from my father. The last thing I wanted was for him to start wondering why I had healed so fast. But I could easily fake it. Gods knew I was used to pretending all kinds of things my whole life.

"You know your father," my friend continued, brushing dust off his pants. "He's going to send an imperial physician to check your leg under the guise of concern for your well-being."

Shit! He was right. I wouldn't be surprised if I got a visit from one of his trusted doctors first thing in the morning. This was why I had never allowed my father to know about my own magic powers. "I will have to persuade the doctor into believing it's irreparably broken."

I had lured Cahki that night at the harbor and then captured her with the same magic. I had often tried to use it on my father, but his minions—some of whom had significant powers even if he himself didn't—had built some kind of protection around him that I had never been able to breach. But I could easily convince the doctor that I was damaged goods.

"What if the doctor has a protection like your father?" Hwarang asked, biting a nail.

"Doubtful," I said, hoping to all the gods in heaven that I wasn't being overly optimistic. "He wouldn't waste precious magic on a minion visiting his worthless son." He had often told me that very thing—that I wasn't worth much in his eyes, just an heir, a necessary evil for any ruler. Fortunately he had never been able to produce other children after my brother. My mother used to say he was so rotten inside that his sperm had shriveled up and died from his toxic fumes. If I had more siblings, I would most likely be dead by now. He'd have had no reason to keep alive the rebel son who could never be what he wanted.

Hwarang threw a glance at Cahki, who still slept on, blissfully ignorant of the conversation. "What about her? What do we do?"

I looked down at her face and brushed my fingers over her cheek. "She's my wife, Hwarang, and I love her," I admitted, not expecting to surprise my best friend who knew me better than I knew myself. "So what do we do about her? We protect her, brother."

My friend nodded in agreement. "We protect her," he repeated, straightening his back. "We will protect her with our lives."

Chapter 24
Whispering Love

The room was dark when I woke up. For a moment, I thought it was the middle of the night, but I saw light coming through the cracks in the shutters. I sat up in bed, letting my eyes adapt to the darkness, and searched for Sung-jin. He was nowhere to be seen. Why were men so stubborn? I had specifically told him he should rest his leg as much as possible for a few days to make sure the healing was complete. So where the fuck had he gone?

My stomach growled as I swung my legs over the edge of the bed. Why was I so hungry? I had just eaten a few hours ago. At least I thought I had. I searched my memory for what I had been doing before falling asleep.

"Whispering," I exclaimed. I had been healing my husband's leg. So I must have been asleep for a long time. I had pushed myself harder than I would normally do. Knowing the emperor was out of town for at least a couple days and that Sung-jin had some tough decisions to make in the near future, I had decided to heal him in one session. I must have been severely depleted of energy afterward. The question was, how long had I been asleep?

The door opened, letting the brightness of the outside in. I blinked and shaded my eyes.

"You're awake." I couldn't see him clearly because of the glare, but his voice was so familiar now, I would recognize it no matter what.

Sung-jin walked across the room and began opening the shutters. "Did you rest well? Are you recovered?"

The sunshine hurt my eyes but warmed my skin. "I feel great," I said, still holding my palm over my eyes. "But I am hungry."

He chuckled, striding in my direction. "You would be. You've been asleep for two whole days with no food." He sat next to me, holding my hand in his. "I've asked a servant to bring you some food."

"How's your leg?" I blinked away the rest of the glare and stared at my husband. "I hope you've been taking it easy."

He nodded. "It's perfect. Hwarang has brought a wheelchair and a pair of crutches for when I have visitors or have to go outside our courtyard. My father's doctor reported my total disability to him." He grinned, the face of a little boy whose silly prank had worked to perfection. My heart melted a little, and I had to fight the urge to hug him. "He has no idea I am fit and able."

There was a hint of naughtiness in his voice, and I was just about to respond when a maidservant walked in with a tray piled high with food. My stomach growled again as the delicious aroma hit my nose.

"Put it down on the table," Sung-jin ordered. "And get some of the good wine, please."

The girl did as requested and then left in search of the drink. Sung-jin held my hand tighter and led me to the table. The colors, the smell—everything looked tantalizing, and I didn't waste any time; I dug in with all the enthusiasm of a woman marooned on a deserted island.

Sung-jin laughed. "Slow down, Cahki, you'll choke," he said, using his chopsticks to select some of the foods and place them in my bowl. "More vegetables, less meat. Your stomach is empty, so you have to be careful."

The maidservant came back with a pitcher of wine and poured two full glasses for us before leaving us again. "It's pretty mild wine. Low alcohol," he said. "You can drink quite a bit without getting drunk."

At that point, I didn't care. I was hungry, thirsty, and full of a nervous energy I couldn't quite explain but suspected had something to do with the man sitting next to me. I wanted to taste his lips again, touch the scars on his lovely back, pull down his pants and—

What was I thinking? Had the effort from the forced healing messed with my hormones? To avoid answering that question even to myself, I stuffed my mouth with a steamed bun and almost choked on it when my imagination and libido turned it into a certain part of his male anatomy.

Sung-jin, unaware of what was going on in my head, patted my back. "See? You're eating too fast," he said. I would have burst out laughing if it weren't for the fact that I was too busy coughing. "The food is not going anywhere. Take it slowly."

I wiped my mouth on a napkin and stood up. Sun-jin looked at me as if I had grown an extra set of arms. I took a step closer to him, and before he could react, I straddled him and wrapped my hands behind his neck. "Don't tell me what to do, husband." He opened his mouth to say something, but I filled it with my tongue, pressing his face against mine, crazy with desire.

His reaction was almost instantaneous as he swelled beneath me, his hardness growing against my softness. He moaned into my mouth, his own hands now cupping my butt, pulling me closer. I obliged, wiggling on his lap, making him harder.

When he stood up with his hands under my behind, I wrapped my legs tightly around his hips, and he carried me like that to the bed where he gently deposited me before taking a step back. "You're so beautiful, Cahki," he said, awe in his voice. He stood before me, flushed and wide-eyed, his lips parted as if he was about to say something else.

"What are you going to do about that?" I asked, pointing at his obvious state of arousal. I had never been good with sentimentality, and no one other than my parents had ever looked at me with that much adoration in their eyes. I didn't know how to act.

I needn't have worried. He threw his head back and roared in laughter. "That's my Cahki, forever practical," he said with a hungry glance at me. "Why don't we start with this?"

He bent a knee on the edge of the bed and, leaning over, began untying my dress. I didn't wear much unless I was working at the imperial palace, so it only took him a few seconds to free my body from all the clothing. I lay naked before him, and he drank me in with his nearly closed eyes, beautifully shaped and reminiscent of his smile. Bowing over my body, he trailed kisses from my neck down, lingering over my breasts before continuing its way lower. Gently, he pried my thighs apart and settled between them. My whole body shook in anticipation, and when his lips found that part of me that ached for him, I thought I'd shoot into the air like a firecracker. Hot blood raced through me as he created magic with his tongue, his hands softly rubbing my outer thighs. My back arched to meet his mouth and the wonder of his touch.

When I thought I would fly to the stars and never come back down, I pulled away, overtaken by the need to have him inside me, to be one with him. I had never connected at that level with anyone, nor had I thought I'd ever want to. But I did now. I wanted to be everything for this prince—the sun, the moon, and the stars. The waves of the ocean and the comfort of the hearth. I wanted to be his world.

Sung-jin read my mind, like he often did, and discarded all his clothes in a heap on the floor, wasting no time in hovering over me, lowering himself between my legs until I could feel his desire against mine—hardness pressing against softness with the gentlest of touches at first, but soon wild and out of control like a fire. He filled me completely, and I welcomed him with a moan that sounded more like a purr.

"I love you," he said, voice hoarse and thick with yearning.

I met each movement of his hips with mine, and just as I was about to explode into a million points of light, I heard myself say, "I love you too."

"Do these hurt?" I asked as I traced one of the many scars on Sung-jin's back. He was lying on his stomach, his left arm cushioning his head. He blinked and smiled at me. "Well, do they?"

"Sometimes," he said, turning onto his side to better face me. "But the pain is a good reminder and motivator to keep going. My father must be stopped."

Leaning forward, I kissed his nose. "He will," I promised, even though I had no idea how to accomplish such a thing. "Good will prevail." That silly romantic core I kept well hidden inside crept out every time I was around this man.

Sung-jin smiled again, his whole face opening. "You do realize you told me you love me, right?"

A wave of heat flooded my cheeks. "Blame it on your excellent lovemaking," I quipped, still unwilling to fully accept the fact I did love him.

I had been taught to stay aloof, to not trust anyone, to rely only on myself. "You must keep yourself and your heart a secret, my child." I had heard that since my mother—my nanny—had brought me to the fjords. She'd rescued me from certain death at the hands of the traitors and hid me well all those years. "Love makes you vulnerable, makes you visible," she used to say.

"I am pretty good, right?" Sung-jin said with a wink, brushing a stray hair from my face.

I chuckled. "Don't be too cocky. I've had better." As soon as the words were out of my mouth, I wished them retracted.

A shadow crossed my lover's eyes. "Have you had many lovers?" he whispered, his hand trailing down my arm in a sweet caress that made me shiver.

"I've had a few," I admitted.

Not lovers. The word implied there were feelings between us. All my previous lovers were prostitutes from the local pleasure house, the famous—or infamous, depending on who you asked—Himmel Hus. The name of the place, a large, beautiful house with walls covered in erotic art and diaphanous fabric panels, literally translated to Heaven House. I had made friends there—or at least, the closest thing to a friend I was going to get. Not the kind you confide in with your deepest secrets, but the type you can at least talk to, someone to keep you company, to hold you through the night when you're scared and can't let anyone know. I had a couple favorite prostitutes in the Himmel Hus, beautiful males who were more than willing to make me feel wanted and alive for a handful of coins. But beyond our paid relationship, there was nothing else. After a night or two in the Hus, I'd return home, where my parents and a few villagers were my only company. Back then I'd thought it would be enough, but now that I had met my prince, I wasn't so sure anymore.

"They didn't mean much," I continued, watching for his reaction. "Company and physical pleasure. Nothing emotional. Being the Whisperer does not lend oneself to lasting and true loving relationships. My best friends were the wild animals in the fjord." I chuckled softly, remembering the arctic foxes that used to follow me around and the snow-white rabbits that always came calling, knowing all too well I'd feed them and provide an ear rub. I squinted at him. "Are you jealous?"

He smiled, and my heart turned liquid again. Sung-jin was so beautiful and so genuine when he smiled. "Maybe a little," he said, tapping my nose with his finger. "Will I have to kill them to make sure I have no competition?"

Rising up onto my elbow, I pretended to be shocked. "Don't you dare, Sung-jin. They are kindhearted people who do not deserve to die."

"Now, I'm really jealous," he said, supporting his head on his bent arm. We locked eyes for a moment, my heart pit-a-patting in my chest. "I'm sorry, Cahki," he said, suddenly serious.

"For what?" I knew what he was about to say. I saw it in his eyes every time he looked at me: guilt and regret.

"For forcing you into this marriage. For putting you in such a dangerous position." He reached out to touch my face. "For having a cruel and ruthless father who thinks of no one but himself."

I couldn't help it. The pain in his voice, the sincerity in his gaze, it was all too much for Cahki the Cold. All my defensive ice thawed out, and I shamelessly threw myself into his arms, drawing him close to me until our skins melded together and I could feel his heart beating in tandem with mine. Was this love? I wasn't sure how I felt about it, never having loved anyone before but my parents and my furry friends. Now my heart overflowed with love for this man who was nothing but a stranger a few weeks ago and then an enemy, someone I had planned to kill sooner or later.

I'd now sooner kill myself than my lovely prince.

Talk about a plot twist.

Chapter 25
Taking Risks

H warang's normally jovial expression was nowhere to be seen. Instead, his features were a canvas on which every sign of worry—creased brow, pinched lips, narrowed eyes—was painted. I had never seen my friend like this, which was a sure sign that the situation was indeed dire.

"If we don't hear from the Island Nations soon, we may be too late to stop your father," he said, pointing at a spot on the map that covered the tabletop. "He has amassed an alarming number of men and weapons, including ships, in just the last few days."

I swept my hand through my disheveled hair. Hwarang had wrenched me out of bed, and I hadn't had the time to gather my hair into my usual top bun. "But these are mostly untrained men," I countered, desperate to find the silver lining in the situation. "It will take time to train them properly."

A bitter chuckle escaped my friend's mouth. "Who are we kidding? Your father only needs bodies to hold the guns and serve as an armor of sorts." He sobered up quickly. "He will use these untrained soldiers as a wall between the enemy and the real troops. He doesn't care if they all die as long as they take the bullets aimed at the soldiers who can actually defeat the enemy."

It was a horrifying thought that carried my father's personal signature. I knew Hwarang was right; my father would send all those untrained men into slaughter to protect the ones hiding behind them. The enemy would waste so much ammunition and energy on the sheer numbers of sacrificial lambs that by the time the real threat emerged from the carnage, they would be spent and ready for the plucking. The emperor was a diabolic genius, the scariest of all villains.

"What do we do?" My voice sounded the way I felt: discouraged and desperate.

"We give them hell!" My beautiful wife crossed the threshold, a fierce scowl on her face. "We find a way to win."

Easier said than done, especially if we didn't succeed in securing the help of the Island Nations, the only people who had a strong enough navy to fight and win against my father's. "How?" Even my years of experience participating in battles didn't help me come up with a viable solution.

Cahki approached the table we had the map stretched out on. She studied it for a moment in silence. "Do we know what his plan of attack is? Where is he heading, exactly?" she asked, raising her gaze to mine.

I shook my head, and Hwarang answered, "We don't know yet. He's keeping the plans well hidden. Even my spies haven't been able to set eyes on it. He must be keeping the war room under lock and key."

She circled the table, her eyes back on the map as she trailed a finger over it. "How long is he away?"

"At least until Saturday," I said. "Maybe even Sunday."

Silence fell over us again while my wife bit her bottom lip, lost in thought. "I have an idea," she finally said. "But it's risky."

Everything about this situation was risky, but if I had been determined before to stop this invasion and depose the tyrant who had fathered me, I was a million times more driven now that Cahki's secret—her life—was at stake. I was not going to let anything bad happen to my love.

"Let's have it," Hwarang said. "You're crazy, but you have good ideas sometimes."

Cahki narrowed her eyes at my friend before continuing. "We sneak into the war room and take a peek at the plans."

Hwarang slapped his thigh. "Brilliant! Why didn't I think of that?" There was so much sarcasm in his voice, you could almost smell it. "Which part of 'under lock and key' didn't you understand?"

My wife scowled at him, and I interrupted before they started fighting again. "There are guards at the door and a lock for which we don't have the key. Neither does anyone in the palace. My father would have taken both copies with him." His suspicious personality wouldn't let him trust even a close government or military official with something that important.

"The lock isn't an issue," she said, waving a hand dismissively. "The question is, will you be able to do your magic and put the guards to sleep if it comes to that?"

What was she plotting? I nodded. Putting them to sleep wouldn't be a problem at all, but the room was deep inside the imperial palace, and we would have to cross a couple courtyards that were heavily guarded day and night. Even if we weren't stopped, my father would find out we had been prowling in his palace. I told her that much.

"Where's your sense of adventure, my husband?" Cahki said, stepping closer enough to me to place her hand on my chest while running her gaze up to my eyes. Heat erupted in my cheeks and other inconvenient parts of my body. "When I say we sneak in, I mean remain undetected." She threw a glare at Hwarang. "Your idiot friend can be the lookout, since he doesn't seem to have the balls for this."

Despite the seriousness of what we were discussing, a chuckle escaped me. Cahki rewarded me with one of her almost feline smiles.

"Wait!" Hwarang exclaimed, cocking his head to the side. "You guys did it." Heavens above, I'd never hear the end of this. "You consummated."

"None of your business, asshole." Cahki rose on her tiptoes and planted a kiss on my cheek. "But yes, we did." She turned suddenly toward him. "Are you jealous?"

My friend tried to say something, but all he could do was sputter some nonsense with his hands on his hips and the most confused expression I had ever seen on his face.

"I thought so," my wife continued. "I'm sure you will find a Mrs. Asshole to keep your bed warm someday. Even though some women in the Northern Lands keep more than one husband, I am a one-man girl."

I knew she was just teasing my friend, but her last words brought a stupid smile to my lips that stayed there for the rest of the day.

"This is a terrible idea," Hwarang moaned behind us for the third or fourth time. Cahki half turned around to punch his arm and shush him. "Ouch, woman. Beating me is not going to change the fact that we are in way over our heads here."

The glare she threw at my friend could melt a whole fjord. "Keep your whining down, idiot. They will hear us." She pointed in the general direction of the map room, still one courtyard away.

Sneaking around seemed to be another of my wife's many talents; she navigated dark corners and hidden paths with the agility and stealth of a thief. She would make an excellent military spy.

Hwarang muttered something under his breath, but he followed Cahki as she dashed across the courtyard, pausing briefly behind trees and bushes while keeping a steady eye on the patrol guards who walked the perimeter. I was just a couple steps behind her, bringing up the rear. My best friend was a top-notch soldier, but he was not made for this, it seemed. Give him an army of thousands any day of the week, and he will not even flinch, but put him in front of a couple sleepy guards, and the man lost his composure. I knew that he was more concerned about what would happen to me if we were caught than he was about himself. Always my protector, Hwarang didn't like this a bit.

Confirming my thoughts, he whispered, "If the emperor gets a whiff of this, you will be beheaded before you can even blink." I knew he was right, but this was bigger than me or him. "Is it worth it?" Of course it was. This involved my wife's safety, among other things. As a soldier and a royal, I knew better than to put the safety of one ahead of many no matter how much I loved her, but this also involved our people and other nations.

I nodded. "I know it's risky, but Cahki has a point," I whispered, keeping a wary eye on the retreating guards. "If we know exactly where my father is planning on attacking, we might have a chance at beating him."

The silence of the night was suddenly broken by a loud cracking sound. Cahki and I instantly turned to Hwarang, who was gingerly lifting his foot from a large broken branch. My wife opened her mouth to chide him, but the words never left her. Two of the patrol guards also heard the loud sound and turned toward us with alarm on their faces.

"Who's there?" one of them yelled before taking off at a run in our direction.

"Shit!" Cahki exclaimed between her teeth. She didn't waste any time. Bending further down behind the large bush we were using as a hiding place, she picked up a rock and threw it with all her might in the opposite direction. The rock flew in a high arc and slammed loudly into one of the columns that held up the roof of the wraparound walkway. The soldiers heard it and changed directions, following the decoy. "Let's go."

We all dashed toward the gateway to the next courtyard, hoping no guards had picked that exact moment to do the same. But the guards' screams had alerted another patrol unit who then sprinted through the opening so fast, they almost stumbled over us three, leaving us with a window of only a few seconds in which to dive behind the bushes with all the speed and abandon we could muster. The pebbles covering the small garden plot's planting soil felt like shards of glass slashing my hands and wrists as I slid over it. I hoped that Cahki had fared better. Female clothing was not as thick and protective as that of males, but I didn't have time to worry about that as more than one group of patrol guards ran past our poorly hidden bodies to help their peers.

"Fuck, that hurt," Hwarang muttered beside me, his black-clad body almost invisible in the darkness.

"Stop whining and let's go," Cahki grumbled. "They're all distracted. This is our chance."

She was right. We had inadvertently created a diversion, as all the guards were gathered on the opposite side of the courtyard, leaving the next one unguarded for a while. As if of one mind, we all stood up and bolted through the gateway and across the next courtyard. We ran all the way to the door of the map room. Even the two guards who normally protected the building were off chasing the decoy. Cahki didn't waste any time and immediately started working on the lock, using one of her long hair pins.

"How are you going to open a high-security lock with a hair decoration?" Hwarang asked, blowing on his scratched hands.

A telling click echoed through the empty courtyard. Cahki glowered at my friend as she removed the lock and opened the door. "Oh, ye of little faith," she whispered, stepping into the dark room and gesturing for us to follow her. "I have a large bag of tricks."

Hwarang's face, barely illuminated by the glow of the moon, wore a comical expression, a mixture of awe and suspicion. "How in all the heavens did you do that?"

"Stop talking and get in here," she ordered, grabbing his wrist and pulling him in after us. "I have to put the lock back before they return."

As she somehow managed to close the door and make it look as if it had never been unlocked, Hwarang was still foolishly trying to get the last word. "And now, how are we ever going to get out of here?"

My wife clicked her tongue. "You have a serious lack of imagination, idiot," she said, burying the pin back in her top bun. "No wonder you don't have a girlfriend."

The familiar sputter that I had long ago come to recognize as outrage erupted from my friend's lips, and I knew I had to stop their bickering before it got out of hand. "Less talk," I said, magicking a glowing light in my hand. My mother had taught it to me as a very young boy who was terrified of the dark, and it had come in handy many times over the years.

I glanced around me, searching for the large table my father used as the staging map. It wasn't hard to find, as it was a massive square structure that occupied most of the space. I rushed toward it, my heart beating so fast, I thought I'd pass out.

Cahki got there first, her keen eyes taking it all in, analyzing and memorizing. "We can't stay long, so study it carefully and remember all the details. We'll draw our own once we go back."

For someone who had never left the Northern Lands, Cahki was an expert at reading maps, plotting routes, and forming attack strategies. She had the true soul of a soldier, as if she had been imbued with it at birth. Maybe she was. Maybe she was given this gift along with her whispering magic, a protection of sorts. Or maybe she was in fact trained for it, having had such a tough childhood and having been brought up by a pirate. Her fighting skills were impeccable, and her strength belied her slim frame.

Silence fell as each one of us learned the map by heart, collecting all the information and storing it in our memory for later use. But one thing became quickly apparent. There was a huge flaw in their plans.

Chapter 26
The Flaw

"I told you we could get out easily," I told Hwarang, a spark of cockiness in my voice. Unlocking one of the large windows at the back of the building and escaping over the wall had been a piece of cake compared to getting in. I was gratified by my husband's right-hand man's unusual silence, a sure sign he was impressed.

Sung-jin checked the doors and then made a tiny gesture with his hand—creating a sound shield, I guessed. I cleared the table and unrolled a map that Hwarang had dug up from one of my husband's many storage baskets. I waited until Sung-jin joined us by the table and then pointed at the map. "Did you notice their mistake?" I asked.

Both men nodded. "To save time they are going through one of the straits instead of going the long way around," Sung-jin said, pointing at the strait in question, a narrow passage between two of the Island Nations we were trying to get support from.

Hwarang added, "If we plan well, we can trap their ships before they reach the Northern Sea."

"But it won't do us any good if we can't get the Island Nations' support," Sung-jin said. "Or at least a guarantee that they won't ally themselves with the emperor."

I shook my head. "Now that we know the route the imperial navy will take, we can send warnings to my father," I said, a crazy plot brewing in my head. "As an ex-pirate, he can probably enlist his old cronies to protect the northern coast. Only a small group of them work for the queen. The others are not in her pocket, and though they are not known for working together, give them a strong financial motivation, and they will stick to each other like glue. If your father takes over the Northern Lands, their days are numbered. Preventing that will be highly motivational for the fjord pirates."

"In the meantime, I will talk to the Island Nations representatives again," Hwarang said. "Shouldn't we warn the Northern capital?"

"Not if we can avoid it," I said. "Our queen is not much better than the emperor, and we can't trust she'll do the right thing. Besides, if we cut them off here, Queen Risberg will never know anything happened." I waved a finger at the northern end of the Strait of Lys, and a droplet of blood fell on the map.

Sung-jin grabbed my hand. "Why are you bleeding?" he asked, concern in his voice. He turned my hand around to look at the palm. I had several deep cuts across it from when we had slid over the pebbles earlier, but in the adrenaline rush of the escape, I had forgotten about it. "You need to treat these."

With a shrug, I tried to pull my hand away, but he held it fast. "It's nothing. I have had worse cuts from the ice." It was true. Ice was treacherous, and I had cut myself many times in the past.

My husband ordered his friend to fetch the medicine kit, his dark eyebrows knitted together in worry or anger, I couldn't tell which. "Are you crazy? You're losing blood. Can you heal yourself?"

I shook my head. My gift could not be used on myself.

Hwarang came back from the next room with the small box of medicine my husband always kept around, undoubtedly because he had to treat his own injuries so often. Sung-jin opened it and picked out a small round container. "This will hurt a bit," he warned, dipping a piece of cloth inside the container. "It's a disinfectant."

He was not kidding. Whatever that white liquid was, it felt as if he were setting my palm on fire. I yelled, and Sung-jin threw me a worried glance. Embarrassed by my show of weakness, I cleared my throat and took a deep breath as my cheeks burned as much as the palm of my hand. But whatever pain I was in began to fade into the background as my husband brushed his thumb ever so gently over the wounds, little shivers of pleasure replacing the sting of the disinfectant. I chanced a glance at Sung-jin, whose eyes were on my hand as he caressed it rather than treated it.

As other more intimate parts of my body lit up in flames, I shifted on my seat, embarrassed by my feelings and hoping Hwarang was none the wiser. "What are you doing?" I asked the prince, my instincts begging me to pull my hand away from him, but I was unable to do so. I liked what he was doing. This was a new feeling for me, a mixture of lust and something much deeper I thought might be love. I both loved and hated it. It made me vulnerable.

Sung-jin lifted his beautiful eyes to mine, and his lips tilted up at the corners. "Why? Doesn't it feel good? I'm just taking care of my wife."

Damn it, husband!

Our eyes locked, and for a moment, there was nothing else in the world. Hwarang vanished, the emperor ceased to exist, as did the world outside this bubble of feeling that enveloped the two of us.

Hwarang busted it.

"What the hell are you doing?" he asked, stepping closer to us, his hands firmly on his hips. "When did you get so lovey-dovey? It's pretty sickening, you know? And totally inappropriate, considering what we're planning here."

We both looked up at him, snapping out of our love daze. Sung-jin was still holding my hand, his fingers drawing circles over the sensitive skin of my palm and releasing a meteor shower of pleasure throughout my whole body.

I forced myself to look unaffected as I frowned at Hwarang. "Are you jealous again?" I quipped, crossing my legs under the table in a futile attempt at controlling the heat pooling between my thighs. "I told you: there's zero chance between us, and I don't think you hold a chance with your friend either."

To his credit, Hwarang didn't even blink. "Like I'd want to," he said. "You guys are both rather pitiful in different ways. I'm looking for someone a bit more put together." He pointed at the map. "Can we go back to our plans?"

What I wanted to do was kick him out of the room, straddle my prince, and show him a thing or two the prostitutes in Hvithet had taught me. But Hwarang was right; there were more pressing things to think about than the burning in my gut. We had to come up with a perfect plan and execute it flawlessly.

We had to win this war.

Everything was in place.

Messages had been sent to my father, reassuring him of my relative safety and relating what was about to hit the Northern Lands. I had no doubt that he would do exactly what I suggested. He had spent the last twenty-odd years of his life leading a small community in a gods' forsaken ice kingdom in order to protect me and my mother. He wouldn't allow a foreign despot to place it all in jeopardy.

Hwarang was still working on the Island Nations. Used to their autonomy and isolation from the rest of the world, they were a tough nut to crack. We had the commitment of Solrig Island, which had agreed to help us by guarding its coast and not providing shelter for the imperial navy, but Skygge Island—just across from Solrig—had yet to profess its support. Frosset Island was too far north to be of much help, but it had offered a few ships to add to however many others would be protecting the Northern Sea.

"My father has added many mercenaries to his army," Sung-jin said. "A good thing for us because once things go sour, those soldiers will be the first ones to defect. They like the money but prefer to be alive to spend it."

Many innocent people who had been unfortunate enough to be conscripted into the army by force to serve as a human barrier would die, but there was no other way. Our only hope was that the battle would not last long enough to claim too many lives.

Now we waited.

Nothing could be done until we had received confirmation from my father and hopefully a vow of alliance from the rulers of Skygge Island. The emperor had returned, and I was back to my daily duties of providing tea, pastries, and sensual entertainment to him and his friends. No alarm had been raised about a break-in to the map room, but I still felt as if I were walking on eggshells every time I set foot in the imperial palace. Thankfully the emperor seemed distracted by whatever war machinations made him tick, and he barely noticed me as I fluttered around him in my simplest and plainest of dresses, pouring tea or wine in a never-ending flow.

I kept my ears sharp, making sure to walk on my tiptoes, always on the lookout for any bit of information we may be able to use. We needed a date—we knew the incursion was eminent, but we didn't know the precise day. But whatever it was, they were keeping tight-lipped about it.

"I wish you didn't have to go to the palace," Sung-jin said while wrapping my hand in a bandage. The wounds from the day we sneaked into the map room were taking their sweet time to heal.

"We still don't know when he's planning to attack," I said, marveling at the care and gentleness of his touch. Who knew that a seasoned warrior like him could be so loving? "As much as I hate it, I have to go."

He sighed, inspecting the dressing one last time before dropping my hand. "Your wounds will never heal if you continue to carry heavy trays laden with crockery all day." He was right about that. The simple act of carrying a tray was torture for my sore palms and fingers. I would sooner have a leg injury. Sung-jin looked up at me. "Promise me you'll be careful." His voice had gone even softer.

I smiled, my heart so full it could burst. "I will do my best to meld with the walls," I promised, stepping closer to him until our bodies touched. "You know...," I breathed, wrapping the ties of his tunic around my finger, "I might need some comforting when I come back." His eyes lit up, and I slid my other hand around his hip and laid it flat on his ass. "Do you think you can manage that?"

We hadn't been intimate since that first time almost a week ago. This business with the upcoming invasion and the spying was putting a serious damper on our love life. The one I didn't know I wanted until recently.

"I can't think of anything better I'd like to do," he whispered, voice thick with desire. He leaned over until his lips touched my earlobe. "Now I won't be able to focus on anything," he said.

I chuckled. "I'll make it worth the wait," I promised, sliding my hand from his chest to the front of his pants. He was already hard, and for a crazy moment, I considered throwing caution and sense to the wind and staying home to indulge in the loveliness that was my husband. But something larger than the two of us was at stake. I let out a deep sigh. "Fuck, Sung-jin, why did you make me love you like this?"

His eyes rounded and his jaw slackened. Before he could respond to my declaration of love, I rushed out of the room, uncomfortably hot and frustrated but with a smile on my face.

Tonight couldn't come fast enough.

Chapter 27
Love War

Normally, I'd feel tendrils of excitement wrapping themselves around me as I held a man at swordpoint, defeated and in my control. But today all I felt was anxiety. Not even the fighting practice with Hwarang could distract me from the fact that my wife was in the palace, alone and defenseless against my father.

To keep up the pretense that I could no longer walk properly, I couldn't show my face at the training field to practice with the other soldiers. Hwarang came every afternoon to spar with me, but it wasn't the same thing as fighting two or three other warriors at the same time. Today it was even worse with my head full of Cahki and all the terrible things that might happen to her in the palace.

"You're not focused today," my friend said, dropping the sword in frustration. "Where is your head, brother?"

I took a deep breath. "With Cahki and the emperor," I admitted, wiping the sweat from my brow with the edge of my sleeve. "My wife takes unnecessary risks sometimes." Hwarang nodded, dropping onto a chair on the makeshift sparing stage in the courtyard. It had been unseasonably warm for the past couple days and even more unusually dry. "She is reckless, and my father is not to be underestimated."

"I agree that she's reckless," my friend said, pouring cool water into a glass. "But Cahki is also smart. She won't do anything she'll regret."

"I knew it!" Cahki's voice exploded behind me. "You are so in love with me, Hwarang. But I already told you it's not possible between us."

Spinning around to face her, I couldn't help myself: I smiled like a fool, so relieved to see her back safe and sound—and belligerent as usual. "Cahki, you're here," I announced unnecessarily. "Are you okay?"

In a couple of wide strides, she threw herself at me, wrapping her arms around my neck. I was so surprised, I almost dropped her. "Been thinking of you all day," she whispered in my ear, and my blood turned to lava.

"I'll go somewhere and poke my eyes out now," Hwarang said, rising from the chair and shaking his head. "You guys went from mind-blowing hate to nauseating love in no time. How did you manage that?"

I chuckled softly as Cahki unwrapped herself from my neck. "Anything new?" I asked, wanting nothing else than to scoop her into my arms and carry her to our bed.

My wife sat down on the chair Hwarang had been occupying a few seconds earlier and sniffed his cup of water. "Did you drink from this?" she asked my friend. He nodded and she frowned, setting the cup back down. "I did learn something," she added, leaning against the backrest of the chair. "I can't promise this is the exact date for the attack, but the way they hushed up every time they mentioned it and how careful they were not to be specific about what will happen on that day makes me think that's exactly what it is."

I slid down onto the chair next to her, and Hwarang stepped closer. "What is it?"

"The emperor's minions kept referring to 'two weeks from today' and 'the big day' as a day of celebration and victory," Cahki explained.

"They would say something like, 'Everything must be ready in two weeks for the great celebration.' Except I took a peek at the emperor's calendar, and there are no celebrations in sight." I exchanged a glance with my friend. "I'm willing to bet that's when they are planning the attack."

I couldn't agree more. The good news was that we now had an approximate date. The bad news was that it didn't leave us a long time to prepare. "They didn't see you checking out the calendar, did they?" I asked my wife.

She shook her head. "No, I was invisible." I had to smile. With her snow-white hair—even if coiled tightly into a top bun—and porcelain complexion, she was anything but invisible. She leaned forward, resting her elbows on her knees. "Husband, we should spar. Serving tea all day makes me itch for violence."

Hwarang snorted. "Hell, I wouldn't fight her now if you offered me a ton of money," he said. "I can only imagine how murderous she feels after spending the day serving your father."

Cahki scowled at him. "Maybe fighting you would be a better choice," she growled. "It would give me great pleasure to damage that pretty face of yours."

My friend rushed to hide behind me like a child, his hands on my shoulders. "Protect me, brother," he said. "She's too violent even for me."

I shook him off with a chuckle. "I'll be glad to spar with you, my wife," I said, bending down to pick up Hwarang's discarded sword and hand it to her. "You can use his weapon. It's nice and sharp."

Jumping to her feet, she reminded me of a wildcat ready to pounce on her enemy. She accepted the sword and twirled it a couple times in her still-bandaged hands. "I promise not to hurt you, Sung-jin." She raised her pale eyes to me, the corners of her lips tweaking upwards. "At least, not too much."

A few weeks ago, those words would have me worried. It was no secret she had been very willing to end my life as soon as the opportunity arose, but now I knew she wouldn't hurt me if her life depended on it. She had tended to me so lovingly when I was wounded, I doubted she would want to hurt me now.

I unsheathed my sword and pointed it at her. "I'm ready."

She didn't wait, immediately lunging at me, sword pointed at my chest. My wife didn't fool around. I dodged the hit and parried the blow, rolling her blade away from me. Cahki stepped backwards before swinging her sword and slicing into my upper arm. A quick look of concern clouded her eyes before she yelled out at me, "Stop coddling me. Fight like a soldier."

I obliged, and we parred savagely for a few minutes, nicking each other a few times until I finally got the upper hand, pinning her down on the ground with the tip of my sword.

Anger darkened her face for a moment, but it was quickly replaced by a chuckle. "Well done, my husband," she said. "You're a worthy opponent indeed."

Offering her my hand, I pulled her to her feet, belatedly worried about the blood on her clothes, a cut on her arm, and another on her hand. "Let me clean those wounds," I said, waving at Hwarang, who had already run inside to get the medical kit. "You're too reckless, Cahki. I could have killed you."

She smoothed the wrinkles in her dress and laughed. "But you didn't, did you? I'm not such easy prey."

I opened the kit and took out the disinfectant. "Of course you're not," I said, holding her wounded hand in mine and examining it. My blade had cut through the existing bandage. It was a mere scratch, and it would heal in no time, but I hated myself for it. I loved this crazy woman and didn't want to hurt her in any way. "But why look for trouble when it's not necessary?"

She covered my hand with her other and took a step closer. "It makes life interesting," she whispered for my ears only, her eyes diving into mine so deep, I'm sure she saw my soul. "Send Hwarang on an errand. I want you all to myself."

She didn't have to ask me twice.

With Hwarang on a mission to check on the status of our negotiations with Skygge Island, we were alone in our room. Funny how I could feel so nervous around my own wife. Not nervous because I was worried she would stab me when I least expected it—even though that had been a real possibility not that long ago—but because my insides turned to mush every time I looked at her. And when I touched her... sirens rang in my head and fire ran through my veins, making me wonder how I managed to stay alive when every inch of my body and soul ached for her.

Ever since we consummated our marriage, Cahki had lost her reserved veneer when alone with me. Just as I suspected, there was fire beneath her icy surface and a warm, tender heart. My ever-growing feelings for her did not help me deal with the guilt of having forced her hand into this marriage. Even when reason told me marriage was better than the alternative for her, that nagging, gnawing shame came flooding in. I hadn't expected to fall for her. I certainly never considered consummating our relationship. Gods! I never expected we'd *have* a relationship.

"What's on your mind, Sung-jin?" Cahki had inched closer to me until I could feel her body heat. "Are you still worried about the upcoming battle?"

That was the farthest thing from my mind at the moment. My head was filled with awe and a bit of fear for the overwhelming love I felt for my wife. With such a crucial battle ahead, one that brought all my carefully and patiently drawn plans to a climax, all I could think about was her safety. What would happen to her if things went horribly wrong? What if I didn't survive this thing? With me out of the way, the emperor would be free to do what he wanted to her.

"I'm just worried about you, Cahki," I admitted. Despite everything, I wanted our marriage to be honest, with no secrets between us. "I'll be leaving with the ships in two weeks, and you'll be here alone with my father."

Cahki smiled, flattening her hand on my chest. "You can always take me with you," she said, raising her eyes to mine. "I'm no fragile flower, you know."

Despite my worry, I chuckled. "Don't I know it," I said. "But you won't be going into battle with me." She opened her mouth to protest, but I stopped her. "No argument. This is all part of the plan. We need you here to keep the illusion that I am still at home, disabled and harmless." She stomped her foot like a child. I brushed my fingers over her beautiful white hair, pulling out one of the pins that held her bun coiled on the top of her head. "Let's not talk about war right now," I begged, watching as her hair fell in a snowy cascade over her shoulders. "I want to show you how much I love you again."

There was a glint of something mischievous in her eyes as she held her bottom lip between her teeth. "Can't wait," she whispered, taking a step closer. "Wait until I show you how much *I* love you."

It was still strange to hear her confessing her love for me, but her words were fuel added to a fire that was already roaring inside me. I wrapped her slim waist with my hands and drew her to me in a tight embrace. "Should we make this a competition?" I whispered in her ear, my lips touching her earlobe. The way she shuddered against me was a powerful aphrodisiac, and it was all I could do not to rip off her clothes and make her mine right there.

"Challenge accepted," she breathed, bracing both hands on my chest and pushing me hard until my back hit the wall. "You're not to move, you hear?"

My heart slammed against my chest bone as I watched my wife undo my outer garment, pull the flaps apart, and cover my bare chest with kisses. While her mouth explored my torso, her hands were busy undoing the ties on my pants. When I reached out to pull her to me, she stopped me, pinning one of my arms to the wall. With my pants undone, she let them slide down my hips and all the way to my ankles before letting go of my arm.

"Don't move," she demanded again, her eyes seeking mine for a moment. Then her eyes disappeared from my sight as she dropped to her knees. "I'm very competitive," she said, and the next thing I knew, I had ascended to the heavens with her lips latched around my erection, her tongue warm and exciting against my sensitive skin.

I wouldn't begrudge her the win this time.

Chapter 28
Battle Mode

Sung-jin, Hwarang, and their men had left at dawn, riding their horses away from the capital toward the secret rendezvous with their army and allied navy. The plan was for their ships to be in place before the emperor's navy left the harbor so they could surround it on all sides once the ships had entered the strait. My job was to stay home and pretend nothing was amiss.

It was harder than it sounded.

When the men had gathered their horses and their gear just outside our back gate while the rest of the world still slept that morning, it had shattered me into a cloud of painful and unfamiliar emotions. When Sun-jin came to stand before me, dressed in his dark battle leathers and ready to go, it was as if someone had buried a dagger in my chest and left me bleeding out.

"I want to go with you," I had whispered, knowing all too well that I couldn't. Our carefully devised plan would fall apart if I left, obliterating the illusion that life went on as normal in our courtyard. I glanced up at him under the dim light of the crescent moon, hoping he couldn't see the tears flooding my eyes.

He pulled off his heavy riding gloves and held them in one hand as he drew me in and held me tightly against him. "I don't know what's worse, Cahki," he confessed in a soft voice. "To leave you here alone or take you into the danger of battle. I wish there was a third option."

He knew that there was. I could forget about these last few months, forget how our hate and suspicion had turned into love and trust, forget it all and run. By the time the emperor realized I was gone, and with a battle looming on the horizon, it was doubtful he would waste his resources to pursue me. But that meant betraying the man I now loved as fiercely as I had hated him back then, and I couldn't do that. He was a part of me I could no longer do without.

We stood in our embrace for a few minutes, my head against his chest, the sound of his beating heart coming loud and clear through the thick clothing. I sighed, and, gathering all the strength I could muster, I pushed away from him.

"You've got to go," I said unnecessarily as all the other men were already waiting on horseback. "You'd better come back to me in one piece, you hear?" I poked him hard on the chest, making sure he knew I meant it. "If you think death would end this thing we have together, think again. I will follow you to the Other Side and give you a serious thrashing for disobeying me."

He chuckled, and then, bending down slightly, he kissed my lips long and desperately, as if letting go would end us right there and then. When we parted, a chunk of my heart was wrenched from my chest.

I had to let him go.

Hours had passed, and I was still reeling from the shock of how my heart ached watching my husband leave and not knowing whether I'd ever see him again. How was it possible that the same man I wanted to kill a while back was now so intricately connected to my soul that the mere thought of losing him tore me apart? I had stood at the back gate of our courtyard for a long time after his horse vanished into the horizon, waiting and wanting—yearning to be with him. If we were to die, I wanted to die beside him, not hundreds of miles away and in the company of his ruthless father.

But duty called.

I got dressed, supervised the making of the morning meal for my husband, carried it on a tray to our bedroom like I did every morning while he sat with his friend, going over the plans for the battle. Except he wasn't there today. The room had never looked emptier. I closed the doors behind me, set the tray down on the table, and sighed, placing a hand on my aching chest. It was a good thing Sung-jin had a very small staff—a couple maids, a cook, and an errand boy. The smaller the number of people, the easier it was to keep the illusion he was still there. For the past few weeks, my husband had limited himself to staying in our room, only leaving it when the staff was not around, and even then, not going any farther than the courtyard for his daily sparring with Hwarang. As far as the staff knew, he was still in his room, hiding from a world he was no longer able to participate in.

If only they knew....

Soon, it was time to go to the emperor and follow the usual dreadful routine of serving him and his inner circle. Today even the palace courtyards looked empty, and it took me a while to figure out that it wasn't because of the emptiness inside me, that void I was finding so hard to deal with. Something *was* different, and it had nothing to do with the way I felt.

"What's going on?" I asked one of the maids who populated the grounds, always busy running errands back and forth, carrying food and clothes, cleaning, and trying to be as invisible as they could.

The girl curtsied, lowering her eyes to the basket of clean clothing she was carrying. "*Wang-Gwan Gongju*, the emperor and his men have gone to the harbor," she said.

My heart somersaulted. "Why?" Stupid question. I was pretty sure I knew why. But it was too soon. Would Sung-jin and his allies make it to their destination before the imperial navy? It was over an hour's horse ride to the secret meeting place, which meant that they only had a very brief headway. "Is there a place where I can see the harbor from the palace?"

The maid pointed to the left. "You can see it clearly from the tower," she said.

I thanked her and took off running. I had to see it with my own eyes. I skipped steps to the top of the tower, too anxious to worry about how my legs would feel later. The girl had been right—the view from the top was clear. The harbor extended and curved along the coastline just below, the bright blue water peppered with warships.

They hadn't left yet.

I let out the breath I was holding. The bright imperial colors—gold and purple—flapped in the wind, hanging on masts and from the tips of the soldiers' lances. I was relieved to see that the soldiers had not yet boarded the ships and were still gathered on the port, lined up like the pieces on a chessboard, their faces all turned the same way, toward where a golden carriage stood. The emperor must have been addressing his men.

"Good. Take your time, Your Royal Rottenness," I uttered under my breath. Hopefully Sung-jin's navy had been on its way for at least a couple hours. His ships were smaller but faster than the clunky, ostentatious imperial navy vessels that had been built more for show than actual action. We had to win this.

I'm not sure how long I was up there, mesmerized and terrified by the show developing before me. The emperor had hundreds of troops, maybe more than a thousand, while Sung-jin could barely boast a force of five hundred men. Yes, he had the support of several other nations, and, if everything had gone according to plan, he was backed up by the mighty strength of the pirate fleet, a force to be reckoned with. But those were all wild odds that we still could not be certain of even now as my husband sailed away to set up the trap. There were too many unknown variables in this. It made me feel itchy.

It scared me.

The courtyard and the house felt haunted by my fears when I returned. Even though I knew I had an important mission—a role to play—I felt helpless, useless. What would I do if things went terribly wrong? What would I do if Sung-jin never came back? I'd always depended on me and myself alone. It wasn't as if I needed him to survive. In fact, this was the perfect time to escape this kingdom. The bulk of the imperial forces were deployed in this attack. Only a few soldiers had been left behind to protect the emperor. Sung-jin must have realized this, yet he trusted me enough not to betray him. It was tempting to leave all this behind and go back home. If I went the northeastern path—however much longer it was—I could avoid the battle and all its dangers. I could be home, safe and sound, in a few weeks.

I'd be leaving the man I loved to his own fate.

I couldn't do that. No matter how much I wanted to see all of this behind me, my happiness was too dependent on the soul I was now linked to. It was useless to fight it. I'd sooner die than betray Sung-jin.

The summons came the next morning. I had hoped the emperor would be too anxious and excited about the incursion to care about tea and biscuits, but as it turned out, he wanted me doing my daily job even then. When I arrived with the tray laden with teapots and cups, two of his usual cronies were already in attendance and sitting around the round table with the emperor.

"How's my son doing?" The question took me by surprise, and the crockery rattled on the tray as I fought for a better hold. He had never asked such a thing. In fact, sometimes I wondered whether he even remembered he had a son. Did he suspect something?

I bowed my head, avoiding his eyes. "He's recovering," I said, my mind racing to find ways not to arouse his suspicions. "He can't walk without the help of the crutches, but otherwise, he's eating well and adapting to his new circumstances."

From beneath my lashes, I watched as his lips curled into a vicious smile. "Unfortunate for you to find yourself married to an invalid," he commented, leaning over slightly. "I hope he can still perform his marital duties."

The other two ministers snickered at the insinuation, and the part of me that I normally kept buried deep inside while in the emperor's presence clawed its way to the surface. "His legs might not work as they used to, Your Majesty, but the rest of him works perfectly fine." I shouldn't have said that. Bringing up anything even remotely sexual in front of the imperial pervert was not wise. Even less so if it sounded as if I was correcting him.

The emperor straightened, the smile dying on his lips. I watched with a mixture of satisfaction and apprehension as he took a moment to recover from my biting remark. The asshole really hoped his son wouldn't be able to perform because of the injury that his own father caused. Even more disturbing was the fact that the emperor took obvious pleasure in it.

"He's never been much of a man," he said, once he collected himself. He turned to the man on his left, a middle-aged minister who always wore a strange cloth hat that resembled a large knitted sock even when it was hot. "*Chinhwassi,* do you remember when I had him taken to a brothel on his thirteenth birthday?" The other man chuckled. "How the guards told me afterward he refused to fuck the whores?"

My stomach filled with acid, and I bit my tongue so hard, the taste of rust took over my senses. I couldn't say anything. He was egging me on, hoping I'd say something that would justify punishing me or my husband. I had to keep my cool.

"He wouldn't perform, not even under the threat of a whipping." The emperor sighed. "But since he was my son, I was merciful and had him whipped only ten times."

The fjord wolf inside me roared, hungry for Emperor Min's flesh. I could take him easily. The man had gone soft through a lifetime of sitting around, eating and drinking, while plotting everyone's demise. I would wager that underneath those rich velvets and damask, there was not much muscle to speak of. But he was surrounded by guards, some in plain sight, but many more hidden. I knew he hadn't sent these men with the expedition, and should I attack him, they would be on me faster than I could bat my lashes.

"When he turned fifteen, I tried again," he continued, oblivious to my murderous thoughts. "I rented out a whole brothel just for him and put the most sought-after prostitute in charge of making him a man. The whore later reported to me that the boy cried like a baby through the whole thing."

My fingers were wrapped so tightly around the edges of the tray that my knuckles hurt. If he thought telling me these horror stories would make me love and respect my husband less, he was sadly mistaken. With every word he said, my love for Sung-jin grew. Despite my background, I had a good childhood, adored by my adoptive parents and cherished by a small but loving community. Sung-jin had known nothing but hate and pain his whole life. Every time he had someone he loved and who loved him, the emperor had made sure to take them away. Other than Hwarang, the crown prince had nobody.

But he had me now. The woman who stood here swallowing the blood I drew from my own tongue and struggling not to lash out at the bastard who had fathered him.

The emperor waved me closer, and I couldn't refuse. I took two steps to stand a couple feet away from him. He leaned toward me over the side of the chair. "You let me know if he can't please you properly, won't you?"

"He pleases me just fine, Your Majesty," I said, summoning all the control I could muster. "Your son is a fantastic lover. You need not worry about his sexual prowess."

But you should indeed worry about his intelligence and his resolve to depose you, Your Imperial Asshole!

With a glare, he dismissed me, obviously unhappy with my reaction. Did he really expect me to agree with him? To somehow side with the man who had tortured my husband since birth and had me kidnapped and brought to this land to be his sexual slave? Could he be that delusional?

For the rest of the day, the emperor sequestered himself with a few ministers, and I was free to go home. Strange how I now thought of the courtyard I shared with Sung-jin as my home, and I had to wonder—not for the first time—whether I would be able to leave it behind once Sung-jin had ascended to the throne and our deal came to its conclusion. Could I ever get out of this enchanted marriage? And even more pressing, did I really want to?

The answer came to me immediately. It was a simple and emphatic "No."

Chapter 29
Victory & Defeat

W ar was by no means pretty, but as I stood on the main deck, looking out over the railing onto the ocean, I couldn't help being awed by the sheer beauty and majesty of those waters. Thankfully we'd had calm seas all the way to the northern mouth of the Strait of Lys. Now the ocean was dotted with warships, their colorful flags representing us and our allies.

We quickly moved into position, spreading out and hiding along the northern coast of Skygge Island as our allies from Solrig were left to defend the southern exit. A couple of our men had been dispatched to the island of Solrig to keep an eye on the imperial navy and give us a sign once it had entered the strait. I exhaled in relief when I spotted the pirate flag flying above the ships on the northern coast of Solrig. They had answered the call like Cahki predicted they would.

My heart tightened. It had only been a few days, and I already missed my wife, worried about what might be happening at home. What if my father discovered I wasn't in my courtyard? What would he do to Cahki? Despite the curse, there were so many ways he could still hurt her. I knew that she was more than capable, but the huge force of the emperor's brutal guards shadowed him day and night.... No, I wouldn't think about that. I had to focus on this battle. My father's ships should come soon, according to the intel we had received from our people in the Southern Kingdom, and my focus had to be razor sharp if I wanted to win this war.

I didn't know how long I had been standing at the bow, staring at the ocean and waiting for the sign, but it eventually came, a humble shower of light. As instructed, our lookouts had released a flare indicating that the imperial navy was now well into the narrow stretch of water and ripe for the trap. The horn wailed, and our ships converged at the mouth of the sound, ready for battle. I saw the pirate ships open their gunports in the distance, their mighty cannons peeking through the holes. If everything went as planned, Solrigen ships should be approaching from the south, effectively trapping the imperial navy. The only wild card was the Skyggen, who might not have refused to help us but had also not pledged their support. Had they cast their lot with my father's navy?

"Hwarang," I yelled out, trying to get a visual of my friend. "Are we ready?"

"Ready to roll," he replied with a wave.

My friend, who was an excellent diplomat besides being a first-rate soldier, had secured the cooperation of several men who possessed the same powerful magic that we had. This small group, which included me, was our defense system. We had placed a couple of these men in each of our ships to create protective shields once the battle began. I would not waste any lives if at all possible. We were as ready as we were going to get.

We had sailed for less than an hour when we saw the purple-and-gold flags. This was it, the moment I had been preparing for my whole adult life, my one and only opportunity to rid my kingdom of its tormentor and gift my people with a brighter, kinder future. I knew that if things went wrong, I wouldn't survive long enough to find out what happened to my wife, a fact that threw a shadow over everything. But in war, sacrifices were always on the menu, as any soldier knew. My wife was smart and strong. I had every confidence that should we lose this battle, she would find a way to escape before my father captured her. I had to believe that.

"They saw us," Hwarang announced.

"Wait until they are within firing range," I said. We couldn't tell how long we would be able to hold the magic shields, so we had to be cautious and use our time wisely.

I could feel the tension across the deck as if it were something solid. Even nature had fallen silent. Gone was the whispering of the wind, the screeching of the gulls, and the splashing of the waves against the sides of the ship. All I could hear was the sound of my own breathing and the beating of my heart against the metal plate of my armor. Seconds became eternities as we watched the enemy ships slowly approaching. My father's navy was mostly composed of large, heavy ships that carried a lot of weaponry and men but moved far too slowly to be fully effective in a battle by themselves. His ego had not allowed him the wisdom of adding a few frigates to his battle group, smaller vessels that didn't look like much but could attack in advance of those clumsy giants and strike killing blows before retreating, taking full advantage of their speed and agility.

As the minutes ticked, the din of my heartbeat became deafening. I wanted to turn the ship around and run, but I reminded myself of each scar on my back and legs, each unnecessary death among the people of my kingdom, the masses of starved and orphaned children who roamed the streets of each city, and my resolve surged back tenfold. I was going to make sure that man I called father would never hurt anyone ever again.

I spotted a puff of smoke as the cannons on the nearest ships began to fire.

"Now!" I screamed, and Hwarang closed his eyes, focusing on building a shield to protect our ship from the cannons about to blast us. I would wait until his magic was exhausted and then replace him. The slight reddish fog rising from each of my ships told me the other men were doing the same. The magical shields couldn't protect us forever, but they would allow us to get close enough to the imperial ships to do major damage before they could do the same to us.

"Aim at the ships, not the men," I ordered, knowing all too well that most of the men on the first line of ships were lambs to the slaughter. The ships were close enough to the coast that if they sank, there was a good chance they could swim to safety on the closest island and have a chance at survival. They owed the emperor no loyalty, and they sure as hell held no love for him. Once they reached land, they would run for it. That would leave us with the real navy. We were strong and had plenty of experienced sailors to take care of them.

The silence of a few minutes ago was replaced with the deafening sound of blasting cannons and the buzzing of flying arrows.

We braced ourselves for the impact, but even though the ship shook, the shield held steady. The cannonballs hit the reddish mist and slid harmlessly into the sea.

The enemy ships were not so lucky. The first few blasts of our cannons pierced their hulls right at the waterline. I watched in morbid fascination as the sailors began abandoning ship, some taking the time to lower small lifeboats into the waters while others just dove into the freezing ocean in a panic. I wished them all the luck in the world. They were but victims of my father's cruelty.

More danger awaited behind the first line of sinking ships, but just as the smoke cleared, I realized I need not fear. Our allies were attacking from the south, and the slow-moving giants had not had time to turn around to defend themselves. One was already sinking, and the other had raised a white flag. Against all odds, the battle was over, and we won with no losses of ships or men.

Hwarang and I exchanged a quick glance, and then, throwing our heads back, we howled like we had never howled before.

Our ship was fast, but I wanted it to fly, and it couldn't.

After the enemy's fleet surrendered, there had been major chaos—some of the prisoners of war had jumped, trying to swim to Skygge Island, only to be captured along the coast by the local soldiers. It turned out that the Skyggen might not have pledged their alliance to us, but they were also not willing to allow our enemies on their land. There was, however, a good chance someone might have escaped both our people and the Skyggen coastal forces, and if so, they might return to the Southern Kingdom earlier than us and warn my father.

Cahki would be in danger.

"Can't this damned ship go any faster?" I yelled, standing at the bow, frantically searching for land. We had left the other ships behind to clean up the mess and deal with the hundreds of prisoners. The pirates and, soon after, the Solrigen had joined our men in securing and manning the two remaining imperial vessels so that they could be returned home. I was worried about what could happen if one of the imperial minions got to the emperor first.

I couldn't stand still and paced on deck from bow to stern, pausing by the rail to watch the horizon, hoping—wishing—to see land.

"You're making me nervous, brother," Hwarang said, laying a hand on my shoulder. "Being this anxious is not going to get us there any faster."

I slammed my palm on the wooden railing, barely registering the pain that echoed up my arm. "I swear I'll kill him if he so much touches a hair on her head."

Hwarang squeezed my shoulder. "He won't. Your father is too cowardly to risk the wrath of the gods."

"But he's conniving enough to find a loophole, some other way to hurt her without bringing consequences to himself," I said, anxiety blurring my vision. "If the news of our victory reaches him before we do, he'll do something desperate."

"Why don't you go rest?" my friend suggested. "I'll come call you when we spot land."

I hadn't slept in two days, but I would never be able to rest as long as I feared for Cahki's safety. I shook my head and squeezed the railing until my knuckles turned white.

"We're going as fast as we can, brother," Hwarang said, patting me on the back. "She'll be all right. She's tough and wicked." He chuckled softly. "She can hold her own."

I knew she could, but the emperor had the numbers on his side. "I won't be able to relax until I have her safely in my arms."

When the sailor in the crow's nest yelled, "Land ho!" I thought my heart would explode right out of my chest. I fought the urge to jump off the ship and swim the last couple miles, ridiculously thinking I could be faster than our frigate. I watched the coast approach way too slowly for my taste, the few buildings along the waterside becoming gradually clearer and more defined. I could now see the watchtower in the distance, perched on top of the hill overlooking the harbor. Would my father have a guard there watching out for the returning fleet? He wouldn't expect it back this early. If we hadn't intercepted it, they would still be attacking the Northern Kingdom. The Northerners might not have been prepared for the attack, but they had enough armed forces to resist for a while. My father knew that, so hopefully he didn't have anyone watching the harbor yet. Not that a small frigate like mine would cause him too much alarm, but I wanted to surprise him and not allow him any time to realize his mistake. Cahki's life might very well depend on it.

As soon as the ship was moored, I left a few sailors behind to secure the ship while the rest of my soldiers, Hwarang, and I rushed up the hill to the palace. We were all armed and armored, prepared to give the imperial guards all we had. Two of the other men who possessed magic had sailed back with us just in case we needed a little extra help, but I wasn't anticipating major problems. The imperial guards were well trained but poorly protected by ornamental armor that was heavy and clunky. They also had no particular love for their sovereign, who was cruel and unfair to all equally, even those he unwisely expected to protect him. Faced with our small but mighty force, they would be more than willing to drop their weapons and surrender.

Our journey up the hill was uneventful. The common people of our city gave us a wide berth, recognizing trouble immediately and rushing back to the marginal safety of their homes. I was glad they did. The emperor was our target, and the fewer innocent bystanders caught in the fray, the better. Beads of sweat rolled down my forehead from underneath the metal helmet I was wearing, but I didn't notice the heat. The rainy season was practically over, and the heat was coming back with a vengeance. Despite our situation a smile crept over my lips at the memory of Hwarang's words to Cahki shortly after we had first met her. She'd been complaining about the never-ending rainfall, and Hwarang had warned her that once the rain stopped, she'd be wishing it hadn't. I wondered how Cahki, who grew up in an extremely cold climate, was dealing with the intense heat of our summer.

Cahki, my love!

I picked up the pace, flying rather than walking the last few yards up the hill and entering the palace grounds. "Hwarang, go check on Cahki," I ordered as we crossed our courtyard. As much as I wanted to, I couldn't stop to do it myself. I couldn't give my father the chance to go into hiding.

Hwarang broke from our group and headed toward our home while we continued on our way to my father's courtyard. As expected, there were a few guards at the gate who stood no chance against us. A few of my men took care of them, and the rest of us barely paused. I climbed the stairs to the imperial palace, skipping steps, the muffled clanking of our armor filling the silence of the summer day. It was too quiet, I realized belatedly. The ministers, servants, and courtiers who normally buzzed on the palace grounds were nowhere to be seen.

My heart plummeted.

"Something's up!" I yelled at my men. I heard my name and turned around to see my friend racing toward us. "What's wrong, Hwarang?"

The deafening sound of my heart barely allowed me to hear his words. "She's not there, brother. Cahki is not at home."

Chapter 30
Dagger

The cold metal of the small but lethal blade sent shivers of panic through my whole body.

The emperor held me against him, one arm tightly wrapped around my waist and the other holding the dagger against my neck. It took me a moment to calm myself down enough so I could analyze the situation and come up with a plan. The man had no hard muscle, that much was clear. Even though his whole body was taut with tension and fear, the softness of neglected muscle was still apparent through his thick clothes. I could take him easily—well, in theory. After all, he was armed, and I wasn't. The guards had come so suddenly into my courtyard, I didn't have the time to grab my knife.

"The crown prince is not here," one of the guards had yelled after searching our rooms.

They knew! I barely had time to wonder how they had found out before they dragged me to the imperial palace and threw me on my knees before Emperor Min.

"Where's my son?" the emperor asked, his face looking like a tomato fresh from the garden. In two strides he was close enough to slap me across the face. "Where is Sung-jin? Answer me!"

It was obvious he knew what was coming already. There was no reason to hide it. "He's coming for you, Your Majesty." I offered him a smirk, giving him a peek at the old Cahki, the one who took no shit from anyone.

He slapped me again. Harder. My face burned, and stars crossed my vision as my head snapped to the side with the force of his hit.

I cackled, unwilling to give him the satisfaction of seeing me cower before him. "You don't scare me, Your Royal Pervert," I spat. It was unwise to poke the wasp's nest, but I had been forced to put up with him for months now. I'd had it. "You're so done."

I braced myself for another slap, and I wasn't disappointed. This time he punched me instead. His hard knuckles exploded against my left eye, pain spreading out like thin rays of electricity, leaving me lightheaded and dizzy.

Before I could recover, he had grabbed me and thrown me across the few steps up to the throne. With my head still swimming among the stars, I couldn't find the strength and the balance to stand up, and it rankled. I growled, keeping my head low and my eyes closed.

"You're very feisty for someone who has no one to protect her, my dear," he said, crouching near me. I opened my eyes long enough to see his shiny shoes mere inches away from my head. I could grab his legs and throw him on his ass—if I wasn't so dizzy. Another growl escaped my lips. "I can crush you like a bug, white-haired beauty, or even better, fuck you right here in front of my guards to show you who is in control."

That made my eyes snap open so fast I saw the world tilt. "Go ahead, do it!" I challenged him, my unsteady voice dripping with poison. "Our wedding curse will then take care of you. I'm willing to sacrifice myself. Do it!" The bravado in my words didn't match the shaking of my hands, the crushing anxiety in my gut, and the overwhelming sadness in my heart. Was this the end for me and Sung-jin? My heart bled at the thought.

His fist came down on the side of my neck this time, and the last thing I heard was "Bitch, you'll get your wish soon enough." Blissful darkness fell upon me then.

I woke up to a knife on my throat. Sung-jin must be close.

"You move, bitch, and I cut you just enough to make it hurt," the emperor whispered in my ear. "Then, I'll cut you again, a little deeper this time, letting the blade linger inside your flesh. Maybe twisting it a bit. Doesn't it sound like fun?"

My head pounded and my eyes were still not completely focused, but I spat out, "You're despicable." Not that you could hurt a psycho like him with words, but it helped me release the anger that threatened to explode inside me and tear me into shreds. "Where are your *faithful* ministers? Your cronies?" Satisfaction made me grin as I felt his hand shake a little. "They're hiding in their holes, not willing to stick it out with you, right? No one is loyal to you, Your Majesty. No one. You'll die alone."

He snorted, but his voice was not as steady as before. He was cruel and ruthless but not stupid. He must have noticed how no one other than himself and a handful of guards were in the throne room, that no one had run to his rescue or given him protection. "I have you, my little whore," he said, tightening his hold on me. "I go, you'll go first."

"Do you think holding me hostage is going to save you?" I said, the need to keep talking too overwhelming. If I stopped, I'd give away to the fear that froze my legs and my arms, that made me quiver inside. "Your son doesn't love me. He married me to spy on you. Do you think he cares that I live or die?" I so hoped he did, but what if I had been fooling myself all this time? What if he really only stuck by me because he needed me to depose his father?

The emperor barked a loud laugh. "I've seen the way he looks at you," he said, pressing the blade harder against my skin. I felt something warm drip down my neck. "He's in love with you, bitch, and I'm glad because I can use that against him. He won't sacrifice you even for the throne."

I begged to differ. Even if Sung-jin was indeed in love with me like I hoped he was, he had a mission—one larger than himself, larger than me. He wanted to rid his people of this tyrant, and I believed he was willing to sacrifice his own heart if necessary.

"Let go of her!" My eyes tried to home in on the tall, familiar figure in the doorway, the light of the summer sun framing him like a magical halo. My prince was here, and my heart both shivered in delight and panic. "Let go of my wife, and I will consider sparing your life."

Emperor Min laughed, a lunatic cackle that echoed against the high ceilings of the throne room. "Come and get her," he said. "Remember what happened to your mother?" I felt rather than saw my husband stiffen. "And Chae-yeong? I guess you didn't get enough and want to watch it again."

Gods! Was this what he had done to Sung-jin's fiancée? Had he killed her in front of his own son? Was this man even human?

"Kill the bastard," I yelled. "Don't worry about me, Sung-jin. Get this bastard once and for all."

Pain radiated from the spot on my neck where he held the knife and down the rest of my body. He was going to kill me. He was so desperate that he was willing to face the consequences of the curse. I could feel a thicker stream of blood running down my neck.

"Sung-jin, kill him for me," I said, voice choked by the pain. "I love you."

I closed my eyes and waited for my death.

A sudden burst of air zoomed close to my head, and I held my breath. Surely it was an angel from the Other Side coming to collect my soul. I waited to be pulled away from the ground beneath me and carried away into the Heavens above. Instead, I felt the emperor's hand dropping from my waist and the blade sliding away from where it had been pressed against my throat and falling with a clank onto the marble floors.

I opened my eyes just as another set of arms came around my body and held me up. My legs had gone soft, I realized with a weird, detached interest, and the world around me had gone blurry as if I were looking at it through the agitated waters of the ocean.

"Cahki." My name was a welcome whisper in my ear even as I felt consciousness slipping away from me. "Speak to me, my love."

I tried. I opened my mouth, but no words came out. The burning pain in my neck was quickly fading away, but so was the room around me and everyone else in it. I smiled instead—a grateful smile at the man who, against all odds, had become more important to me than anything else in this world. The man who, despite everything, was my soulmate, my heart. My eyes fluttered and my arms were filled with lead.

"No, Cahki, no," Sung-jin yelled, holding me tighter, struggling to hold me up as my body went boneless. "Stay with me, my love. Don't leave me." I couldn't keep my eyes open any longer, but I was still smiling. I might be dying, but I had been happy these past few months. Very happy. "I love you, Cahki, but don't you dare leave me."

I found the strength for a last feeble chuckle before I faded into oblivion.

Chapter 31
Long Live the Emperor

H er skin had gone so pale, she was transparent. As I held her in my arms, I could see the dark veins just underneath the skin of her cheeks, her forehead, her neck.... Blood, obscenely bright against her pallor, poured from the cut on her throat and dripped over her white nightclothes and my hands as I tried in vain to stop it.

"Hwarang, go get the doctor," I yelled unnecessarily because my friend had already whirled on his feet and was racing out of the throne room.

I pressed my hand over the wound harder, knowing all too well that she was bleeding out faster than I could control. My chest hurt with the pressure of fear. If I lost my wife, all of what I had just done would have been for nothing. Funny how things worked out, how things changed. For most of my adult life, I had been planning this coup to bring change to my people. For years that was all I lived for. And now that I had finally achieved it, all I could think of was Cahki and how life would be unbearable without her.

It couldn't have taken more than five minutes, but it felt like an eternity had passed before the doctor arrived, running across the large space toward the dais where I still kneeled, holding my unconscious wife. The man dropped his bag on one of the steps and immediately checked her pulse. "She's alive," he said, turning around to open the bag. "Let me check the wound."

My hand was still firmly pressed against her neck, her precious blood slipping between my fingers. I whimpered as the doctor pried my hand away from her. "*Jeonha*, I need to check the wound," the man repeated, and I realized I was still holding on to her.

I removed my hand and held my breath, afraid her life would rush out of her through the cut now that I wasn't covering it any longer. Sitting back on my haunches, I watched him as he examined my wife. He worked fast and efficiently but still too slowly for me. Nausea gurgled up my throat. I hugged myself, my arms burning and cramping.

She couldn't die. Cahki couldn't leave me.

For the first time since childhood, I muttered a prayer to whatever gods were willing to listen to me. "Save my wife, please. Take me instead."

Hwarang closed his hand over my shoulder. "She'll be okay," he said. "She's a fighter and too stubborn to let your father win."

A sob escaped my lips mixed with a chuckle. Cahki was indeed a warrior, braver and more determined that many soldiers. She could kick death's ass.

"Extraordinary," the doctor exclaimed, kneeling beside Cahki. "I have never seen anything like it."

Hwarang and I both leaned forward. "What is it?" I asked, panic rising in my throat.

"The wound on her neck," the doctor said, blanching. He paused before turning and looking at me, eyes wide in wonder. "It's healing itself. The blood is already clotting, and the flesh is knitting itself together. How is this possible?"

My heart almost jumped off my chest. Her gift! Could it be?

I shuffled closer and leaned over her. She was still very pale, but there was a hint of color returning to her cheeks, and her breathing was no longer as shallow as before. "Cahki," I called, not really expecting her to answer but wanting her to hear my voice. "Love, you're healing yourself. You'll be all right."

I exchanged a glance with Hwarang who immediately helped the doctor to his feet. "Doctor, can we have a word in private?" The doctor complied, mouth slack and eyes still focused on the prone figure of my wife. Had he even noticed the dead body of the emperor lying just beside Cahki, an arrow still sticking out from his neck?

The sight of my father's dead body should have garnered some reaction from me, but I found that I felt nothing. Nothing at all other than repugnance for what he had symbolized for decades. I stood up and crossed the few feet between us to move his corpse away from my wife. I dragged him up to and unceremoniously dropped him at the foot of his gaudy throne. Good riddance. No one would be crying for him, and that thought finally brought a sliver of sympathy to my heart. How sad to die alone with no one—not even your children—to mourn you.

A low moan shook me out of my reverie. A quick glance at Cahki told me she was coming to. Forgetting my dead father, I rushed to her, crouching beside her body. "Cahki, you're awake," I whispered, afraid of startling her. Her eyes fluttered open, sky blue staring up at me. A smile stretched across my lips. "Move slowly. You lost a lot of blood."

She moaned again and brought a hand to her neck, gingerly touching where my father had cut her. The wound had been almost completely replaced with a slightly raised scar that I was guessing would also vanish eventually as her blood worked its magic. "Where's the asshole?"

Relief washed over me. My wife was back. "He's dead, my love," I told her, helping her sit up. "Are you okay?"

She leaned against my chest. "Dead?" she repeated. "I thought I was the one dying. What happened?"

"Hwarang shot him," I told her, a shiver running through me. It had been a risky move. My friend was an amazing shot, but Cahki had been so close to the emperor, his body completely blocked by hers. The only vulnerable place had been his neck, inches away from my wife's head. "Maybe you should stop calling him an idiot now."

Cahki turned her face up to mine and smiled. "All right, from now on I'll call him a nincompoop instead."

What had started as laughter quickly turned into sobs as we held each other tightly, overwhelmed by a tidal wave of emotions—anger, relief, happiness... and love.

A voice rose from the door to the throne room, loud and clear, and was soon followed by many more. They echoed against the walls and ceilings of the space, laced with awe and joy.

"The emperor is dead, long live Emperor Sung-jin Min!"

"Stop fidgeting, Your Imperial Pain in the Ass." Cahki slapped my hand away from my head where she had placed the imperial crown. It was such an insanely cumbersome contraption, one had to wonder who the idiot was who came up with such a design. She stood on her tiptoes, straightening the tall thin gold cuff that held my long hair in a top bun. She laughed. "Move slowly, or these dangling things will hit you in the eye."

I sighed, watching as the curtain of gold chains and beads that hung from the crown swung wildly in front of my eyes. It was going to be a long day.

"Can we just skip this?" I whined, knowing all too well that we couldn't. How could I possibly miss my own coronation?

"Well, you are the emperor," Cahki said, capturing her lower lip between her teeth for a moment. "I guess you could write an edict ending such ceremonial events. But it might be a little too late at the moment. You're supposed to be at that throne in half an hour."

Her smirk made me huff like a toddler. "Don't mock me. After all, you still have to put your crown on, too, and yours is much heavier than mine." I pointed at the mentioned accessory set on a red velvet cushion on the table.

Cahki took a peek and wrinkled her nose. "I demand a divorce," she said, stomping her foot. "I don't want to wear that, not even for minute."

As I pulled her into my arms, the hanging ornaments fell onto her head, making us both laugh. "You're my empress. You have to," I said. "The ceremony is more for the people than for us. I promise I'll cut it down to less than an hour."

She raised her head, and one of the chain ornaments got stuck in her hair. "Fucking thing," she spat, halfway between amusement and annoyance. "How long do these things normally last?"

I managed to untangle the chain from her head. "Over three hours."

"No way!" She looked so outraged, I couldn't help but burst out laughing again. "Why so long?"

I shrugged. "Tradition, I guess. I will make sure we do the actual coronation and cut down on the other stuff," I promised, not one hundred percent sure how I'd manage that. "We'll move all the speeches and stuff to during the banquet. That way, we can get rid of these crowns at least."

A maidservant walked in. "Your Imperial Majesties," she said, bowing to both of us and then addressing my wife with a frown. "You're not ready yet, and they are waiting in the throne room."

They were all the ministers and courtiers of the kingdom. Breaking with tradition, I had also invited the soldiers and sailors who had fought on my side, and I opened the imperial courtyards to the populace. This was all for them, so it stood to reason they should be able to watch it if they chose to do so.

"Can you help her with the crown?" I asked the young woman, who wasted no time doing just that.

Cahki looked beautiful in a dress she had picked herself to match better with her own nation's traditions. It was cut from cerulean blue silk and draped with a translucent blue lace overdress. Compared to the fussy, heavy Southern style, it was simple, but it fit her perfectly. Around her neck she wore a lapis lazuli teardrop necklace that brought out the blue of her eyes. With her white hair combed into braids coiled around her head and topped by the elaborate imperial crown, she looked stunning. My wife, the empress.

"Ready?" I asked once the crown was well settled on her head. I was already melting beneath the heavy imperial cloak, but I'd endure it. This was a special occasion, and I was not going to spoil my people's fun because of my discomfort.

My wife nodded, the crown shaking precariously on her head. "Ready, my handsome imperial husband," she said, holding out her hand to me. I grasped it and led her out of our rooms.

Hwarang was waiting outside with an escort of loyal soldiers who had been with me for years. As soon as he set eyes on us, he whistled. "Holy fuck. The wild woman from the North cleans up nicely."

"I'm your empress now, nincompoop," Cahki barked back, daggers in her eyes. "You better watch your mouth."

My friend bowed to her with a grin. "Your Imperial Majesty, I will watch it closely and never allow it to express any disrespect." Both Cahki and I snorted at the same time. "What? You don't believe me?" Hwarang's innocent expression was not fooling anyone.

We proceeded to the imperial palace, a grand procession in the suffocating heat of the Southern summer. In front of us, two young women dressed in blue to match Cahki's attire carried glowing golden lanterns hanging like flags from long rods, and behind us two more girls were carrying unlit lanterns. Most of the ceremonial pomp was just that—meaningless ways of showing off one's power. But my wife had added her flavor to the ceremony.

"A new emperor with a new philosophy of governing needs his own traditions," she had said. And so, the girls with the lanterns were added to the procession. "The girls in front represent the future, and the girls in the back, the past. The future is bright as we leave the darkness of the past," she had explained. "A future where women are included in every aspect of society, not just in men's beds." I couldn't argue with that.

The imperial courtyard was packed with people, the guards barely able to keep the path clear for us to pass through. People oohed and whispered as we walked by, hand in hand with smiles on our faces. Cahki waved a few times, and the crowd went crazy with excitement. My wife sure could work an audience.

Slowly, we climbed the stairs to the throne room, my desire to throw the cloak onto the steps almost stronger than the resolve to act dignified. Inside, the new thrones awaited. Shortly after my father's death, I had his throne melted and the gold distributed among the poor. Then I commissioned a local craftsman to build us a set of simple thrones. The pieces were both pleasing to the eye and comfortable with their cushioned round seats and high heart-shaped backs.

As we both sat down, I glanced at Cahki and whispered, "Are you ready to be the empress?"

She snorted. "Just about as ready as I am to swallow a handful of nettles." I cocked my head with a smile. "But don't worry, I'll be the best empress this kingdom ever had, or my name is not Cahki Aros."

I had no doubt in my mind she'd be an amazing empress, but her name was now Cahki Min, Empress of the Southern Kingdom.

Chapter 32
The Cold North

"Why do you have to be so stubborn?"

My father's exasperated voice soothed a rough spot in my heart I hadn't even noticed was there. So much had happened since I'd been taken away to the Northern Kingdom that missing my parents had been put aside. But now that I was here in Hvithet, sitting in this familiar kitchen with my mom and dad, sipping on hot goat milk, all those suppressed feelings of yearning and pain exploded inside me.

A smile stretched my lips even as tears burned behind my eyes. "I will take him to the fjord hut," I insisted, my voice surprisingly steady, considering the knot in my throat.

"The man will die," my father said, glancing at my mother—a silent plea for support. "He's not used to our climate. Do you want to kill your husband?"

I swallowed my unshed tears and replied, "He's a warrior. He can do it." The truth was that the same doubts had crossed my mind more than once as I planned our excursion up the mountain to my lonely, freezing outpost. But Sung-jin insisted he wanted to see it, and I wanted to share it with him too.

We had been in Hvithet for almost a week, and things couldn't have gone smoother. My husband was a hit with my mother, who couldn't stop praising his looks.

"He's so handsome, Cahki," she kept repeating. "That long dark hair and those gorgeous eyes—how beautiful!"

Gods, did I have to be jealous of my own mother now? She was so infatuated with Sung-jin, I swear I saw twinkling stars in her eyes every time she looked at him.

My father, the former fjord pirate, couldn't praise him enough either. "Sung-jin is such a great warrior," "Your husband is so strong," "His skills with the sword are amazing." It was all rather sickening, really. You'd think my husband was a son they'd spawned themselves.

I opened my mouth to argue with my father, but Sung-jin spoke instead. "I want to be there with your daughter, sir. We're husband and wife, and she's been part of my world for months now. I want to be part of hers too, and if that means being uncomfortable, so be it."

My mother snorted. "Uncomfortable? Boy, you have no idea." Leave it to my mom to address the ruler of a mighty kingdom as a boy. "That level of cold can easily kill anyone who's not used to it."

Sung-jin chuckled. "I'm tougher than I look," he said. "Besides, your daughter will protect me."

An involuntary grin followed by a wave of heat spread over my face. I loved that he thought of me as someone capable of protecting him.

He made a lunge for my hand, squeezing it inside his. "We're a formidable team, Cahki and I. We can handle anything."

After all, if we had somehow survived a depraved, cruel, and powerful man like Sung-jin's father, we could survive a journey to the fjords.

"*Glem det*!" my mother finally exclaimed. "We might as well give up and just have warm clothing made for our son-in-law so he doesn't freeze his crown jewels. I want grandchildren."

Yes, my mother had taught me the art of being inappropriate.

Sung-jin broke into a cough attack, spitting out the hot goat milk he had been sipping on.

My father, oblivious to my husband's discomfort, slapped his knee and exclaimed, "Right! Protect the jewels at all costs." Sung-jin had turned a strange shade of purple and was still sputtering milk onto the palm of his hand. "Cahki, go call Ingrid and tell her to make extra warm underpants for the boy."

Afraid that my poor husband couldn't handle much more of this vicious attack on his private parts—however well intended—I pulled him toward the door. "Come on, I'll save you," I whispered. "I'll show you to a secret place."

Still coughing, Sung-jin set his mug down, waved at my parents, and followed me outdoors. The icy air hit us like a rock. After months in the hot and humid climate of the Northern Kingdom, even my body had trouble dealing with it. I shivered, already tingling in anticipation of where I was taking my husband.

We walked hand in hand across the main square toward the foothills where there were few buildings and the snow was gathered in large piles thanks to the drifting wind.

"Where are you going?" Sung-jin asked me, his lips already a sickly shade of blue.

I should have grabbed a face covering on my way out, but we were less than a minute away from the caves, so I pressed on.

"There!" I pointed at the entrance of a cave half obscured by an evergreen that grew defiantly from the frozen ground. Sung-jin glanced at me in a silent question. "You'll see. Let's get out of the cold."

The cave entrance was low, so we ducked on the way in, but the ceiling grew higher until we could walk upright just a few feet in.

"Why is it warm in here?" my husband asked, unwrapping the woolen scarf from around his neck.

The tunnel opened suddenly into an almost round chamber, heat and humidity hanging in the air as thick as the gauze my mother used to make cheese. In the center of the room, there was a large rock that hid what was just beyond it. I pulled Sung-jin in that direction, sweat already beading on my forehead.

We turned the corner around the rock, and there, in all its lovely warm and wet glory, was my own hot spring, my one and only luxury.

"Is that a bathtub?" Sung-jin asked, his narrow eyes widening in surprise.

I dropped his hand and began disrobing, throwing my clothes into a pile on top of the rock.

"It's a hot spring, dummy." I yelled as the last piece of clothing followed the others. "Get rid of those clothes and join me."

I didn't linger to see if he obeyed me. Instead, I climbed up on one of the rocks and slid carefully into the hot water, vapor wafting up to wrap me in a cozy and comforting cocoon. A moment later, a splash told me my husband had indeed joined me. Two strong arms enveloped my midsection and pulled me closer. Every muscle in my body immediately relaxed from both the touch of the hot water and my husband's equally hot body. If anyone had told me just a few months ago that the touch of a loved one could be this miraculous, I would have laughed in their faces. Now, I was a believer.

"You're full of surprises, my wife," he whispered in my ear, his lips brushing against my skin.

"What do you mean? This hot spring?" My clueless act was not fooling anyone. "I thought everyone had one."

Sung-jin chuckled. "That and the fact that you never told me your mom was the queen in your house."

It was my turn to laugh. "Who do you think taught me every-thing?" I twisted in his embrace to face him. "Wait! I'm lying. My father did teach me how to fight, and the prostitutes taught me how to f—" He stopped me with a kiss, squeezing me so tightly against him,

I couldn't miss his state of arousal. I relished his lips, his tongue and flavor, growling in disappointment when he pulled away.

"Don't ever mention that again," he whispered, his lips still touching mine. "It makes me insanely jealous that I wasn't the one to teach you."

I melted in his arms, feeling at home and never wanting to leave. "Silly. They may have taught me the skills, but you get to enjoy them for the rest of your life," I said with a tiny giggle. I nipped his lower lip. "Unless, of course…"

He pulled away a bit to look me in the eyes. "Unless what?"

I licked my lips, my eyes devouring him. "Unless you do lose your jewels at the fjords."

The glare he gave me told me he was about to prove to me how perfectly his jewels still worked.

Bring it on, my love. Bring it on.

Sung-jin's nose was a worrisome shade of purple, his teeth chattering so hard, I could hear it over the howling wind. I didn't know whether to laugh or feel sorry for him.

"How do people live here?" he said, his voice coming out in spurts. "Northerners are not humans."

I did laugh then, throwing my arms around him to warm him up, his puffy fur coat and scarf making it nearly impossible to get close to him. "It's not that cold, wimp." I knew it was. I could stand it easily enough because I had grown up in this weather, among the fjords where only the hardiest of plants and animals survived. Poor Sung-jin was used to hot, humid weather and was not built to withstand the freezing cold. "We're almost there," I promised.

My husband nodded—at least I thought he did. It was hard to tell with all the shivering—and we resumed our walk up the fjord. My winter hut was just another half mile or so up the icy slopes of Mount Kulde, but I was beginning to fear that the new Emperor of the Southern Kingdom wouldn't make it. I held his arm and stopped him, pulling him down enough so I could whisper into his mouth.

"I'm flattered," he said, his voice faltering a little less. "But it's hardly the time, is it?"

I snorted, pulling away from him, my lips already missing his. "You should be so lucky. I just whispered some heat into you, Your Majesty."

He smiled, color returning to his cheeks. "Thank you, Cahki," he said, his words getting swallowed by a gust of wind.

With the wind picking up, I had to slow down our pace. My husband was not used to striding through the soft, thick covering while fighting the snowdrifts, and I could tell how much of a toll it was taking on him. But we did eventually arrive at the small cabin where I had stayed so many times during my trips to collect the valuable and rare plants that grew there despite the climate.

I wasted no time building up a roaring fire in the hearth, the biggest feature of my small hut for a very good reason. Soon, the room was warm, and even my shivering man was comfortable enough to remove his outerwear. While he sat by the fire, his shaking hands turned toward the flames, I busied myself preparing us a small meal. The advantage of being in the fjords was that food was easily preserved in the ice, and even meat lasted for a very long time. It had been months since I had been up here, yet I found my usual stock of meat and root vegetables under the mound of snow just outside the front door.

"We'll have snow rabbit stew with mountain potatoes and snow-berries," I announced, dropping my stash on top of the small table to the left of the hearth. "It's delicious."

Sung-jin didn't look like his usual self. He was pale and still trembling like a leaf, and for the first time today, I truly worried about him. The smile on his face didn't quite reach his dark eyes. "I'm sure it will be," he said.

"Come with me," I said, crossing the space to grab his arm. He stumbled getting to his feet, and my worry increased tenfold. Was he getting hypothermia? "Let's get you into bed and under a pile of warm blankets."

He didn't fight me, which in and of itself was a sure sign he wasn't feeling well. I helped him remove his fur-lined boots and was startled at how cold his feet felt in my hands. Shit! He really was not made for these temperatures.

He slipped in between the sheets, and I piled three down duvets over him before hanging a pan of water over the fire. Tea would come in handy just about now while I prepared the stew.

"I'm sorry, Cahki," my husband said as I threw all my ingredients into the pan. Because I always had to use them frozen, I prepared the meats and vegetables ahead of time so there was no need to cut through the frozen provisions.

I glanced at him, momentarily forgetting my cooking. "What for?" I asked.

"For being such a weakling," he said with a gentle chuckle. "Who would have thought a mighty warrior and emperor like me would not be able to handle the cold of the fjords?"

I laughed, stirring in a few spices and adding water. "Good thing you have me to protect you." We laughed together while I hung the pot over the fire. The water was boiling, so I poured it over the tea leaves inside the mugs and carried his to him in bed. "Give it a couple minutes before drinking it. It will warm you inside."

I was so glad that Sung-jin had agreed to travel across the ocean to meet my family. My husband wanted to meet my parents and to thank the pirates who had helped him defeat the imperial navy as well, and messages had been sent ahead to my father to arrange a meeting. But more than anything, I wanted to show him where I spent a lot of my time before being taken away by the emperor's men. I felt as if he couldn't truly know me unless he could see it, feel it, understand the solitude and majesty of the fjords. Now I was beginning to regret that decision. He looked so uncomfortable, so sick, guilt began gnawing at me. Had I been too selfish?

"If you're thinking you shouldn't have brought me here, don't." I hated it when he could read my mind. "I wanted to come. I wanted to know more about your past, about what made you who you are. I love you, so how can I not want to share your life even if it is uncomfortable for me?"

A smile tugged at the corners of my mouth. "I'm glad you said that," I said, sitting on the edge of the bed and sipping my tea. "Because I'm planning to take you to the pleasure house to meet the prostitutes who taught me all my bedroom skills."

The little color that had returned to his cheeks left him completely as he choked on his tea.

"You may want to thank them, after all."

The communal hall had never looked so small. Dozens of people crowded inside for a chance at meeting the man who had defeated Emperor Min. My father had already dismissed many guests, but no matter how many people left the building, as many or more replaced them inside.

"*Fanden*!!" my father cursed as a new wave of people slipped through the guards at the main doors and into the room. He rubbed his forehead as if a headache was coming. "They're not listening to me."

I smiled, knowing all too well what was coming.

My tiny mother, wearing her usual humble blue gown and not a stitch of makeup, stepped up to the dais where my husband and I had been put on display, opened her arms wide, and yelled, "People of Hvithet, stop acting like children and listen up!" The whole room went silent, faces turning slowly to my mother who, with hands on her hips, was easily the smallest adult in that hall. "That's more like it." The last whispers of noise evaporated, and every eye was now fixed on Edel Aros, half of their leadership team. "Emperor Sung-jin Min is here to thank a few people for all their help during the Battle of Lys. He will attend our town celebration later today, so if you are not a fjord pirate, get out of here right now." Her voice, usually gentle, left no margin for argument. "*Gå ud!*"

People started filing out of the hall, throwing longing glances at us. I hid my chuckle behind my hand.

"I see where you get your fierceness," Sung-jin whispered at my side. She might not be my biological mother, but I had learned everything I knew from her. "I'm a little intimidated myself."

The pirates who had been lost in the crowd were herded and organized into rows before the dais by my father and his men. My mother dropped her hands from her hips and looked at us. "I will go get you something to drink," she said with a smile that belied her previous outburst.

My husband and I exchanged a look and burst out laughing. "I warned you about my family," I said, trying to compose myself, as all the pirates were now waiting for whatever my imperial man was about to tell them.

We both took a moment and some deep breaths before Sung-jin addressed the men who stood before us, some obviously not accustomed to standing so still for that long. "Brave men of the fjords," my husband began. "I'm here to give you my official thanks for your support during the naval battle. Without you I'm not sure we would have been successful." The men shifted and wiggled like children who had been sitting for too long. "But since words are cheap, I brought you proof of my gratitude." He waved to one of our attendants who had been standing to the side of the dais. The man came around, followed by a few other men carrying two heavy wooden chests. "This is a humble thank-you gift from the Southern Kingdom that I hope you will accept." The chests were placed in front of the pirates and opened to reveal pieces of gold and precious jewels inside. The men sucked in a loud collective breath. "I understand there were two crews involved, so here are two chests of equal value for you."

Two older men—the captains of the mentioned crews—stepped forward, looking dazed. They had not been promised anything, so to be presented with such riches had taken them by surprise. They stared at the contents of the chests before kneeling and bowing their heads. "We accept and thank you for the generous gift, Your Imperial Majesty," the taller of the two said.

Taking the cue, all the other men fell to their knees with dry thuds and bowed, words of thanks in a few different dialects wafting around them like bubbles.

"It is I who should thank you," Sung-jin insisted. Before I realized what he was about to do, he stood up and then fell into a deep bow on his knees, eliciting a loud gasp from the audience. "*Jeg er evigt taknemmelig*," he said in a heavy accent while still on his knees. "I'm eternally grateful."

I stared at my husband, a mighty emperor humbling himself to men who by all criteria were mere outlaws. Outlaws who had done the right thing at the right moment. My heart overflowed with love for that beautiful man I had married. I would never have thought that what started as a marriage of convenience—or desperation, depending on how you looked at it—would become something so warm, so fulfilling.

Moments later, the crowd dispersed to join the rest of the populace in the main square for the celebration my parents and the other elders had organized. We both stood up and joined my mother, who had been waiting for us by one of the front doors.

"Isn't it too cold to be outside?" my Southern husband asked, wincing a bit and undoubtedly remembering our excursion to the fjords.

I looped my arm through his and pulled him to me. "Don't be stupid," I said with a chuckle. "We have our ways."

Even though he looked skeptical, he allowed me to lead him outside as my mother laughed quietly behind us. "I'm almost sorry for you, Your Majesty," she said. Sung-jin threw her a questioning glance, but she waved her hands in front of her. "No, nothing to worry about, really."

Sung-jin and I hurried to the main square just a few yards away from the hall, and if I didn't know any better, I would have believed his legs had frozen as soon as we entered the public space. The square was indeed just that: a wide square framed by rows of homes on all sides to protect it from the cold winds. Colorful awnings jutted out from the ground floors where stores were located.

But that was not what had made my husband freeze.

On the red and dark blue roofs, and defying everything my husband had ever known, the best kept secret of the fjords stood, breathing hot air onto the square.

"What the fuck are those?" Sung-jin exclaimed, pointing at the large creatures that sat on the roofs. Their bodies glittered in the moonlight, their scales competing with the Aurora Borealis that painted the skies.

I laid my head on his shoulder. "Those, my love, are dragons."

Chapter 33
Karma

Everyone calls her Cahki, an old-language word that means hard and icy. Cruel.

It's hard not to protest that assessment of my wife's personality as I watched her hand out food to the orphans and widows in the slums of the imperial city, a sunny smile stretched on her lips as she hugged the urchins and whispered comforting words to the women. My wife might wear an outer layer of ice, but inside she was pure warmth, pure love.

We'd stood in the icy harbor of Hvithet a few weeks back, saying our goodbyes to her parents when I pledged to protect Cahki and her secrets once more. She was such a part of who I was now that I couldn't hurt her any more than I could hurt myself. She's in my heart and in my soul, and nothing or anyone will ever be able to tear us apart.

My name is Sung-jin, an old Southern name that means true successor—or as I prefer to think of it, follower of truth.

I started my reign as the new Emperor of the Southern Kingdom, hoping that my name held true, that I might indeed be the tyrant's successor, but one who follows the truth and fights for his people. Helping those who were the most impacted by my father's greed and cruelty was the first step in the right direction, and Cahki, my fierce wife, was with me every step of the way.

In the whirlwind of the aftermath of my father's death, so many things had been set in place. Along with Hwarang, Cahki was now in charge of plans to rehabilitate a vast number of our population who suffered in silence and survived on the scraps of generous people.

"That empty field south of the city—what's it called, Hwarang?" my wife had asked a few days ago, a large piece of paper unrolled on top of the table between us.

"The Divide," my best friend replied, pointing at the area of the map that separated the city and the next village to the south. "It's been left abandoned for decades."

Cahki nodded. "But the land is actually very fertile," she said. "After being laid fallow for so long, with only grasses and wildflowers grow-ing there, the land is now full of the necessary nutrients to grow fruits and vegetables." She raised her eyes and threw me one of her gorgeous smiles. "And there's plenty of room to build homes for our destitute to live in."

Like everything Cahki did, it was a solid plan, and one that wouldn't even cost too much. There was enough gold in the imperial treasury to cover all of it with plenty left over. My father had been a miser with his riches, a fact that only reconfirmed his cruelty. With as many people suffering from lack of income in the kingdom, why had he stuffed his coffers to that extent? It was a rhetorical question, one to which I knew the answer too well. It was for the same reason he had so often beaten me: thirst for power and an extreme craving for control.

I rushed home today with an extra spring in my step. I had what I hoped would be exciting news for my wife. The guards at the gates to our courtyard bowed awkwardly as I flew by, waving at them in response, no time for the usual chitchat. These were mostly men who had fought under my command, and I rewarded their loyalty and faith in me the only way I could—by treating them like family.

Dashing through the front doors of our rooms—the same ones we had occupied before the coronation—I yelled Cahki's name, excitement tingling in my fingertips. "Where are you, wife?"

"In here," she said, her voice slightly muffled. *Here* was her favorite room, the one she called the Plotting Cave. Shortly after the coronation, she announced she would like to have a room adjacent to our sleeping quarters where she could plot all kinds of things in peace and quiet. She had furnished the bright space with a couple tile-top tables, a few chairs, a bed that doubled as a couch and eating space, plus a few shelves that she quickly filled with books, paper, pens, and other miscellaneous, mysterious, and whimsical artifacts I could only guess the function of.

I walked into a disaster—not an unusual thing in that room. There were papers on the floor, on the bed, and spread out over the tabletops. My wife had her sleeves rolled to her elbows and her skirts gathered on one side with a ribbon of some kind, her legs bare to the knee.

"Wife, you're not even decent," I exclaimed, repressing a chuckle. "What if Hwarang walked in here and saw you half naked like that?"

She didn't bother to look at me, preoccupied with some document on one of the chairs. "I'm hardly naked, and if he did, who's to blame? He should have knocked."

My best friend had quickly learned to never walk in on my wife without warning. Cahki, now that she didn't have to fear my father, had the habit of walking around in different stages of dishabille—too hot for all the clothing, she always claimed—and if we were together, there was always the chance Hwarang could walk into something he'd sooner not see.

"I have a surprise that I think you'll love," I said, not able to keep it in any longer.

She finally looked up at me, blinked a couple times, and threw herself into my arms, wrapping her legs around my waist and her arms around my neck. "What is it? Am I going to love it? Can I eat it?"

I laughed, kissing her nose. "So many questions," I said. "Guess who just arrived in town?"

Her beautiful blue eyes opened wide. "Your brother?" she wondered. I had sent men to the far end of the kingdom to fetch my brother a couple weeks prior.

"No. Not him," I replied. "Guess again."

She bit her lip in deep thought. Then her shoulders slumped. "Fuck, no idea. Who?"

The news played in my brain and on my tongue, tasting like a piece of deliciously spicy meat. "Old friends of yours," I quipped.

She cocked her head to the side. "Friends? The Hvithet prostitutes who taught me how to—" I laid a finger across her lips. Naughty woman, always bringing that up, knowing all too well it made me insanely jealous. She smiled wickedly. "All right, no clue. Who are these friends of mine?"

I kissed her again but on the lips, and with feeling this time. Her kisses always left me breathless. I had to take a moment before I could say, "The guys who brought you to the Southern Kingdom."

Cahki slid down my body until she was standing on her own two feet before me, opening her eyes so wide, I thought they would tear at the corners. "The traffickers?"

I nodded enthusiastically. "They brought a new stash of women from the West this time," I explained. "They thought I'd continue my father's practice of collecting sex slaves for my harem, so they very generously came to offer me their wares."

She was silent for a moment and closed her eyes, biting her upper lip. "Are you giving them to me?"

I flicked her chin with my index finger. "All yours, my wife," I said. "Let's say it's a belated wedding gift."

She whooped, wrapped her arms around my neck again, and kissed me. "You're the best husband ever, Sung-jin." She turned around to leave, but at the last minute, she looked at me and winked. "I will show you tonight how much I appreciate this gift."

Fire erupted in my belly and other parts of my lower body. "Promise?"

"It will be epic," she said with another wink and a quirk of her lips. "After I take care of those *jævler* and make sure the women are placed in comfort and fed properly, I will be full of energy for you, my husband. I love you."

She ran off, not caring that her legs were still bare to the world. "I love you too," I yelled after her.

I smiled and scratched my head as Hwarang walked in, looking confused. "Where the hell is she going in such a hurry?" he asked.

"Going to give those traffickers what they deserve," I replied, chuckling. "Want some tea?"

I was almost sorry for the seafaring devils who waited anxiously in the harbor for the payment I had promised them.

Almost.

"Tea? Are you fucking kidding me?" Hwarang said. "I'm going down to the harbor. No way in hell I will miss this."

He was right, of course. I wouldn't either.

Not delaying another minute, we both took off at a trot out of the rooms and across the courtyard in the direction of the harbor where a group of assholes were about to learn why kidnapping Cahki had been the worst mistake of their lives.

<<<<>>>>

Glossary of Terms

HOUSE OF BLOOD AND WHISPERS

SOUTHERN KINGDOM LANGUAGE (inspired by Korean)

Jeonha - Your Highness

Abeoji - Father

Gongjunim - Princess

Wang-gwan gongju - Crown princess

Dang-Gui - Angelica root

Il-eona - Get up

Gamsahabnida - Thank you

Hangug-eo - Language of the Southern Kingdom

Boricha - Barley tea

NORTHERN KINGDOM LANGUAGE (inspired by Danish)

Jævel(s) jævler(pl) - Bastard(s)

Drage - Dragon

Kanin - Rabbit

Jeg er evigt taknemmelig - I am eternally grateful

Fanden - F**k

Gå ud! - Get out

Acknowledgements

Every time I sit down to write one of these, I freeze. I have so many people to thank and I'm always terrified to forget someone. So consider this as an act of bravery from this writer who is grateful to every single person who has ever helped her one way or another, even if it was simply by offering me a smile when I was feeling discouraged.

This was such a fun story to write, but the encouragement I received from the wonderful people in my critique group (you know who you are) made it that much more exciting. To experience their pleasure when reading excerpts from my story was the best gift and the best motivation to keep going.

Writers are often told to write what they know, which is the worst advice ever unless you're a nonfiction writer. Where would we get all those fantastic, out-of-this-world stories we so love if writers only wrote about what they knew? Anyone who has met me knows I am rather shy and come across as cold and unassertive. But they can't see the *me* that lives inside. Even though Cahki might seem as the opposite of me, she really isn't. Inside I also have a kickass Cahki who kicks and screams against all injustices. I just don't curse like her, lol.

But kidding aside, the cast of characters in this book was inspired by the fantasy books, movies, and TV shows I have been fortunate enough to read and watch throughout my life. I have to thank all the creatives who pour their hearts and souls into all those wonderful stories. I have truly lived a thousand lives through them.

Thanks go to my awesome editors at Hot Tree Editing who are more than just editors, cheering me on all the way through the process. I couldn't do it without you.

J.P. Kemp drew a fabulous map of the Land of Whispers for which I am so thankful. It's so thrilling to see my imaginary world coming to life on paper.

A heartfelt thank you to A.L.Vincent (AKA Jolie) who is always ready to listen to me and offer me advice just about on anything and everything. You have no idea what it means to me to have someone to turn to with writer's questions.

And finally, I couldn't do any of this without my family, here and in Europe, and you, my lovely readers everywhere in the world. You make it all worthwhile. Thank you.

About the Author

Natalina Reis is an international bestseller who wrote her first romance at the age of thirteen. Since then she has published many romances that defy the boundaries of her genre. She enjoys writing all kinds of rebels and outcasts into her stories and she always roots for the underdog.

Natalina doesn't believe you can have too many books or too much coffee. Art and dance make her happy and she is pretty sure she could survive on lobster and bananas alone. When she is not writing or stressing over lesson plans, she shares her life with her husband and two adult sons.

Follow the Author

To keep up with Natalina's news and books, follow her on the web:

Website/Blog

I'd like to thank you ahead for leaving a review of this book on Amazon, Goodreads and/or Bookbub. Or anywhere else, really. Readers rock!

DON'T MISS THE PREQUEL TO
HOUSE OF BLOOD AND WHISPERS

HOUSE OF BLOOD AND PIRATES

Coming Soon!